The Choice

Acclaim for
The Choice

"An extraordinary novel. The story compels you to finish. You are swiftly drawn into Mina's life—a caring geriatric nurse who after six years of marriage realizes she is attracted to women and is unable to deny it any longer. Mina falls in love with Regan, causing her to leave her husband Sean. Ciletti guides the reader through this painful process with caring, humor, and sensitivity. Once introduced, the characters become real—their feelings and challenges captivate throughout.

Ciletti's genuine gift is that she's given us a good 'read.' *The Choice* guides us to understand that although we have been brought up to believe that we choose our sexual preference—perhaps we don't. That realization becomes clear as Mina's new life begins—we can only hope that Ciletti doesn't leave us hanging and creates a subsequent novel with the same energy that will unfold Chapter Two in Mina's life."

—K.J. Satrum, MA
Retired, Executive Director for Student Services,
Youngstown State University

"The novel's gentle and unassuming prose makes it easy to identify with and care for every single character and their plight. There are no easy answers in this triangle with a twist, only the realization that we all must follow our path. At the heart of this extraordinary novel lies Mina's inner journey toward acceptance of her sexual orientation, despite the cost involved to herself and the people she loves. While *The Choice* is first and foremost the story of a lesbian woman coming into her own, it is also the universal story of a human being able to acknowledge and accept her own true identity."

—Helga Schier, PhD
Editor, *WithPenAndPaper*

NOTES FOR PROFESSIONAL LIBRARIANS
AND LIBRARY USERS

This is an original book title published by Alice Street Editions™, Harrington Park Press®, the trade division of The Haworth Press, Inc. Unless otherwise noted in specific chapters with attribution, materials in this book have not been previously published elsewhere in any format or language.

CONSERVATION AND PRESERVATION NOTES

All books published by The Haworth Press, Inc. and its imprints are printed on certified pH neutral, acid-free book grade paper. This paper meets the minimum requirements of American National Standard for Information Sciences-Permanence of Paper for Printed Material, ANSI Z39.48-1984.

DIGITAL OBJECT IDENTIFIER (DOI) LINKING

The Haworth Press is participating in reference linking for elements of our original books. (For more information on reference linking initiatives, please consult the CrossRef Web site at www.crossref.org.) When citing an element of this book such as a chapter, include the element's Digital Object Identifier (DOI) as the last item of the reference. A Digital Object Identifier is a persistent, authoritative, and unique identifier that a publisher assigns to each element of a book. Because of its persistence, DOIs will enable The Haworth Press and other publishers to link to the element referenced, and the link will not break over time. This will be a great resource in scholarly research.

The Choice

Maria V. Ciletti

Alice Street Editions™
Harrington Park Press®
The Trade Division of The Haworth Press, Inc.
New York • London • Oxford

For more information on this book or to order, visit
http://www.haworthpress.com/store/product.asp?sku=5791

or call 1-800-HAWORTH (800-429-6784) in the United States and Canada
or (607) 722-5857 outside the United States and Canada

or contact orders@HaworthPress.com

Published by

Alice Street Editions™, Harrington Park Press®, the trade division of The Haworth Press, Inc.,
10 Alice Street, Binghamton, NY 13904-1580.

PUBLISHER'S NOTES
The development, preparation, and publication of this work has been undertaken with great care.
However, the Publisher, employees, editors, and agents of The Haworth Press are not responsible
for any errors contained herein or for consequences that may ensue from use of materials or information contained in this work. The Haworth Press is committed to the dissemination of ideas and
information according to the highest standards of intellectual freedom and the free exchange of
ideas. Statements made and opinions expressed in this publication do not necessarily reflect the
views of the Publisher, Directors, management, or staff of The Haworth Press, Inc., or an en-
dorsement by them.

This is a work of fiction. Names, characters, places, and incidents either are the products of the
author's imagination or are used fictitiously, and any resemblance to actual persons, living or
dead, business establishments, events, or locales is entirely coincidental.

Cover design by Kerry E. Mack.
TR: 3.2.07

Library of Congress Cataloging-in-Publication Data

Ciletti, Maria V.
 The choice / Maria V. Ciletti.
  p. cm.
 ISBN-13: 978-1-56023-638-2 (pbk. : alk. paper)
 ISBN-10: 1-56023-638-8 (pbk. : alk. paper)
 1. Self-actualization (Psychology)—Fiction. 2. Coming out (Sexual orientation)—Fiction.
3. Nurses—Fiction. I. Title.

PS3603.I44C47 2007
813'.6—dc22
                                                                              2006029453

For Aunt Ellie

You showed me truly what unconditional love was.
You never missed an event in my life, no matter how big or small,
and even though you are not here now, there is no way
I wouldn't include you in this one as well.

Editor's Foreword

Alice Street Editions provides a voice for established as well as up-coming lesbian writers, reflecting the diversity of lesbian interests, ethnicities, ages, and class. This cutting-edge series of novels, memoirs, and nonfiction writing welcomes the opportunity to present controversial views, explore multicultural ideas, encourage debate, and inspire creativity from a variety of lesbian perspectives. Through enlightening, illuminating, and provocative writing, Alice Street Editions can make a significant contribution to the visibility and accessibility of lesbian writing and bring lesbian-focused writing to a wider audience. Recognizing our own desires and ideas in print is life sustaining, acknowledging the reality of who we are, as well as our place in the world, individually and collectively.

Judith P. Stelboum
Editor in Chief
Alice Street Editions

The Choice
Published by The Haworth Press, Inc., 2007. All rights reserved.
doi:10.1300/5791_a

Acknowledgments

To my family: To my Dad, Tom Ciletti, who in his short life taught me the important things. To my Mom, Donna Infante, who after becoming a widow at age thirty-six managed on her own to raise three kids, all of whom acquired initials after their names (MD, CPA, and RN). Not too bad for a girl from Mantua. Thanks for always believing in me.

To my brother, Mike, and sister, Traci, for your support, acceptance, and encouragement. You have made my life so easy when it could have been so disastrous.

To Helga Schier, PhD, my first reader who gently taught me a lot about writing and encouraged me when I thought it would never work.

To Kayla, Sara, Jacob, and Katie, for making my life fun. You are all truly amazing and the lights in my life.

To Ken, even though our marriage didn't work out, we didn't lose each other and both walked away with so much more.

Thanks to Judith Stelboum for giving me this opportunity and to Tara, Donna, Amy, Tracy, Robert, and everyone at Haworth for all your help getting me through the publishing process.

And last, but not least, to my partner, Rose. (My Rosetti.) You are truly the love of my life.

The Choice
Published by The Haworth Press, Inc., 2007. All rights reserved.
doi:10.1300/5791_b

Chapter One

I stared at the ceiling as my mind flickered, like a television remote, channel surfing, searching for a fantasy to make this experience some-what pleasurable. Tonight, nothing seemed to help, not even my old standbys of when Sean and I first got together, when we couldn't get enough of each other, and when this didn't feel so much like an obli-gation. I closed my eyes and halfheartedly caressed Sean's strong back and shoulders while enduring each raw thrust. Finally his breathing quickened, his body tensed, and then he collapsed, pinning me to the bed. A few minutes later he rolled off of me and onto his side of the bed. I tenderly kissed the top of his head, and he smiled a lazy, satis-fied smile. When I heard his soft, slow breaths, I knew he was fast asleep, and I crept into the bathroom to wash up. After six years of marriage, the thrill of marital sex was bound to cool off . . . wasn't it?

I awoke with a start as the Baby Ben alarm clock clanged on the night stand. My heart pounded and my face was damp with dewy sweat. I had had the dream again, the exquisite dream about the honey-haired woman. This time the dream was about the woman and me lying naked on a deserted beach somewhere, and when I slid my hand beneath the rumpled sheet, my face wasn't the only thing that was damp.

Feeling guilty over the effect the dream had on me and the lack of effect sex with my husband had on me, I cautiously turned over and was relieved to find that Sean had already left for work. No matter how much I tried to suppress these thoughts, thoughts no married woman should have, they continued to invade my mind. I lingered in bed, putting off having to get up and dressed for work, enjoying the wonderful afterglow the dream had produced. The morning sun fanned its warm rays through the birch trees that stood tall and strong outside our bedroom window in the courtyard of the apart-

The Choice
Published by The Haworth Press, Inc., 2007. All rights reserved.
doi:10.1300/5791_01

ment complex. The sun's glow warmed the room and it promised to
be another gorgeous June day.

Our apartment complex was adjacent to the nursing home where I
worked, so I could sleep in a little longer. After all, it took me only five
minutes to walk there. Sean and I were the youngest tenants in the
complex. Because I worked at the nursing home, the owners gave us a
break with the rent in exchange for my being on call for the old folks
who lived in the complex.

It wasn't unusual for me to have to change a dressing on a diabetic
foot ulcer, check a blood pressure, or give a vitamin B_{12} shot before
my shift started or when I returned home. Sometimes I'd even receive
a 911 call in the middle of the night from across the complex to bandage a skin tear or give an enema. The patients were always so appre-
ciative, and I really didn't mind. Some of the residents would try to
pay me for my services, and when I would decline their monetary of-
ferings they would leave pies, cakes, and cookies on my doorstep.

I stepped off the elevator on the second floor of St. Michael the
Archangel Nursing Home just as the undertaker from Morelli's Funeral Home was about to step on, pushing a gurney shrouded in a maroon velvet blanket. We nodded our silent hellos and I stepped aside
to let him pass. The purity of the soft morning light that filtered
through the thinning sheers hanging on the picture window of the solarium clashed with the ever-present smell of urine and disinfectant
that always seemed strongest in the morning.

Some of the residents were already up and at their places around
the large round table, ready for breakfast. A few of them had drifted
off to sleep again, because the chore of getting up and dressed was like
a whole day's work to their feeble little bodies.

"That's the third death this week," I said as I entered the nurses'
station. The aides and nurse from the midnight shift were bustling
around the desk, wrapping things up. I reached for my Premarin coffee mug, which hung from a wooden rack above the intercom. "Who
was it this time?" I asked.

Suddenly the room had gotten suspiciously quiet; the only sound
was the hum of the fluorescent lights overhead. "Well, who was it?"

Finally, Brenda, the midnight charge nurse, spoke up. "It was Vivian," she said quietly. "I am sorry, Mina."

"Vivian! Not Viv! What happened?" I waited for an answer, even though what had happened needed no further explanation. Vivian was dead.

"She was fine when I left last night. I gave her the bedpan around ten o'clock and then I gave her her sleeping pill at eleven. She was fine," I said.

Vivian was one of my favorite residents. She was eighty-eight years old, a retired elementary school teacher, never married, and consequently had no family to speak of, except Martha, her lifelong friend, who came for a visit every single day.

Vivian was a very proper lady. She insisted on being well dressed every day. No duster and slippers for her; she wore a full undergarment foundation including a 40 DD cup brassiere, a slip, and stockings that attached with a garter belt. Specific accessories went with certain outfits. Dressing Vivian in the morning was like dressing a geriatric Joan Collins.

Now she was dead. Hot tears sprung to my eyes. I headed toward the medication room so no one would see them. Brenda followed me, touching my shoulder as she entered the cramped little room. "I am so sorry, Mina. When I checked on her during two o'clock rounds, she was fine—sound asleep—snoring in fact. When I went back in at four she was gone."

"So, no one was with her," I said sadly.

"I'm afraid not," Brenda whispered, lowering her gaze to the floor.

Vivian had died alone—something I always vowed would never happen to the people I cared for. You don't come into this world alone, and you shouldn't have to leave it alone either.

"How's Martha?" I asked.

Brenda stared at me blankly.

"You did call Martha and let her know, didn't you?" I asked.

"Who's Martha? No one was listed under family or next of kin," Brenda said.

I was angry with Brenda, but knew she was right. Vivian didn't have any family, and friends, no matter how close, didn't count, at least not enough to be listed on a patient's chart to be notified if their condition worsened. Or if they died.

"Martha is her best friend. She comes here every day and helps Vivian with her meals and then she takes her outside. They sit in the courtyard and Martha reads to her."

"I'm sorry, Mina, I didn't know. No one gets visitors on night shift. I had no idea," Brenda said.

I glanced up at the clock. "No sense in waking her at this hour," I said, wanting to spare Martha the heart-wrenching experience of a ringing phone at six in the morning, when you know the only news you are going to get is bad news. And anyway, I didn't want Martha to shoulder this alone. "I guess I'll wait and tell her when she comes in this morning."

Brenda nodded in agreement, relieved, I'm sure, that she didn't have to be the one to deliver the news. That is one of the hardest things about this job, telling people that their loved ones have passed away. You have to talk to daughters, sons, wives, husbands, and sometimes grandchildren, telling them what is too unbearable to hear. That's one thing you never get used to.

I wiped the tears from my eyes and walked back to the locker room behind the nurses' station. I glanced at the schedule on the wall of the locker room to see who I would be working with today. I was grateful to find that it was Peggy. She'd understand what losing Vivian meant to me. This was Peggy's fifth year at the nursing home, and I knew that she had grieved over the loss of many patients. It was nearly impossible doing this job without getting attached to the residents. I also noticed on the schedule that we were going to be orienting a new hire. *Great,* I thought to myself. *Just what I need today is someone tagging along on one of the saddest days of my career.* It would be difficult to focus on anything else today except the fact that Vivian was gone.

When I returned to the desk to get the shift report from Brenda, Peggy was already sitting there. My eyes were still wet and my face flushed from crying.

"You okay, Mina?" Peggy asked, touching my knee as I sat beside her. Her eyes were red rimmed and shiny with unshed tears. I nodded and Brenda began shift report. I was assigned to be the med nurse for the day. This duty was traded off and on between the two nurses on each shift. Peggy would be the charge nurse, responsible for overseeing the operation of the entire unit as well as completing all of the treatments.

The report lasted the usual thirty minutes. Afterward, I counted and logged the narcotics with Brenda, and pushed the large med cart from the nurses' station into the tight medication room to prepare the medications for the eight o'clock round. I scribbled out the list of patients on Digoxin and Lasix that required blood pressure and pulse checks before they could receive their medications, all the while keeping an eye out for Martha.

The nursing unit was eerily quiet. Although a lot of the patients on our unit were confused and disoriented, they seemed to sense when someone passed away. They would retire to their rooms or sit silently in the solarium. I often wondered what went through their minds. Did they wonder if they were next?

It was almost seven thirty and Martha, Vivian's friend, was due any minute. Peggy came into the med room.

"You okay?" she asked again.

I nodded. "Fine. I'm gonna miss her."

"I know. I will too. She was quite a character," Peggy said. "Do you want me to tell Martha about Vivian?" Peggy asked.

"No. It's the least I can do for Viv, since I wasn't there when she needed me the most."

"Mina, you can't beat yourself up over this. You can't be here twenty-four hours a day."

"I know, but I feel so . . . bad."

"Mina, you took good care of her. That's what counts."

I nodded.

A patient call light went on and Peggy turned to answer it. Before she left the room she turned back toward me. "I'm here if you need me," Peggy said.

I smiled at her, and meant it. Her concern was just what I needed.

A few minutes later, I heard the elevator doors open, and Martha stepped off into the solarium. The adrenaline rush from my anxiety about having to tell her that her lifelong friend was gone made my hands shake and my mouth feel cotton dry. I went to the solarium to meet her.

"Good morning, Martha," I said, hesitantly.

"Good morning, honey. How's our girl today?" Martha asked, her expression sunny and carefree. She always seemed so happy to greet a new day.

My hands trembled as I searched for the right words to tell her about Viv. "Martha . . ."

"What is it honey? Is everything okay?"

I shook my head. "No . . ."

"What is it?" Martha demanded. Her eyes searching mine.

"Vivian's gone, Martha. She passed away last night . . . in her sleep."

Martha's knees buckled. I caught her and helped her into a chair. "Gone? No, it can't be. She was fine yesterday. She told me to bring *East of Eden* today to read this afternoon. She loves Steinbeck, you know." Martha said.

I nodded, unable to find any words that would ease the pain of loss.

Martha stared down at her wrinkled hands that rested in her lap. "Did she suffer?" Martha asked.

"No. Not at all. She slipped away peacefully in her sleep. She probably had another stroke. She never knew what happened."

Martha began to cry. I sat down next to her and held her close. I could feel her plump body heave against mine. A few minutes passed before Martha looked up at me, her softly creased face soaked with tears.

"We promised each other that, when the time came, we would be there for each other. But I wasn't there . . . I wasn't there, Mina. I let her down." She spoke those last words almost in a whisper.

"I know what you mean. I feel bad for not being there, too. But we could not have known this was going to happen; there was no warning. There was no way you could've have known it was her time." I knew my words were nothing but a feeble attempt to ease the pangs of guilt we both felt. I probably was talking to myself as much as to Martha. "At least we can take comfort in the fact that she didn't suffer."

A few minutes later Peggy appeared with a box of Kleenex and a glass of water. Martha took a sip.

"Thank you," she whispered.

Peggy crouched down in front of Martha and placed her hand on Martha's. "Martha, I am so sorry for your loss," Peggy said. "Vivian was a wonderful lady."

The three of us huddled together and cried. We passed around the box of Kleenex, dabbing at wet eyes and runny noses. When there seemed to be no more tears left, Peggy and I walked Martha to Vivian's room and helped her pack up Vivian's things. There wasn't much to pack. Everything she owned fit into three cardboard boxes: costume jewelry, lavender talcum powder, books, and a photo album so old that the yellowed black-and-white pictures curled out of the tiny black triangles that were supposed to hold them in place. I flipped open the green leather cover of the photo album. On one of the pages was an eight-by-ten, sepia-colored photograph of Vivian in her twenties and another young woman standing next to her in a field of high grass with a beautiful black stallion in the background. Both women were dressed in dungarees and button-down, plaid shirts.

"Wow, look at this," I said.

Peggy and Martha came over and looked at the picture.

"That's Vivian and me on vacation at a dude ranch in Colorado," Martha said.

"A dude ranch? Vivian? Miss I-have-to-wear-the-turquoise-brace-let-with-the-silver-necklace-or-I-can't-go-down-to-the-dining-room Vivian?" I asked.

Martha chuckled. "Yes, one and the same. You'd be surprised if you knew some of the things our girl used to do in her younger days."

Martha took the photo album from me and flipped a few more pages and then stopped. A warm smile crossed her lips. "I forgot this picture was in here," she whispered. I looked over Martha's stooped shoulder at the picture. It was a photograph taken in a smoky night club of a young Vivian and Martha, their faces shiny with excitement, sporting pageboy hair cuts and dressed in identical men's pin-striped suits. They were laughing and smiling as they held each other close, posing for the camera.

"This was taken in a speakeasy in Harlem the summer Vivian and I spent in Greenwich Village after graduating from college," Martha said. "I remember that night like it was yesterday." Martha ran her hand over the photograph to bring back the moment.

Seeing that picture stirred something in me. Greenwich Village? Could Vivian and Martha have been more than friends? I banished the thought from my mind. These were two very nice, very proper, church-attending, spinster schoolteachers. What was I thinking?

"You and Vivian go back a long time," Peggy said, breaking the silence and my reverie. She picked up one of Vivian's' sweaters, folded it, and put in one of the boxes.

"Yes, all the way back to elementary school," Martha said. "We were the first girls in our families to go to college. Both of us wanted to be teachers. We even taught in the same school for a while. Vivian liked teaching the primary grades, but I preferred high school."

"What subjects did you teach?" Peggy asked.

"English literature," Martha said proudly. "Vivian loved literature, too. We both loved to read." The thought of their afternoon ritual brought new tears back to Martha's eyes, and she quickly turned her attention back to packing.

Most of the contents of the boxes were the books that Martha had read to Vivian during their afternoon visits: John Steinbeck, Edna St. Vincent Millay, and Willa Cather were some of Vivian's favorite authors. When we were finished packing up Vivian's things, Martha took one last look around Vivian's room.

"She didn't want calling hours," Martha said with a wet sigh. "I guess we will just have a small graveside service."

"I'll call the funeral home and make sure they know that," I said, closing the lid on a box of Vivian's clothes.

Peggy and I carried the boxes downstairs and helped load the car. "Are you going to be alright?" I asked, closing the trunk on Martha's gold Oldsmobile Delta Eighty-Eight. It was a tank of a car and I wondered how such a tiny lady could see over the steering wheel.

Martha nodded. "You girls did a wonderful job taking care of her. I know she appreciated everything you did for her, especially you,

Mina. She had a soft spot in her heart for you, dear," Martha reached up and touched my cheek.

My throat twisted. "I cared about her very much," I paused. "I will miss her terribly." Peggy and I hugged Martha good-bye. "Don't be a stranger," I said. "Stop by any time."

Martha drove off and Peggy and I headed back to the second floor. We were already an hour behind schedule, but that didn't seem to matter. We returned to the med room where I finished pouring the morning round of medication and Peggy filled out the vital sign list. As we completed our final checks, there was a knock on the door. Miss Jacobs, the shift supervisor, was standing just outside the med room with a nurse I had never seen before.

"Mina and Peggy, this is Regan Martin. She is one of the new nurses we've hired and today is her first day. She will be spending the entire shift with you today."

This girl could be the poster child for nursing. Her glossy, light brown hair was pulled back tightly into a bun and a white, freshly blocked nurse's cap sat upon the crown of her head. Her makeup was applied impeccably, her uniform dress crisply pressed, and her clinic shoes were pristine white—not stained with prune juice, Betadine, and applesauce like mine and Peggy's.

"Hello," I said, extending my hand to her. She shook it briefly. Her hand was cold and clammy. Then quickly stuffed her hand to the pocket of her stiff uniform. This woman was a walking contradiction. She may have looked the part, but her whole demeanor, especially her large blue eyes gave away her inexperience and uneasiness.

"Regan is a graduate nurse from St. Anne's Nursing School. She graduated with a four-point-o grade average. We are very lucky to have her on board here at our nursing home," Miss Jacobs boasted.

Regan's gaze never lifted from the floor.

"Four-point-o average—that's pretty impressive," I said, trying to make conversation. She did not reply, only nodded and drove her hands deeper into her pockets.

"I trust you and Peggy will show Regan the proper protocols to be followed on this unit," Miss Jacobs said over her shoulder as she walked from the nurses' station to the elevator, clipboard in hand.

Peggy and I looked at each other as the elevator doors yawned open and Jacobs stepped through them. Hearing the elevator doors close behind her, we burst out into wild laughter.

Our laughter seemed to startle Regan. She stepped back, almost hitting her head on the mug rack that hung above the intercom.

"Oh, honey, we're not laughing at you," Peggy said.

Regan blinked eyes wider then before.

"We're laughing at the thought that management would want Mina and me to influence an impressionable new grad like yourself. You see, management doesn't always agree with our rendering of the nursing practice. Isn't that right Mina?"

"That's right," I answered. But Regan obviously had no idea what we were talking about. I felt I owed her an explanation to make sure she wouldn't be too worried about working with us.

"See, Peggy and I are known as the 'dynamic duo.' We practice 'an unorthodox style of nursing,' at least according to administration. All that really means is that we treat all our patients as people, no matter how senile, or combative, or comatose they may be. We care for them as if they were our own family members. So, sometimes we go a little off the protocol we are supposed to be teaching you."

"Isn't that right, Peg?"

"Uh-huh. Just a little off protocol . . . not much," Peggy said with a giggle.

Regan's eyes remained blank. By the look on Regan's face, she didn't approve of our candor. I looked over at Peggy and then back at Regan. Peggy followed my gaze and shrugged her shoulders. "I wonder how long this one will last?" Peggy whispered as she followed me into the med room with an armload of medicine cups and straws.

I pushed the medication cart out into the nurses' station. Peggy was off taking vital signs and checking on our more critical patients. Regan was standing in the far corner with her arms wrapped tightly around her abdomen as if she had a stomachache. After the trauma of losing Vivian this morning, I wasn't quite in the mood to babysit this uptight girl for the entire shift.

"Are you okay?" I asked Regan.

She nodded. "I'm a little nervous, this is my first real nursing job," she said.

"I was a wreck my first few days here too. It's okay to be nervous," I assured her. "Why don't you come with me while I pass out the first round of medication? You can meet the patients and watch what I do. If you have any questions, just ask."

"Okay," she answered softly, and then helped me load the assortment of juices we served during each medication pass: cranberry juice, orange juice, and prune juice. Prune juice was by far the favorite among the residents and the least popular among the nurse's aides. Once the cart was loaded we headed down the hall to room 201, Sara Antonelli's room.

"We are responsible for taking care of forty of the sickest patients in the nursing home. We have patients with anything from mild confusion, to Alzheimer's, to coma. So, right out of nursing school, this job is intimidating," I said as I popped Mrs. Antonelli's Serentil from the unit dose card into the small white soufflé cup.

Regan nodded, but the look of uneasiness never left her face.

"But, it's really not that hard. It's basically doing things at certain times each day. Medications are passed out at specific times each day. Treatments are done at the same time each day. The residents like the routine and it's easier for us, too."

Regan followed ten steps behind me as I entered Mrs. Antonelli's room.

"Good morning, Mrs. Antonelli, how are you today?" I said.

"*Mezzo-mez,*" she said, a frown clouding her normally cheery face.

"What's wrong Mrs. Antonelli? Does something hurt?" I asked.

"No . . . not so much hurta . . . I haven't mova my bowels in two days," she said rubbing her rotund belly.

"Oh . . . okay, wait here, I'll get you something that will help."

"No en-e-ma!" she shouted after me.

"No enema," I said over my shoulder, as I walked back into the hall.

I returned to the med cart, with Regan in tow, and pulled out the thirty-two ounce, cobalt-blue bottle of Phillips' Milk of Magnesia. I poured two tablespoons worth of the thick white liquid into a plastic medicine cup and handed it to Regan. "Hold this for me while I pour her some prune juice."

Regan followed me back into Mrs. Antonelli's room carrying the cupful of Phillips' Milk of Magnesia.

"Mrs. Antonelli, this is Regan. She's a new nurse. She's going to be working with us today."

Mrs. Antonelli's face turned back to its normal friendliness. "A-lo," she said and smiled brightly.

"Hello," Regan said. "It's nice to meet you."

Sticking to the protocol, I checked Mrs. Antonelli's name band even though I had been taking care of her medications for well over a year now. I handed her the soufflé cup. She popped the tiny red pill into her mouth and downed it with a big gulp of prune juice. Regan handed her the medicine cup of milk of magnesia. "This will help you move your bowels," Regan said, timidly.

Mrs. Antonelli looked up at me for reassurance and I nodded. She tossed back the milk of magnesia, swallowing all of it in one gulp. She wiped her lips on the sleeve of her housecoat and handed the empty cup back to Regan.

"Taank you," she said. "You seem a like a nice girrl . . . and pretty too," Mrs. Antonelli said to Regan. And for the first time that day, Regan smiled.

Regan and I returned to the med cart. "If she doesn't move her bowels this morning, we'll give her some warmed up prune juice with her snack this afternoon," I said, pushing the cart forward to the next room.

"Why not warm up the prune juice and give it to her now?" Regan asked.

"Because it would be too harsh on her system with the milk of magnesia we gave her. She has horrible hemorrhoids. I don't want them to flare up causing her even more discomfort. Plus, she doesn't get around too well. I don't want her breaking a hip trying to rush to the bathroom."

"They didn't teach us this in nursing school," Regan said.

"I know. I think I got more of an education working here than in the three years I spent in nursing school. We take care of these people

"Mina, the hospital is on line two," the unit secretary's voice boomed over the intercom.

"I have to take this call. Do you feel confident enough to finish these last two rooms by yourself?" I asked Regan. "Mr. Armstrong and Mr. Miller are very cooperative; I don't think you will have a problem."

"I'll be fine," Regan replied.

"If you come across something you're not sure about, wait until I get back and I'll help you," I hollered over my shoulder as I hurried down the hallway to take the call.

The hospital was calling about a patient I had sent to the hospital the night before with chest pain and shortness of breath. The patient was on alternating doses of Digoxin, and they didn't know if she was due for a dose today. I pulled out her chart and gave them the information they needed.

Heading back down the hall I noticed the medication cart was abandoned at the end of the hall. I looked into Mr. Miller's room when I reached the doorway—no Regan. I turned around and looked into Mr. Armstrong's room—still no Regan.

I yanked on the cart to pull it back to the nurses' station when I found Regan crouched behind it on the floor. Regan's arms were wrapped tight around her abdomen again. She was rocking on her heels, as if she was in terrible pain.

I crouched down next to her. "Are you alright?" I asked. I could see the tears brimming in her eyes.

"I gave Mr. Armstrong his sleeping pill instead of his Micro-K," she blurted out. "The capsules looked almost identical." She buried her face in her hands, muffling her now uninhibited sobs. I stood up and pulled out Mr. Armstrong's medication drawer, and sure enough, there was the orange and white Micro-K capsule, still in its cellophane package. The package, which formerly contained his Dalmane, lay opened and discarded in the small trash bin, which sat atop of the medication cart.

"Regan, it's okay," I said, touching her shoulder in reassurance. Intense feelings of affection swept through my body. This seemed inappropriate and I drew my hand away. Regan may have been uptight, but she seemed so vulnerable too. I wasn't at all upset and not the least bit worried about Mr. Armstrong. I knew the sleeping pill would not harm him; the effects of it would wear off in an hour or two. I was worried about Regan.

"How could I have been so stupid?" Regan said. "They're going to fire me for this, won't they? Oh God, what am going I tell my parents?" Regan was beside herself. I grabbed her by her elbows and pulled her to her feet.

"Regan, listen to me. Giving Mr. Armstrong his sleeping pill early isn't going to hurt him. He'll probably just take an extra long nap this morning. Really, it's—it was an honest mistake. No one is going to fire you over this. Med errors happen."

Her sobbing subsided and she finally slid her hands down from her face, which was wet with tears and melting mascara.

"Really?" she said relief in her voice.

"Yes, really . . . I mean, this is a medication error, so I do have to call his doctor and we have to write up an incident report, but he'll be okay and you won't have to find another—"

I barely got my last sentence out, when she threw her arms around my neck and hugged me tight. "Thank you, thank you. I'll double-check . . . no, I'll triple-check next time, I promise," she said into my shoulder, which was now warm and wet with her tears, snot, and mascara. "Are you sure he will be okay?" she asked again, looking up at me, tears glistening on her long lashes.

Regan's shimmering blue eyes and the vulnerability I saw there touched my heart. I felt an uneasy twinge in the pit of my stomach. My heart fluttered and I couldn't speak. I grabbed her by the shoulders to unlock our embrace. I hadn't been this uncomfortable since the locker room incident in high school when I stepped naked into the shower stall not knowing that Christine Wentworth was still in there showering. After that I couldn't bring myself to look Christine in the eye ever again. I shook the embarrassing memory from my head.

Finally, I found my voice: "Really kid, you gotta get a grip. You don't have to be a rocket scientist to do this job; you just have to use a little common sense."

She stepped back, took a deep breath, and closed her eyes, apparently trying to pull herself together. A few seconds later she opened her eyes, a look of horror on her face.

"What?" I asked.

"Oh my God, look what I've done to your uniform?" she said, pointing at the smeary stain over my left shoulder. "I am so sorry . . ." Regan said and pulled a handful of Kleenex from the dispenser on top of the med cart, and dabbed at the hideous mess.

"It's okay," I said, taking the Kleenex from her and pushing her hand away. I tried to wipe out the stain, but it had already dried.

When I returned the cart to the nurses' station at the end of rounds, Peggy looked up from her charting and did a double take.

"What happened to your uniform?" she asked.

"Aw, nothing . . . must have brushed up against something," I answered, too embarrassed to tell her the truth.

Regan entered the nurses' station close behind me. Peggy looked up again, and with a startled expression noticed that Regan's eyes were red and swollen and her once perfectly applied makeup smeared all over her face. She looked like Tammy Faye Baker caught in a downpour.

Peggy glared at me suspiciously, obviously thinking I had something to do with all this, and I'm sure she was afraid I was going to drag her into something that would need a lot of explaining and hours of paperwork. I turned away from her. What was there to say anyway?

Still ignoring Peggy, I picked up the phone and dialed Harold's doctor's number to report the med error. Dr. Reynolds picked up on the third ring. I explained to him what happened. He didn't yell like a lot of the docs did when we called them with errors. He said the effects would wear off in a few hours. He told me to increase Harold's fluids to ease the effects of the sleeping pill. Then he gave me a one-time order for another sleeping pill tonight just in case Harold needed it.

When I hung up the phone, Peggy redirected her gaze toward me, obviously still looking for an explanation. With my eyes I silently begged her not to ask. She didn't.

Chapter Two

"Rough day?" Sean asked, peering up over top of the newspaper as I trudged into the living room of our third floor apartment. The constant report and static of his police scanner announced a 10-33 (alarm drop) at the Giant Eagle on Fifth and Main.

I smiled wearily at him as I kicked off my clinic shoes and tossed them in the bottom of the coat closet. "What makes you think I had a rough day?"

"You look like hell . . . and what's that all over your uniform? It's not shit again, is it?"

"No, it's not. I had to break in a new nurse today. Her first day on the job and she already went to pieces."

"That doesn't sound good. What happened?" Sean asked.

"She gave one of the patients his sleeping pill at nine this morning."

"She sounds like a real genius."

"I know. She really freaked out about it too. Started blubbering. That's what this is, her mascara."

"How come it's all over you?"

I knew what he was getting at, and instead of an answer, I just gave him an exasperated look.

"Is she cute?" I knew he was teasing me, and so I played along.

"Sean! The stuff that goes through your head sometimes is . . . is sick."

"You know, two girls together . . . that's a big fantasy for a lot of guys."

"One of your fantasies?" I asked, only half joking this time.

He laughed and returned to his paper. I breathed a sigh of relief.

The living room carpet was littered with newspapers, dirty dishes from Sean's little after-work snacks, which would be a three-course

The Choice
Published by The Haworth Press, Inc., 2007. All rights reserved.
doi:10.1300/5791_02

meal for anyone else, and a couple of empty Bud Light cans. I knew that I had left a clean apartment that morning when I went to work.

I kicked a path through the newspapers to the dining room table, where I shrugged off my backpack. It hit the floor with a thud.

"How was your day?" I asked.

"Busy. I arrested a shoplifter in the mall who tried to steal three hundred dollars worth of Calvin Klein underwear by putting all of it on under his clothes."

"People just amaze me," I said as I unpacked my backpack.

"We also had a little four-year-old girl missing. She strayed away from her mom in Sears. We found her wading in the center fountain, collecting the pennies that lay on the bottom."

"Wow, I bet the mother was terrified."

"Yes, frantic. There are a lot of lunatics out there. We were lucky we found her before someone took her. She's a really cute kid."

"What a blessing that you found her," I said, feeling very proud of Sean.

"Meen . . . ?"

"Uh-huh?" I answered, pulling the spaghetti-sauce-stained Tupperware out of my backpack. When I tossed it into the sink some of the sauce accidentally splattered on my uniform. *This uniform is ready for the garbage* I thought. I caught myself smiling, and didn't quite know why.

"When are we going to have one of our own?" Sean's question brought me back.

"Our own what?"

"A kid. When are we going to have a kid of our own?"

The question sent shockwaves of terror through my body. I didn't want kids. Not yet.

"Uh . . . aren't you supposed to be working undercover next week?" I asked, trying to change the subject.

"Yes," he answered, with a hint of exasperation in his voice. He knew I was avoiding his question, again.

"Drug task force?"

"Uh-huh. Headquarters is adding a new officer for this assignment."

"Do I know him?"

"Her," Sean said from behind the safety of his newspaper as if trying to slip the information by me.

"You're kidding! They are hooking you up with a female officer?"

"Uh-huh," Sean said, still trying not to make a big deal of it.

"What's her name?" I asked, curious.

"Rosetti . . . Rosemary Rosetti. She's a sergeant. Transferred to our department from Cleveland PD"

"Why would a sergeant from Cleveland come to a rinky-dink town like ours?"

"I'm not sure. Something about her having family here. Her mother, I think, is ill. I don't know."

"Is she cute?" I teased.

Sean laughed.

"Do you mind if we order in tonight? I'm exhausted and really don't feel like cooking."

"Meen, the last time you cooked was . . . let me think . . . the first week we got back from our honeymoon. Why should tonight be any different?"

I laughed to myself. He was right. Why should tonight be different than any other night in the past six years? Although I am Italian, the cooking gene must have skipped my generation.

"Great. How about Chinese?" I asked. "I'll buy, if you go pick it up."

"Fine. You call and order it," he said from behind his newspaper. "Get me my usual," he said folding the paper into quarter sections and set it on the floor.

I dialed the number for the Asian Moon and ordered sweet and sour chicken, vegetable lo mein, and two egg rolls for Sean. For myself I ordered the usual lunch portion of chicken and Chinese vegetables over steamed rice.

"It'll be ready in fifteen minutes," I shouted from the bedroom where I tossed my dirty uniform into the trash can and pulled on my terry cloth bathrobe. I opened my purse and pulled out a twenty-dollar bill for dinner.

I handed Sean the twenty. "Thanks for going," I said.

He took it from me, and then pulled me down on the couch beside him.

"I'm sorry you had a tough day."

"That's not even the worst of it. Vivian died last night."

"Oh, Meen, I'm sorry. I know how much you liked her."

He pulled me close and I buried my face into his neck. A trace of his Polo cologne still lingered. The familiar smell was so comforting.

"I still can't believe it," I said, feeling the tears starting to well up again in my eyes. "She was all alone."

He held me tight, stroking my hair, wiping away my tears, as if trying to lift away my sadness for Vivian. I smiled at him through damp eyes. I knew I was lucky to have someone like him to come home to.

Sean went to pick up our dinner and returned just a few minutes later. He inhaled his food as if he was afraid someone was going to take it away from him—a trait you can find in most police officers. Their explanation is that they never know when or what the next call will be or when they will get the chance to eat again. It also never ceases to amaze me how much food he can consume without gaining so much weight as an ounce. Most people, including me, would kill to have his metabolism. As soon as he was finished he returned to the living room to watch *Jeopardy!* while I cleaned up the kitchen. We had our routine. It was comfortable, like a favorite old pair of Levi's. I couldn't imagine my life any other way, at least not until that day.

Although we had only been married six years, Sean and I had weathered many storms, which managed to only bring us closer. Our first home was a two-bedroom apartment, which we shared with Sean's eighty-eight year old grandmother, Henrietta. The arrangement was that Henrietta would live with us, I would take care of her, and Sean would get to keep her $284.00 Social Security check. It helped pay the rent while Sean was still working at the gas station for just a little over minimum wage.

Being eighteen, newly married, and the primary caregiver of an obnoxious old woman was no easy task. At night Henrietta took enough medication to sedate an elephant, but the meds never seemed to touch her. She was up at all hours of the night. Each morning around 3:00 a.m. she would get up and stumble around in the hallway. Occasionally she'd mistake our bedroom for the bathroom and subsequently would take a crap in our clothes hamper—not necessarily the notion of wedded bliss I had pictured.

Three months after moving in with us, Henrietta suddenly became ill and passed away. Cause of death: hyperglycemia, probably brought on by the two jelly donuts she'd eat for breakfast each morning. After Henrietta's funeral we moved out of the apartment and into the renovated four-room apartment in the basement of my mother-in-law's house. Out of the frying pan and into the fire!

We lived there for four excruciatingly long years, enduring everything from having to bail muddy water that seeped through the walls of our bedroom every spring to being awakened at 3:00 a.m. by the thud-thud-thud of Sean's mother and her boyfriend having sex in the room above our bedroom. This was enough agony to motivate me to get my nursing degree and get the hell out of there. Sean and I stuck together through the whole ordeal and felt liberated when a week after my graduation from nursing school I got my job at the nursing home and we moved into the apartment we live in today. Two months later, Sean took the civil service test, passed it even without the military points, and was hired by the city police department within six months. Our hard work had paid off. Things had been great ever since.

Most couples at this point in their marriages would be eager to start a family, but I have to admit, the thought of it terrified me. Before we got married Sean and I decided not to have children right away. A good decision, I thought, since we were both so young when we got married. I always thought that in time, when we got more settled, I'd be ready to have a child. But I wasn't. Not that I don't like kids, and I know Sean likes them as well, it is great watching him play with the other officers' kids during the family picnics, but the whole experience, the enormous responsibility, the lack of freedom, let alone the lack of sleep didn't appeal to me one bit. It's nice to be able to play with the kids knowing that someone else will take them home while you return to your nice and quiet apartment. This is a luxury you can't indulge in if they are your own.

It was ten thirty when Sean clicked off the TV and came to bed. My eyes were blurring, as I read the same sentence in *The Summer of '42* three times. It was time to close the book. I reached over to turn off the light on the nightstand and snuggled up to Sean, who got into bed next to me.

"Good night," Sean whispered and kissed me softly on the lips. His strong hand slid over my belly and circled my waist. As he pulled me close, I could feel the firmness of his erection pressing against me: no doubt, a blunt invitation.

"Good night," I whispered, then turned on my side praying for sleep to come.

Sean moved his hand up and cupped my breast through the thin cotton fabric of my nightshirt. I could feel his warm breath on my neck as he held me close. Again, like a secret sign language, he pressed his erection into the back of my thigh. I tried to ignore him, but found it impossible to do so when he started kissing my neck. Pleasant jolts raced through my body, and thoughts of the Regan flickered in my mind. My insides began to warm.

Chapter Three

As I crossed the parking lot of the nursing home on my way to work the next morning I was nearly mowed down by a speeding candy-apple red Mustang. The driver slammed on the brakes, showering me with gravel and dirt, narrowly missing me.

"Oh my God, I am so sorry!" the driver said from behind the wheel. I shaded my eyes and peered through the windshield to see who it was. Regan slowly backed the car away from me, and carefully maneuvered it into a nearby parking space.

"Where are you going in such a hurry?" I asked watching the dust settle around me.

"I didn't want to be late," she said as she climbed out of her car.

"I am glad to see you came back, even if you were trying to kill me in the process." The adrenaline rush was subsiding now. All that remained was a dull headache. "Honestly, I wasn't sure you would come back, you seemed pretty upset yesterday."

"I was," she said. "But I put too much time and effort in becoming a nurse to give up after only one day," she said. "Plus, I have major school loans to pay off; I sure can't do that just lying on a beach somewhere."

"Well, maybe today will be better. Sunday's are always quieter. Some of the residents go home for a few hours," I said.

"I hope so," she answered, smiling faintly.

Regan and I rode up in the elevator together. She fidgeted with her uniform, obviously uncomfortable in my presence, or maybe she was just uncomfortable in general. I was thankful that Peggy would be working again today as well. We worked well together, and whatever catastrophe the new grad stumbled into today, Peggy and I could surely handle it.

The Choice
Published by The Haworth Press, Inc., 2007. All rights reserved.
doi:10.1300/5791_03

The elevator doors slid open, and as I stepped off on to the nursing unit the fetid stench of human feces slapped me in the face. This was something I just couldn't get used to, even after all my time working here.

I stashed my backpack in my locker, retrieved my notebook, and sat down at the desk to receive the shift report. Regan sat down as well, flipping through the pages of her notebook. Peggy hadn't arrived yet. She was probably running late.

"Peggy call off?" I asked Brenda as she sat down to give report.

"Not that I'm aware of," she said. "Do you mind if we get started? I've got to be at graduation by nine thirty. My niece is graduating from high school."

"No, go ahead, I'll catch Peggy up when she gets here," I said and Brenda began report.

"Our census is thirty-six, room 201, Mrs. Antonelli—"

"Hold it," I interrupted. "Thirty-six? Jesus, Bren, you lost another one? I wouldn't be surprised if I came to work one day and found you standing at the front desk wearing a black robe and carrying a sickle."

"It wasn't me this time, it was afternoon shift. Harold Armstrong died at seven thirty, just before the supper trays were picked up. They found him face down in his pudding."

Shock shot through me—not only was I upset about Harold's death, I had forgotten about the incident report. I had never filled it out. Jacobs was going to have my hide. I glanced over at Regan—her eyes were wide with terror. She bolted up from the desk, covering her mouth with her hand. Before I could even get up she ran behind the nurses' station into the staff restroom and slammed the door shut.

"What's wrong with her?" Brenda asked.

"She gave Harold his sleeping pill at nine o'clock in the morning yesterday, thinking it was his Micro-K," I answered.

"Well, the capsules do look alike," Brenda said, nodding with understanding.

"Yes, I know, I told her that. She still took it pretty hard. I also told her that he would just take an extra long nap. I surely didn't think he would be taking 'the big dirt nap.'"

"That's funny, afternoon shift never mentioned a med error or an incident report," Brenda said.

Guilt flushed my face. "I forgot to write up it up," I said, nervously clearing my throat. "Things were so hectic here yesterday, I totally forgot about it," I said.

"You better let the supervisor know, this could put you and Regan in a lot of hot water. It might look like you are trying to cover for her. You know how administration feels about that—Jacobs is going to be pissed," Brenda said.

Brenda was right. I immediately put a page in for the supervisor. A few minutes later the phone rang. "This is Jacobs. Somebody paged me?"

"Sorry to bother you on a Sunday Miss Jacobs . . . it's regarding a med error that occurred yesterday morning." I knew Miss Jacobs's thin lips were tightening in disapproval. "Regan, the new hire you brought up yesterday, gave one of the patients his Dalmane at nine in the morning, thinking it was his Micro-K."

"No one said anything about any med errors occurring yesterday. Where is the incident report?" she asked, obviously irritated.

"I forgot to write one up ma'am . . . it was pretty crazy here yesterday . . . it totally slipped my mind," I said.

"Mina, that's not like you. Is the patient okay?" she asked.

"Well, he was when I left yesterday, but he died in the evening. The patient we're talking about is Harold Armstrong."

"Mina, this doesn't look good! Did you at least notify Doc Reynolds of the med error?" she asked.

Doc Reynolds was the medical director of the nursing home. He took care of all the residents at the nursing home as well as most of the people in town. "Yes ma'am. Doc said Harold was getting such a small dose of the sleeping pill that taking it early in the day wouldn't hurt him. He said the effects would wear off in a few hours but if Harold ran into problems to let him know and he would come in to see him. He even gave me a one-time order for an additional dose for Harold that night," I said.

"That still doesn't mean that this won't be looked into. The fact that the incident report wasn't done until twenty-four hours after the actual incident is, in itself, enough to trigger an investigation. Don't you think it looks a little suspicious when the incident report shows up after the patient's death, Mina?"

"Yes, ma'am."

"Mina, I'm disappointed in you."

"I'm sorry ma'am."

"Mina, make sure everything is charted, especially your phone call to Doc. And get that incident report on my desk by the end of your shift. Let's hope nothing comes of this," she said. "Do you understand me?"

I nodded into the phone. Of course she couldn't see that.

"Mina, is that clear?" Her voice was getting testier by the minute.

"Yes, Miss Jacobs. That's clear."

"Good. Now please pay a little more attention to what's going on up there. You're supposed to be setting an example for the new grad," she warned.

"Yes, ma'am," I said, and then quietly replaced the phone in its cradle. My head was pounding now.

"You in trouble?" Brenda asked.

"Yes. Jacobs is furious."

"How about Regan?"

"Good question," I answered, suddenly realizing that Regan was still barricaded in our bathroom. Brenda and I cautiously approached the door. On the other side we could hear her retching. I tapped on the door lightly.

"Are you okay in there?"

There was more retching, then the flushing of the toilet, and finally the sound of water running into the sink. Slowly the door creaked open and Regan emerged.

"Are you okay?" I asked again. She looked up at me with red-rimmed eyes, wiping her mouth with a wet paper towel.

"You said he would be okay."

"I know—you didn't kill him," I said

"Of course I killed him. I gave him the wrong medicine—now he's dead. I killed him."

"You did not kill him. Sometimes these things happen. It was just his time. Trust me, you had nothing to do with his death. I talked to his doctor yesterday, right after the med error. He said Mr. Armstrong would be fine. He even gave me an order for another sleeping pill for him at bedtime," I said. "If he thought another sleeping pill would hurt Harold do you think he would order him another one?"

Regan blew her nose and then pushed by me on her way back to the desk to hear the rest of the report. As we were finishing up, the phone rang. There was no unit secretary on Sunday, so I answered it.

"Second floor, Thomas, RN."

"Mina, it's Peggy. I am going to be late. My son Johnny jumped off the back porch this morning playing Superman and I think he broke his ankle." *Wonderful,* I thought, *could this day get any better?*

"When do you think you'll be in?" I asked.

"That depends on the emergency room," she said.

"Guess not at all then," I mumbled under my breath. The average wait in the emergency room was anywhere from three to six hours. "Regan is here again . . ." I said and looked over at her, sitting at the desk, gnawing on the cuticle around her thumb. "I'm sure we can muddle through without you today," I said without much confidence.

"Are you sure?" Peggy asked, I'm sure remembering the fiasco of yesterday.

"Yes, I'm sure," I said into the receiver.

"Thanks Mina, I owe you," Peggy said just before the receiver clicked off in my ear.

"Well, I guess it's just you and me today," I said to Regan as I hung up the phone.

"I feel sick," she said.

"I know, Regan, but I really need your help today. I can't do this alone," I said.

"Okay. What do you want me to do?" she asked. I could tell she was really trying to pull herself together.

"You make out the treatment sheet, and I'll pass out the meds and be in charge. How does that sound?" I asked.

"Okay, I guess," she said.

"We'll get through this. It is only eight hours, right?" I said, trying to convince myself as much as Regan.

I showed Regan how to fill out a treatment sheet then went into the med room to prepare for the first medication pass. Alberta, the nurse's aide came into the med room.

"Mina, could you check Rosie in two eighteen? She says she's having chest pains."

"Sure," I draped my stethoscope around my neck and headed down the hall to Rosie's room.

When I got to room 218, Rosie Simpson was having difficulty breathing and her face was ashen gray.

"I don't feel so good, nurse," Rosie said. "Like I need to . . ."

No sooner had she tried to get the word out, the vomit came with it. She upchucked copious amounts of undigested food with tendrils of blood streaked through it into the wastebasket. I checked her pulse: it was 130 and weak. I wrapped the blood pressure cuff around her chubby left arm to check her pressure: it was 70/20.

"Rosie, let's get you into bed and give you a little oxygen," I said, turning on the flow meter above Rosie's bed and slipping the plastic nasal cannula into her nostrils. I took Rosie's cool, clammy hand and helped her out of the chair. She stood up.

"Nurse, I don't feel so goooood . . ." She said and let out a long, low burp. Her body went limp and her knees buckled beneath her. I caught her before she hit the floor, and heaved her 180-pound, limp body onto the bed.

"Rosie, Rosie, are you okay?" I asked shaking her.

No response. I rubbed the middle of her sternum with my knuckle. Still no response. "Rosie?" I put my stethoscope on her chest; she had stopped breathing and her heartbeat was erratic. Apparently the day *could* get worse.

I pushed the emergency call button. "I need help in two eighteen!" I yelled. "And bring the crash cart!"

I heard frantic footsteps and the red Craftsman toolbox that served as our crash cart rumble down the hall. Regan entered the room cautiously after Alberta, who pushed the crash cart next to Rosie's bed. I was cursing under my breath that today of all the days I was stuck with an inexperienced new grad.

"Alberta, call nine one one!" I ordered. "Tell them we have a seventy-two-year-old female in respiratory arrest. Regan, I need your help here. Do you know how to use an Ambu bag?"

Regan shook her head, her eyes wide with fear.

"Okay, I need you to learn fast. Get the Ambu bag out from under the crash cart and start giving Rosie some breaths."

I put my stethoscope back onto to Rosie's chest. Her heartbeats were few and far between, and then nothing. I began CPR compressions immediately.

Regan fumbled with the safety lock on the crash cart, finally cutting it off with her shiny new bandage scissors. "Tilt her head back to open up her airway then put the mask over her mouth and nose." Regan did as instructed. "Okay—good. Now squeeze the bladder, then release it, squeeze and release . . . squeeze and release to a count of a breath every two seconds."

I continued full compressions on Rosie's fleshy chest. It seemed like hours since we had called 911, but I knew it couldn't have been more than a few minutes. I stopped for a minute and placed my fingers against Rosie's neck to see if her pulse had returned: it had not, and so I resumed CPR. Regan, positioned at Rosie's head as I had instructed, diligently squeezed the black rubber bladder of the Ambu bag, keeping Rosie breathing until the squad arrived. I don't know who was paler, Regan or Rosie.

The ambulance finally arrived. Two male paramedics rushed into Rosie's room, dragging a metal gurney and EKG monitor behind them. I gave them an update on her medical history and the event that was unfolding before us. One of the paramedics attached three leads to Rosie's exposed chest. I could see that my compressions were paying off as the green-lighted screen came alive with the beep of Rosie's heartbeat. I stopped compressions again to check her status, but as soon as I stopped the flashing green line faded from a healthy QRS complex to a wavy, flat line. The alarm sounded and I again resumed CPR. One of the paramedics started a saline IV in Rosie's right arm, and pulled four vials of injectable medication from their emergency pack. The first injection they gave Rosie was atropine. Five minutes after the atropine was given, I stopped compressions for the third time. This time the flashing green light did not fade. Rosie was going to make it.

Regan continued squeezing the Ambu bag, still assisting Rosie with her breathing and practically running alongside the gurney as we wheeled Rosie into the elevator and through the downstairs lobby to the waiting ambulance. On three, the four of us lifted Rosie into the ambulance. Chris, one of the paramedics hopped into the back of the ambulance, taking over the Ambu bag duties from Regan. "Thanks, you did a great job," he said, then pulled the two back doors of the ambulance closed. The ambulance sped away with red lights flashing and siren wailing, leaving Regan and I in its wake.

"Well, so much for Sunday being quiet," I said as I turned to head back up to the floor.

Regan stood frozen, still staring after the ambulance, its siren fading. I suspected she was trying to make sense of the overwhelming feelings you experience following the first time you save someone's life.

"Regan . . . you okay?" I asked.

Her reverie broke and she nodded her head. "Yes, I'm fine," she finally answered.

"You did a good job in there. Not bad for your first arrest," I said.

"Really?"

"Yes. You did great. You kept your head, you did what you were told; you were very helpful. I couldn't have gotten through it without you," I said as we stepped onto the awaiting elevator. And it was true. I couldn't have done it without her.

Regan beamed, her ice-blue eyes sparkled, replacing the fear and apprehension I saw there earlier. "Thanks," she said with a modest air of confidence.

Already an hour behind, we split up to get at least the most important things done. I passed the cardiac meds and antibiotics that were to be given on a more precise schedule, while Regan checked our more complicated dressings.

A few minutes later Regan appeared at my med cart as I finished taking Mrs. Webber's pulse before I gave her her Lanoxin.

"Mina, when I checked Ed Smith's decubitis dressing, I found his bed soaking wet with urine."

"Did you check his catheter?"

"I checked the tubing. There was urine in it, but it was cold to touch."

"That could mean only one of two things—either he was having bladder spasms or his catheter was blocked." Knowing this was one of the skills Regan needed to learn to get through her orientation, I told her to get an irrigation set and a Foley catheter tray from the supply closet. "Let me finish these last two patients and I'll go back with you and we'll see if we can irrigate it. If we can't irrigate it and it's blocked, we'll have to change his catheter."

When I finished giving the last antibiotic, I met Regan back in Ed's room, where she had assembled the equipment I had asked her to get. She also had clean linens to change his bed when we were done. I remember thinking how thoughtful that was.

Regan inserted the syringe as I had instructed and tried to irrigate Ed's catheter, but it wouldn't budge. As I suspected, Ed's catheter was blocked and needed changing.

After helping Regan assemble the equipment she needed for the catheterization procedure, I pulled back the sheet that covered our patient's lower body.

"I have never done this before," Regan said meekly.

"I know. I'm going to help you get through it," I said.

"I know . . . but I have never . . ." Regan said.

"Never what?" I asked.

"I've never touched a penis before," Regan said, a shadow of blush crept over her cheeks.

"Oh . . . well, okay, there is nothing to it," I said. Now I was embarrassed.

In nursing school, female student nurses were not required to catheterize male patients, rationalizing that it was too traumatic to the young female student to have to handle male genitals. I guess they assumed that these girls should not be subjected to having to touch a penis, let alone shove a twenty-five inch piece of rubber tubing into it.

Regan gloved up and laid out her sterile field. The rubber catheter shook in her hand as she tried to apply lubricant to the end.

"Okay, once you get the end lubricated, hold his penis up with your left hand," I said.

Regan took a deep breath and gingerly took hold of her patient's flaccid penis. A small amount of urine dribbled out of the opening onto her sterile glove—she looked up at me in horror.

"That's alright," I said. "You only need one hand to be sterile, and that's the hand you are holding the catheter with." Regan took another deep breath, and then inserted the catheter into Ed's urethra. After shoving the catheter in to the hilt, clear golden yellow urine flowed through the plastic catheter tubing—the sweet sign of success.

"See, you did it!" I said, congratulating Regan on her success.

"I did, didn't I," Regan said, seeming in awe of what she had just accomplished.

"So what did you think?" I asked Regan as I helped her change Ed's bed.

Regan giggled girlishly. "It felt kind of weird, not what I expected," she said.

"Inserting the catheter?"

"No." Regan blushed. "His . . . penis."

"Oh! Well, what did you expect?" I asked.

"Something harder," she answered.

"Harder? The guy's in a coma, for Christ's sake."

"So, I thought they were always hard," she continued.

"My gosh girl, you must have lived a sheltered life. No, they are not hard all the time—a lot of the time, but not all of the time," I said. Both of us were giggling now, our faces pink with embarrassment. I couldn't believe how naive she was. I dragged the dirty linen down to the utility room, shaking my head.

Ten hours later our shift was over. All the treatments were done, all the medications were passed, no medication errors were made, and, most important, no one had died. The incident report on Harold Armstrong was complete and on Miss Jacobs's desk as promised. Regan restocked the med cart while I gave the afternoon shift report.

In the locker room, behind the nurses' station, Regan unfastened the bobby pins in her nurse's cap and shook free a beautiful cascade of honey colored, shoulder length hair. I opened my locker to retrieve my backpack. Pulling it down from the shelf, the backpack fell to the floor, spilling car keys, coupons, tampons, and a bottle of White Shoulders perfume onto the tile floor.

Regan picked up the bottle and unscrewed the top. "Mmm, this stuff smells good," she said, ignoring my frantic scrambling to recover my keys, coupons, and tampons. She dabbed the perfume on both wrists and rubbed them together. The scent of the perfume permeated the air around us. Our eyes met and my heart pounded. *Such an attraction could be trouble,* I thought, and as suddenly as it began Regan looked away.

"Here," she said and handed me the bottle of perfume. "You don't want to forget this."

I took the bottle from her. Heaviness centered in my chest.

Regan placed her nurse's cap in a clear round plastic hat bag and zipped it shut. I finished reloading my backpack and we walked out to the parking lot together.

"Thank you for all your help today," I said as we crossed the parking lot. "This being only your second day . . . you did a great job," I said, and I truly meant it.

Regan stopped and turned to me. "You're welcome. Thank you for being so patient with me. You know, to be honest, I did consider not coming back. I'm glad I did," Regan said.

"I'm glad you came back too," I said. My response surprised me a little, but I wasn't sorry I said it. Butterflies fluttered in my stomach as I watched Regan walk the rest of the way to her car. I found myself looking forward to the next time we would work together. I was still watching her, from the safety of the curb, as she drove away. Tires screeched and gravel sprayed as Regan pulled out of the parking lot and onto the main street. I laughed to myself as I walked down the path to my apartment. Regan's nursing skills had improved in the last twelve hours, but I wasn't so sure about her driving skills.

Chapter Four

What Regan lacked in experience, she made up for in compassion. Regan was very attentive and loving with the patients. She became especially fond of one resident, Opal Crenshaw, who, like a lot of our residents, had outlived their friends and family and therefore did not get any visitors. Opal Crenshaw wasn't your typical nursing home patient. At age eighty-one, she still had a slim figure, and preferred slacks and button-down shirts to housedresses or dusters like the other female residents. Just looking at her you would think she was just as lucid as anyone of us, but her incessant inquiring of "Who's going to milk the goats this morning?" and "Is this where I go to catch the school bus?" gave away her mental status. She was as senile as the day was long.

Regan never tired of answering Opal's incessant questions. She actually seemed happy to answer them, never wanting to miss an opportunity to bring Opal back to the present, even if only for a little bit.

It was not unusual for Regan to arrive at work with a new shirt, a cardigan sweater, or lavender-scented soap for Opal. Before our shift would start, Regan would grab Opal and take her back to her room where Regan would then dress her up in the new stuff she had bought her. The week before, Regan had bought Opal a pink-and-white striped Polo shirt. Regan put it on Opal and turned the collar up, giving Opal a preppy-eighties look. When Opal came to the nurses' station to check on the time she was beaming ear to ear, tugging on the collar to make sure it stayed were Regan had put it.

I really liked how Regan cared for Opal, and lots of other things about her. I looked forward to working with her, as much as I looked forward to working with Peggy. Her nursing style was almost as unorthodox as Peggy's and mine, and we seemed to have developed chemistry.

The Choice
Published by The Haworth Press, Inc., 2007. All rights reserved.
doi:10.1300/5791_04

When Anna Bartoli, one of the part-time nurses, invited us to her daughter's graduation party on a Friday night, I asked Regan to come with me. Regan hadn't planned on attending the event, being new and all, but with a little nudging and a promise that I'd pick her up in Sean's Corvette, she agreed to go.

"Is six thirty okay to pick you up tonight?"

"That's fine," Regan said as she finished applying Fungoid Tincture to Otis Jenkins's thick, gnarled toenails. "Can we stop somewhere and eat before the party? I'll be ravenous by seven o'clock. The hors d'oeuvres and cake they serve at these things never seem to be enough to hold me over," Regan said.

"Regan, we are going to an Italian graduation party. There will be more food than you have ever seen in your life."

"Oh, well, excuse me. I've been to graduation parties, but never an *Italian* graduation party," she replied, rolling her eyes.

We finished up Otis's treatments and helped him back into his wheelchair. Regan plopped his signature black Stetson cowboy hat on his head and he was off to wreak havoc in the resident's lounge.

Otis wasn't a real cowboy, although he liked to tell everyone he was. He was actually a retired high school history teacher from Columbus, Ohio. His wife Cora had died of a stroke a few years ago. Otis was doing fine living alone since Cora's death, until one night he put a kettle of water on the stove to make some tea, and at six the next morning he was awakened by the Columbus fire department hacking away at his front door. Thank God the upstairs neighbor had called them when she smelled the smoke coming from Otis's apartment. Two weeks later, Otis arrived here at the nursing home.

At six thirty sharp I pulled the metallic blue Corvette into Regan's driveway. She came out onto the back porch, wearing a pair of impeccably pressed, pastel pink cotton pants and a crisp white oxford shirt. The white shirt made her tan face look even darker and her ice blue eyes luminous. I felt a twinge in the pit of my stomach. She was so beautiful.

"This car is so cool!" she said as she leaned inside the passenger-side window checking out the interior and exposing a flash of suntanned cleavage and white lace. "Do the T-tops come out?"

I nodded, since finding words to answer her question was impossible right at that moment.

"Cool . . ." Regan said. "Wait here. I'll be right back. I want to bring a jacket."

Regan bounced back into the house and I waited in the car, grateful for the time to pull myself together. I was tugging on the passenger's side T-top when I noticed the curtains moved in the kitchen window. As I turned toward the window I could see a woman wearing large framed glasses peeking through the sheers. I raised my hand to wave hello, but as soon as she saw me she pulled back, leaving the sheers swinging in her wake.

Finally Regan appeared at the back door again with a navy blue Windbreaker draped over her arm.

"Sorry I took so long. My mother was in a very talkative mood. I feel bad leaving her home alone."

"Does your mother wear glasses?" I asked, putting the car into reverse and backing out of the driveway.

"Yes, she wears those huge plastic frames that are way too big for her face . . . why?"

"Because she was peeking through the curtains at me. When I waved hello, she disappeared."

"Really? Come to think about it, she was giving me the third degree about where I was going and who I was going with. You'd have thought I was leaving with a strange guy or something," Regan said with a laugh.

As Regan and I headed down Route 46, "Borderline," one of Madonna's hits was playing on the radio. Regan was dancing in her seat, imitating Madonna doing her song in the video. The warm air rushed through our hair as we cruised down the highway. The scent of Johnson's baby shampoo and Regan's Avon Soft Musk cologne permeated the air. When I looked over in Regan's direction, I felt strangely high. Regan was smiling, her head tossed back, her eyes closed, and the warm late afternoon sun was bathing her face. I couldn't help thinking that she was a beautiful woman, beautiful both inside and out.

Suddenly Regan opened her eyes and caught me looking at her.

"What are you looking at?" Regan asked.

I froze, feeling like a kid caught with her hand in the cookie jar. The heat of embarrassment slowly crept up my neck and into my face.

Regan smiled and then reached over and gave my knee a little squeeze, causing my leg to jump so intensely that I lost control of the car. It swerved left, then right, and we were halfway off the road when I finally regained control.

"Boy, you sure are sensitive," she said, clutching onto the door handle.

My face flushed even more.

Gravel crunched beneath the tires as I pulled the Corvette into a parking space of the Italian-American Club. We got out of the car and headed toward the red brick building at the top of the hill. As we walked up the sidewalk, we passed a row of boccie courts. Several older gentlemen were playing.

"What's this?" Regan asked as we approached the boccie courts.

"Boccie. It's a game of skill. Mostly men play it. See that little ball over there? That's called a pallina. *Pallina* means little ball in Italian. My father used to call me 'scorch of the pallinas' when I was little and misbehaving. He used the word referring to his testicles, see, little ball . . . testicles . . . get it?"

Regan looked over at me in total disgust.

"I guess you had to be there to get it. Anyway, the object of the game is to roll the bigger balls closer to the little ball. The team that gets the closest wins."

As we passed the boccie courts, one of the older gentlemen sporting a red beret on top of his balding head called out, *"Bella, bella."* He was looking toward Regan, smiling a broad toothless grin.

Regan clutched onto my arm as we walked up the stone walk to the party. "What's he saying?" Regan asked.

"Bella means beautiful in Italian," I said. "He thinks you're beautiful."

Regan blushed and for the third time that night. So did I. She smiled at me, then lowered her gaze and let go of my arm as if realizing she had done something inappropriate. The old man was still smiling when we turned back toward him. Regan smiled back at him and he put his hands over his heart.

Both of us laughed. We continued up the walkway to the entrance where the party was in full swing. As we approached the door, Anna saw us.

"Hey, Paesans, you made it," she said pulling both of us into a big bear hug, smothering us with her huge bosom.

"This is quite a party, Bartoli," I shouted so she could hear me over the loud accordion music. In the center of the room, a large circle of people had formed to dance the tarantella. In the middle of the circle was Anna's husband, Vito, twirling a red napkin over his head while spinning to the beat of the music.

"Hey Anna, looks like Veet is really getting into it," I said as we watched Anna's husband lock arms with Anna's Aunt Helen and spin her until they both looked like they were gonna fall down.

"Yes, if he doesn't take it easy I'm afraid the fool is going to have another heart attack," Anna said with a laugh.

The room was packed. A lot of people from work were there. Peggy and her brood were plowing their way through the buffet table. It always amazed me how a tiny woman like Peggy would have such large children. Her three boys, all in their teens, were well over six feet tall.

Anna and Vito both came from large, Italian families, explaining all the laughter and shouting. For some reason Italians cannot speak in a normal tone of voice. I think it's because they come from such large families: they have to all talk at the same time and get louder and louder just to be heard.

"I'm glad you could make it," Anna shouted over the music. She led us further inside. "There is plenty of food and an open bar," she said, gesturing toward the far side of the room where a huge buffet table was set up, containing every type of Italian delicacy you could imagine. "Please, *mangia!*" Anna said, herding us over toward the food. "Oh, wait a minute, let me introduce you to my daughter Jessie, first," Anna said as she parted the crowd of people on the dance floor, finding a willowy, dark-haired girl.

"Jessie, I want you to meet Mina and Regan from work."

"Hello, it's nice to meet you. Congratulations," I said, extending my hand to her.

"Thank you," she said, the words barely audible. She took my hand and delicately shook it.

"Congratulations," Regan said.

Jessie smiled shyly, and then slipped back into the sea of people.

"She's pretty shy," Anna explained. "I think she wants to go into nursing though. She gets a kick out of the stories I tell her about work."

We all laughed, acknowledging that indeed every day seemed to be like an adventure. At a nursing home, you never know what will happen next.

Anna excused herself to attend to the other guests. Regan and I waded through the noisy, crowded room. People of all ages, sizes, and shapes were laughing, singing, and dancing. This was definitely a traditional Italian celebration. The music had changed to a polka and everyone on the dance floor paired up and began moving in the same direction. Older women, dressed in traditional black, were dancing with children, swaying them to and fro to the beat of "Tick Tock Polka." Men and women danced, women and women danced, and a group of little girls, dressed in party dresses the color of Sweetarts, laughed and giggled as they spun in circles flaring their skirts out into tiny crinoline parasols. This was all very familiar to me. It felt like home.

Regan's eyes were wide with amazement as she took in the scene.

"Are you hungry?" I asked, bringing her out of her reverie.

"Starved," she answered.

"Let's see what they have."

We turned toward the buffet table and instinctively I put my hand on the small of Regan's back, guiding her through the crowd. Regan looked over her shoulder, apparently surprised at my gesture.

"What are you doing?" Regan asked.

I snatched my hand away as if I had just touched something hot. "Uh . . . I don't know. Sorry, just a reflex I guess," I said. *Jesus, where did that come from?*

We reached the buffet table, which was actually four tables long, and began filling our plates. The first table contained two large brass kettles of spaghetti and a platter of meatballs and Italian sausage. The next table contained a huge wicker breadbasket overflowing with warm rolls and loaves of freshly baked Italian bread. Next to the breadbasket were sweet red peppers and a platter of braciola, which is an Italian delicacy, made with eggs and flavored bread crumbs, rolled up in chuck steak and cooked in tomato sauce until the steak is so tender it melts in your mouth. The rest of the buffet contained fresh garden salad, cut up cantaloupe wrapped in proscuitto, and at the end, small desert cups filled with spumoni for desert.

"Looks like all the seats are taken," I said, looking over the tables in the crowded room. "Let's see if there is somewhere to sit out back." As we headed toward the back entrance, I grabbed two glasses of Chianti off the bar. I pushed open the wooden screen door with my elbow to reveal a courtyard, overgrown with wild roses and weeds. In the middle of the courtyard was a gray stone bench and a weathered statue of the Blessed Mother.

"Is this okay?" I asked holding the screen door open to let Regan pass through. She brushed passed me, leaving the scent of her perfume in her wake. *She smelled so good.*

"This is fine," she said, tiptoeing her way down the crabgrass-infested brick walk.

We sat on the cool cement bench and started to eat. The sun was making its descent and the sky was turning pink. The air was heavy with the thick scent of roses from the bushes surrounding the statue of the Blessed Mother. The warm breeze gently caressed our skin, and I couldn't remember the last time I felt this good. But I couldn't help wondering if Regan enjoyed being here as much as I did.

"You haven't said much since we've gotten here. Anything wrong?" I asked.

"I've never been to anything like this," she said. "My family is pretty stoic. They would never celebrate anything with this much enthusiasm. And they are definitely not as physical with one another, like these people." Regan said, spearing a leaf of Romaine lettuce with her fork.

"That's how Italian families are," I said. "They are always hugging, or touching, or pinching one another. How do you think I got these cheeks?" I gestured to my face with both hands.

Regan laughed, practically spitting her Chianti across the court-yard. Her eyes sparkled when she laughed. I loved making her laugh. She had a great laugh, and when she smiled, my heart flew.

Our conversation was lively as usual and never seemed to get bor-ing. After we ate, we stayed in the garden, sipped our wine, and en-joyed the sunset. I wanted to know everything I could about Regan Martin and she seemed just as interested in me. But when she con-fided in me that she felt comfortable in her career choice and now wanted to find a nice guy and settle down, I felt a twinge of disap-pointment in the pit of my stomach.

"I've always dreamed how it would be," Regan said with a heavy sigh. "Mr. Right would come along and sweep me off my feet. It would all be so magical and nothing like I have ever felt before. That magical feeling is the key to knowing that that person is the one," Regan said, with dreaminess to her voice.

I toed a corner of a broken brick that protruded from the walk. I didn't know what to say, and feared saying the wrong thing consider-ing how bewildered I felt inside.

"Isn't that what it was like for you and Sean?" Regan asked.

I thought about this for a moment. Magical? I'm not sure it was magical. Practical, maybe. Did I know Sean was the one when we met? Do I know Sean is the one now? Well, the only thing I knew for sure was that Sean was the only one.

"Mina?"

I looked up and found Regan staring at me, apparently waiting for an answer. "Ah . . . I guess so," I said. "I didn't really date much in school, so I don't have a lot to compare to," I confessed.

"Mina, you're so cute. That surprises me," Regan said.

I didn't know whether it was the Chianti or her comment, but my face felt on fire again.

"Mina, are you okay? Your face is as red as a beet."

"Yes, I'm fine," I said, fanning my face with my hands. "I think the wine is getting to me," I set the glass down, smiling at her.

"I can't believe you didn't date much in school," Regan continued.

"Well, Sean and I met when I was a junior and he was a senior. We dated off and on for a year, and then during my senior year things got serious. That was the same year my father died."

"Your father must have been pretty young when he died. What happened?"

"He had Lou Gehrig's disease. He contracted it when he turned forty and died two months after his forty-second birthday. My father never got to see any of his three children graduate from anything, except kindergarten."

"That's so sad," Regan said. "I'm so sorry."

"Thanks," I answered, feeling her sincerity.

"Sean and my dad never got along. My dad thought I should be dating a nice Italian boy or a football player; someone *he* could relate to—not a grease monkey who worked five nights a week at a gas station until ten o'clock at night. But Sean showed up at my father's funeral, anyway. In my heart, I knew how difficult that was for him, especially after he had just buried his sixteen-year-old brother who had died in an accident the year before. That gesture alone made me fall in love with him. When he asked me to marry him after graduation, I couldn't say no."

"Is that why you went into nursing? Because of your dad?" Regan asked.

"Yes, I guess it is. I helped my dad as much as I could. I got a lot out of that, so why not make it my profession? I really wanted to go to medical school, but my grades weren't good enough to get in."

"You're a good nurse, Mina, and I think you'd make a good doctor too someday," Regan said and took another sip of her wine.

"Thanks," I said, feeling a little self-conscious. I wanted to change the subject.

"So . . . how 'bout you? Did you date a lot in high school?" I asked.

Regan tucked her legs beneath her on the cement bench. "Well, actually, I wasn't allowed to date in high school," Regan said. "My parents are pretty strict."

"You didn't date at all in high school? What about the prom or winter formal? You didn't get to go to any of those?"

Regan shook her head.

"I bet once you got out of high school, you felt like you had been paroled."

Regan laughed. "Not exactly. I did go out a few times in college, but nothing to brag about. Either I lost interest by the second or third date, or the guys lost interest when they didn't get what they wanted."

"You mean they lost interest when you wouldn't put out?"

Regan blushed. She nodded and took another sip of her wine.

"So, what about now?" I asked.

"What kind of girl do you think I am?" Regan answered, annoyed. Suddenly I realized she misunderstood my question.

"Oh no . . . I'm sorry, I didn't mean it that way. Oh gosh, how embarrassing. I meant are you dating now?"

We both laughed at the ridiculousness of my comment. I think we were both feeling the effects of the wine now.

"Well, since you've asked. Chris, the paramedic that came when Rosie crashed, asked me out last weekend."

"Really?" I said, surprised that Regan hadn't mentioned this before now.

"Yes. I ran into him at the mall a few weeks ago. He's very nice . . . and cute too," she said.

"Hmmm," was all I could manage trying hard to cover my unease. "So did you go out?"

"Yes, we went to see a movie . . . I wanted to see *Hannah and Her Sisters* but he insisted the we see *Aliens*. He said he saw the first one, *Alien,* a few years ago and had been waiting to see this sequel, so I gave in. I thought the movie was scary, but he seemed to enjoy it."

"Did you have a good time?" I asked, for some reason hoping she hadn't.

"Yes, it was nice."

I picked up my wineglass again and swirled the last of the wine and then took a big swig. "So, do you think he's the one?" I boldly asked.

"Huh?"

"Do you think Chris is . . . you know . . . The One?" I repeated, setting the wineglass down and forming quotation marks in the air with the index and middle fingers of both hands.

"Oh, I don't know. He's nice and all. And very polite . . ."

"Polite is always good," I chimed in.

"I don't know if I'm supposed to be able to tell after one date."

"Maybe you need to sleep with him." I couldn't believe I said this out loud, considering her reaction only a few minutes ago to the same subject. Maybe it was the wine that was making me so bold. Bold to the point of being obnoxious.

"Why does everyone think that sex is the most important thing in a relationship?" Regan asked, clearly annoyed by my suggestion. I didn't blame her.

"To see if you're compatible. Don't you think that's important? To be sexually compatible?" I continued against my better judgment.

"You know, sex isn't everything. Anyway, I was taught that sex is something you saved for your husband on your wedding night," she answered sternly. She was clearly taken aback by my forward behavior. "Giving yourself to someone in that way is the ultimate gift. You can only give it once, and that person is supposed to be the one you spend the rest of your life with. You're Catholic, I'm sure you can understand that," she said.

"Well . . ." I replied, looking at the ground, searching for an acceptable answer. "I was taught that . . . I mean the nuns and priests preached that to us, but . . ." I could see the statue of the Virgin Mary out of the corner of my eye, mocking me. "I guess I'm not that good of a Catholic."

"You mean you weren't a virgin on your wedding night?"

"No, not exactly."

"What does that mean? 'Not exactly'? You're either a virgin or your not; there's no in between here. "

"Well, then no."

We sat in awkward silence for a moment, and then Regan piped up: "Please tell me at least that it was with Sean."

"Yes, it was Sean. We used protection . . . and I was on the pill. At least give me credit for that."

"Birth control. You really aren't a good Catholic are you?" Regan said with a chuckle. She took another sip of her wine. "Well, spill the beans. When was the first time?" she asked as casually as if she were asking me where I bought my new Calvin Klein jeans. She too was finding courage in the bottom of her wineglass.

"Easter break of my junior year in high school."

"High school! Oh my gosh, you had sex when you were sixteen years old? I can't imagine doing it now, let alone in high school," she said. Regan leaned forward and lowered her voice. "How did you know you were ready?"

"I was sixteen. What did I know? It felt like it was something I had to do . . . find out what it was like for myself. You know, kind of a right of passage."

"Was it what you thought it would be?"

"No, not at all."

"So what was it like?" Regan asked as she drew her knees up, hugging them to her chest. She picked up her glass to take another sip of wine and looked surprised to find that the glass was now empty. She set the empty glass on the bench beside her.

"Well, there was no romance that I can recall; no candlelight, no soft music. It happened on a freezing cold night behind the bowling alley in the backseat of a 1971 Chrysler Newport."

Regan listened intently, so I continued. "The first time I felt his erection, I thought he was deformed because his penis was pointing straight up."

"It points straight up?" Regan shrieked and then covered her mouth with her hand.

"Yes, when it's hard, it points straight up," I said, sending us both into a fit of drunken giggles.

"Sorry," Regan said, steadying herself on the bench trying to regain her composure. She brought her hand to her mouth as if trying to wipe away the smirk on her face. "Go ahead, I didn't mean to interrupt."

"After the shock wore off, Sean and I ended up in the backseat. The only thing I remember was that it hurt."

"There's pain?" Regan asked, astonished. I couldn't believe how naive she seemed to be.

"Yes, but not only from doing it, I had a terrible headache from my head being slammed repeatedly into the armrest of the back door every time he would push into me."

We were laughing uncontrollably now, tears blinded my sight. Regan sat bent over on the bench, clutching her knees when Anna pushed open the screen door and joined us in the courtyard. "Sounds like you two are having a better time out here," Anna said as she sat down next to Regan.

"What's so funny?" Anna asked as she slipped off her pink sandal and rubbed the instep of right foot. The party was winding down and I'm sure her feet were killing her, having walked around in heels all day.

"Nothing really . . . just girl talk," I said.

"Girl talk and a little too much wine," Regan chimed in with a snort.

Anna shook her head as if she'd seen this behavior before. "I wish I could have spent more time with you guys, it's just that . . ."

"We understand, Bartoli. No problem. It was a nice party," I said, trying to relieve Anna of the natural guilt feeling instilled in all of us Italian girls.

"We better get going," Regan said. "It's getting late. This was a great party, Anna, thank you for inviting me."

"Yeah, thanks Bartoli. See you at work tomorrow?" I asked.

"Yes, I'll be there. I tried to get a day off, but we are short staffed, so my request got denied."

"That's okay, we'll have a good time anyway. I hear that the Dairy Queen is having a sale on Peanut Buster Parfaits. We can sneak out at lunch, okay?"

Bartoli nodded and laughed.

I drove Regan home and deposited her safely on her doorstep. I waited until she was safely inside before I drove away. It was the beginning of summer. The evenings were lazy and long, and that night, the first night of many nights to come, I wished had never ended.

Chapter Five

When I did get home from Bartoli's party, the apartment was completely dark. I flipped on the dinning room light and found the note Sean had left on the kitchen table letting me know he got called out to work. Sean is on the crime scene investigation unit, so he frequently gets called out at all hours during the night. Nothing takes the fun out of the holidays or any other special occasion like a homicide.

I had trouble falling asleep that night, but I wasn't sure if it was because my husband was out on an investigation, with a new partner who happened to be a woman, or because I couldn't stop thinking about Regan and the great time we had had that night.

Police officers' marriages are supposedly difficult because of the high stress level on the job. The infidelity rate is pretty much through the roof. It seems that every officer on the force has had an extramarital affair at some point in his life. Sean and I discussed this matter when he first joined the police department. He assured me that he loved me very much and that there was nothing I'd ever have to worry about. So when he told me his new partner was a woman, I didn't worry. Okay, well maybe a little.

I had never met or even heard of this woman officer. Was she an older and experienced police officer or a young hotshot with something to prove? What did she look like? Single? Married? And what was the real reason behind her leaving a big city like Cleveland to come to our little town? All these questions rummaged through my overloaded head.

It was five in the morning when Sean returned home. I felt him slip into bed next to me.

"How was your night?" I asked gently, hoping we could connect and he'd ease my uncertainties.

"Long," he said.

The Choice
Published by The Haworth Press, Inc., 2007. All rights reserved.
doi:10.1300/5791_05

"Another coroner's case?"

"Uh-huh. Thirty-seven-year-old male. Poor guy's wife found him hanging with a nylon ski rope around his neck in the upstairs eaves of his house. Looks like he killed himself jacking off"

"What?"

"Autoerotic asphyxiation. These guys try to get a more intense orgasm by tying something around their neck to cut off the circulation to their brains. He slipped, lost his balance, and hung himself."

"How do you know that's what he was doing?" I asked.

"There were *Penthouse* and *Hustler* magazines stained with semen on the floor underneath him. What do you think?"

"I think that's pretty gruesome."

"Yes, you should have been there."

I ran my fingers through Sean's blonde hair. He turned over onto his side and spooned me. He pulled the white sheet over his muscular shoulders and circled his arm around my waist, pulling me close. Minutes later he had fallen asleep.

I lay awake, stroking Sean's arm and watching the silver morning light creep into the room. I wondered how he could deal with some of the terrible things that he saw and not let it affect him.

Sean would be leaving later that day for a seminar at the police academy in Columbus. I had to work again that weekend, so Sean had decided to go to Columbus earlier, get registered for the seminar, and then spend some leisure time with a couple of his buddies from the police academy. The seminar, an advanced course on crime scene investigation, was to be six weeks long. This would be the longest time we had ever spent apart. I couldn't help but wonder if the new female officer would be attending the seminar as well.

I slipped out of bed and padded to the kitchen to make some coffee. I pulled a clean uniform out of the closet and showered. After my shower, cup of coffee in hand, I stuffed my clinic shoes and two cans of Diet Coke into my already overloaded backpack.

Knowing I probably wouldn't see Sean before he left for Columbus, I pulled out a sheet of notebook paper and wrote a note:

Dear Sean, Six weeks is a long time. We have never been apart for this long and I know I will miss you terribly. Maybe I can come down on a weekend some time soon. Please be careful. You aren't as invincible as you think sometimes. Have a good trip. Love, Mina

Sean and I wrote notes to each other all the time. It started when I was in nursing school. Because of our conflicting schedules, notes were sometimes our only means of communication for days on end. Out of habit I started saving the notes Sean would write, so I could read and reread them when I was working a double or knew I wouldn't see him for a few days. If I was having a bad day, I would pull out one of Sean's notes, read it, and I would feel better. Any job that requires your husband to carry a gun makes you worry in the back of your mind that when you say good-bye to him in the morning it might be the last time you see him. Keeping his notes with me made me feel that a part of him was with me all the time.

I folded the note in half and spritzed it with my White Shoulder's perfume: a little something to remember me by. As I propped the note against Sean's car keys on the dining room table I felt a twinge of guilt. I'd miss Sean, sure, but I was really looking forward to having some time to myself. I grabbed my backpack and quietly slipped into the hallway, gently closing the door behind me.

When I got to the nursing unit Regan was already sitting in the so-larium with Opal, giving her a much-needed manicure. I watched as Regan gingerly painted one, then another of Opal's' fingernails Peony Pink, gently blowing on each one to speed up the drying process.

"Hey, you're here early," I said.

"I couldn't sleep, so I thought I would get an early start. You know, do some of the things we don't normally have time to do," Regan said.

She finished Opal's' manicure, then joined Brenda and I at the desk for report. Regan sat next to me. The scent of her freshly washed hair made me swoon. She smelled so good, so clean. I shook my head to clear it so I'd be able to focus on report.

"Mina, are you okay?" Brenda asked.

"Yes, fine. Why?"

"You seemed a little distracted in report," she said as she stuffed her stethoscope and notebook into her scuffed-up, PBS tote bag.

"I'm okay. I guess I have a lot on my mind. Sean's leaving today for a six-week seminar in Columbus."

"Wow. I wish my husband would leave for six weeks," Brenda joked.

We both laughed.

"It's weird. I mean, this will be the longest we have ever spent apart." I didn't mention the new female partner. I didn't want to appear too insecure.

"I know," Brenda said. "But when my Charlie had his hernia repaired last year, those three days he was in the hospital were three of the most relaxing days of my life. Don't get me wrong, I love Charlie, but you know, sometimes you just need time for yourself. Do you know what I'm sayin'?"

"Yes, I think I do," I said, trying not to show that deep down inside, I was indeed quite happy he would be gone. "Thanks."

"Do something for yourself. Get a massage, or a pedicure. There is that new place just outside of town; I think it's called Xanadu. It's a day spa where you can check in for an hour or a day and get all the pampering you can imagine."

Regan stood at the med cart, filling out the vital sign sheet for the day, well within earshot of our conversation. Brenda unpinned her nurse's cap from her short-cropped red hair, picked up her industrial size coffee thermos, and headed for the elevator.

"Really Mina, you should give it a try. If I had the fifty dollars for an hour, I'd do it in a minute," Brenda said as she waited for the elevator.

"Fifty bucks an hour?" I said out loud. "That's a lot of money."

"Not really," Regan chimed in. "I've always wanted to go to one of those places. I think it would be great, don't you?"

"I don't know. I mean, I've never had a massage, have you?"

"No, but it sounds wonderful. We should do it Mina," Regan said bursting with enthusiasm.

I thought about this for a moment. What did I have to lose except fifty bucks? "Okay, let's do it," I said. "How about next Saturday? I'm off. Are you?"

"Yes, Saturday will be great," Regan said. "I'll call and make us both a reservation."

"Hey, I thought Bartoli was working with us today?" I shouted to Brenda just as the elevator doors opened.

"Jacobs gave her a day off. The census is down, so they didn't need her after all."

"That's good. I know she was pretty tired after the party last night. I'll miss her though; we were going to make a run for Peanut Buster Parfaits this afternoon."

Brenda shook her head. "I don't know how you guys get away with that stuff."

I shrugged and we both laughed. "See you tomorrow," Brenda said as she disappeared into the elevator.

The morning started off quiet. Regan and I even had time to sit down and join some of the patients in the lounge for a second cup of coffee after the first morning med pass, but by the time two-thirty rolled around, Regan and I were both exhausted. Three admissions and a hospital transfer had put us an hour behind schedule. Afternoon turn came on and started rounds before I could sit down and give them report.

"Boy, I'm really looking forward to that massage on Saturday," Regan said as we walked out to the parking lot.

"Yes, me too, especially after a day like today. My feet are killing me."

Regan smiled, and again I felt that strange flutter in the pit of my stomach. "See you tomorrow," she said as she unlocked her car door and got in.

"See you tomorrow," I answered and headed toward the path that took me home.

I trudged up the three flights of stairs to my apartment. Once inside, my heart sank. Sean had apparently left for Columbus in a hurry, leaving the apartment in shambles. His clothes were strewn from the bedroom to the bathroom. His breakfast dishes were stacked in a sink full of cold dirty dishwater, and the smell of burnt toast still lingered in the air.

Sean left me a note taped to the microwave oven. It said,

Left at one o'clock, should get to Columbus by five. I'll call you when I get in. Have a good weekend. Love, Sean. P.S., I took the last tube of tooth-paste; you might want to pick some more up.

I pulled the note off the microwave, folded it into four small squares, and tucked it into my pocket.

I started on the clothing trail, picking up sweatpants, a white T-shirt, and a pair of Fruit of the Loom briefs. Once in the bathroom I discovered two sopping wet bath towels on the floor next to the com-mode, where Sean had left them in haste.

When I bent down to retrieve the towels I discovered the note I had left Sean earlier that day, crumpled at the bottom of the wastebasket. I tossed the wet towels into the hamper with the rest of the clothes and sat down on the commode. I retrieved the note from the bottom of the wastebasket and smoothed out the crinkles on my leg. I felt like a disappointed five-year-old who discovers a prized picture she has drawn for her dad carelessly tossed into the garbage can.

I wrote the note hoping he would take it with him. This hurt. I was surprised at how much it hurt. I folded the note and tucked it into the same pocket I put the one he had left me. Something was changing in our relationship, and apparently I wasn't the only one who felt it.

I finished straightening up the rest of the apartment, feeling sorry for myself, and wondering when things had changed. I was about to pop a Weight Watcher's frozen dinner in the microwave when the phone rang.

"Hello," I said, hoping it was Sean letting me know that he got to Columbus safely and to apologize about tossing the note.

"Mina, it's Regan. Are you busy?"

"No, I was just cleaning up a little," I said, trying to hide the disap-pointment in my voice.

"Have you eaten dinner yet?" Regan asked.

"No, I was just going to throw something into the microwave."

"My parents went to my sister's for the weekend, and I didn't want to cook for myself. Would you like to go out and get something to eat?"

I looked at the frozen dinner in my hand and quickly accepted her invitation.

"Great, I'll be over in about half an hour," Regan said, and then the phone clicked dead.

I took a quick shower, pulled on a pair of acid-washed denim shorts and a navy blue T-shirt. I was blow-drying my hair when the doorbell rang. I pushed the buzzer to unlock the security door downstairs, and I opened the apartment door, leaving it ajar for Regan to come in. I went back to drying my hair.

"Anybody home?" Regan shouted over the hum of the blow dryer.

I stuck my head into the living room. Regan was dressed in faded jeans and a white polo shirt. I immediately felt self-conscious about wearing shorts; my legs were okay . . . but not the greatest. It was too late to change. Anyway, I didn't want her to think I was so insecure that I couldn't stick to my fashion decision.

"Hi," I said, suddenly nervous. "I'll be out in a minute."

"Take your time," she said, and sat on the sofa, leafing through one of the magazines on the coffee table. I finished drying my hair and then joined her in the living room.

"Hi," she said, standing up when I entered the room. "I hope you don't mind the last-minute call. I just didn't feel like staying home alone tonight.

"It's Saturday night. No date with what's-his-name? The paramedic?"

"Chris? No . . . I think things are starting to fizzle there," Regan said quietly. "I haven't heard from him in over a week."

"I'm sorry to hear that," I said, but I really wasn't. Even though I didn't know Chris that well, I didn't think he was the one for Regan.

"Anyway, as they say, there are a lot of fish in the sea. Right?" Regan said as we descended the three flights of stairs leaving my apartment.

"Right," I answered. "The right one will come along, when you least expect it," I said.

"Whatever you say. I'm just afraid I'll be doing something else when it happens," Regan said with a chuckle.

Regan put her key into the passenger's side door and held the door open for me as I slid into the velour-covered bucket seat. It had been awhile since anyone opened a car door for me. I was lucky sometimes if Sean would bring the car to a complete stop, let alone open my door for me. It felt especially odd to have a woman perform this gesture for me, but in a way, I liked it.

I reached over and unlocked the driver's side door. Regan opened it and plopped into the driver's seat next to me. She put the key in the ignition and started the car. "You seem kind of down. Are you still upset over Sean's leaving?" Regan asked.

"No, it's not that so much," I said, embarrassed that she noticed. "It's kind of silly."

"What? What is it?" Regan said, encouraging me to talk.

"It's stupid."

"So tell me anyway."

"Oh, all right."

Regan nodded, encouraged.

"Before I left for work this morning, I wrote him a note telling him how much I would miss him and maybe I could come down and spend some time with him."

"Sounds okay so far."

"Then, I sprayed the note with my perfume, hoping he would take it with him to Columbus . . . you know, as something to remember me by."

"That's so romantic," Regan said.

I felt my face flush. "But when I got home from work, I was picking up his wet towels off the bathroom floor and found the note crumpled up in the wastebasket. It really bothered me. I mean I know it's petty, but it hurt."

Regan was quite for a moment. I could see that she was turning this information over in her mind trying to come up with a reasonable explanation. Finally she spoke: "I don't think guys get it sometimes," Regan said. "I don't think guys pay attention to the details like women do."

"Do you think that's all it is?" I asked.

"Sure. I guess that's why I get disillusioned with dating. Just when I think I've found the right guy, something happens. We seem to value different things. That note meant one thing to you and another thing to Sean. I'm not saying that it didn't mean anything to him, but it meant a lot to you. Do you see what I'm saying? It's like we are on two different wavelengths."

I nodded. For someone who didn't have a lot of dating experience, she seemed to know what she was talking about.

"Sometimes I don't think I'll ever learn how to be in a relationship with a guy," Regan said. "I'm afraid I may end up single for the rest of my life."

"Come on, you are only, what? Twenty-three, twenty-four years old?."

"Twenty-five," she corrected.

"You've got your whole life ahead of you and so much to offer. Plus, I don't think spinsterhood sets in until you are at least thirty," I said.

We both laughed. Both of our moods improved in less than a minute. Gone was my heavy heart, and I was looking forward to our dinner out.

Regan stopped the car at a small roadside diner called Milo's Grill. Milo's was the first "burger joint" in our town, even before McDonald's came into the area. The smell of burgers and grilled onions greeted us as soon as we stepped out of the car.

We sat in one of the cracked and faded red leather booths in front of the picture window with "'Milo's Grill" painted across it. Antique ceiling fans creaked overhead, stirring the warm, humid air around us. I think Milo's' was the only restaurant in the tri-county area that wasn't air-conditioned, but most folks didn't care because the food was so good.

Pools of sweat were forming under my legs where my thighs stuck to the leather seat as we looked over our menus. I ordered a hamburger with mustard, lettuce, and tomato. Regan ordered a cheeseburger with lettuce, tomato, ketchup, and onion. We split an order of chili-cheese fries. This was much better than a Weight Watchers frozen dinner, although I knew this meant an extra session with my Jane Fonda workout tapes.

I watched as Regan picked up her cheeseburger and took a bite. Her facial features were dainty, her wrists small, but her well-manicured fingers were tapered and strong. Ketchup smeared at the corners of her pink-lip-glossed mouth. She wiped the ketchup away with her napkin and smiled at me from across the table.

"You haven't even touched your burger," Regan said. "Isn't it done enough?"

"Oh . . . no . . . it's fine," I said, picking up the sandwich and taking a bite. "Mmm . . . delicious."

Regan and I talked all though dinner and all the way home. Time seemed to fly by when we were together. It was eleven thirty when we found ourselves sitting in her car in the parking lot of my apartment complex.

"Well, I guess I better go in," I said. "It's getting late."

"Yeah," she looked at her purple Swatch watch. "Wow, it's almost midnight," she said with a yawn and then stretched her arms over her head. As she stretched, I couldn't help noticing the swell of her perfect-sized breasts. I turned and looked out the passenger's side window. This moment suddenly felt awkward. Like the end of a date where you're not sure whether to shake hands, kiss, or just bolt out of the car running for the front door. I wanted to do all three, and it disturbed me. I thanked her for asking me to dinner and settled for just saying good night.

Regan waited until I was safely inside my apartment. I waved at her through the dining room window and watched as she drove away. I felt inexplicably on cloud nine, that is until I checked the answering machine before going to bed. There were three messages—all from Sean. The first one was at seven thirty letting me know that he arrived okay, two hours late. The second one was at nine fifteen, which said he was just checking in and to call him when I got in. The third one was short and abrupt. It said, "It's after eleven, where are you? Call me when you get in."

I wasn't used to Sean using this tone with me. He rarely did. But then again, I had never been out that late when he didn't know where I was. I called the number he left on the message. He picked up on the first ring.

"Sean, it's Mina."

"Where have you been? It's almost midnight?"

"Regan and I went out to eat."

"Where the hell did you go? Cleveland?"

"No. We went to Milo's. Sean, what's wrong with you?"

"What's wrong? I leave town and the next thing I know is you're out running around with your girlfriends."

"I went to dinner with a friend. What's wrong with that?"

He was silent for a moment.

"I'm sorry Meen," he said quietly into the phone.

"Sean, what's the matter?"

"Nothing . . . I don't know. You're such a homebody. I'm lucky if I can get you to stay out past ten o'clock on a Saturday night. When you weren't home, I got scared."

"Scared of what?"

"Scared that something was wrong or that you might . . . "

"Might what?"

"I don't know . . . I'm sorry."

"Sean, don't be ridiculous. I love you and I miss you. Didn't you even read the note I left for you? I was hoping you would keep it with you."

"I did read it and I do have it with me. It's right here in my wallet."

"No, it's not, Sean. I found it in the wastebasket in the bathroom."

"No sir. It's right here." I could hear him fumbling for his wallet. "I could have sworn I put it in here," he said. "Mina, I'm sorry. I'm acting like a jerk."

By the end of the conversation I was feeling relieved. It was one thirty by the time I got into bed. I had to be up in three hours for work. I lay in bed as memories of the day filed through my head like microfiche on a reel. The images faded, and the next thing I knew the alarm clock sounded the beginning of another day.

Chapter Six

Sean had called a handful of times throughout the week to check on things and to ask me to wire him some more money. Apparently, he had underestimated how much he would need for living expenses down there. Or maybe he was out every night, having a good time with his buddies or his new female partner. I tried to push those thoughts out of my mind, but curiosity had gotten the better of me and one time he called I couldn't help but to ask.

"Is Rosetti attending the seminar?" I asked, trying to sound as casual as I could manage.

"She's on the roster, but not due to come down until the last two weeks. She took this course already, but needs to recertify, so she's only coming down for the testing. Why?" Sean asked.

"Oh, no reason . . . just curious," I said, relieved, and then gently changed the subject.

Sean assumed I'd be working the weekends that he was away, so I didn't bother to tell him I'd be gone most of Saturday. I didn't want him asking questions or getting upset over the cost of the spa day Regan and I had planned: what he didn't know wouldn't hurt him, right? Anyway I would pay for the spa treatment with money I kept hidden in my underwear drawer for things I wanted but didn't want to go to him and ask him for. The things Regan and I did together seemed special. I wanted to keep this experience private, for myself.

Saturday morning came. It was raining, and for the end of June, unseasonably cold. In spite of the cold, damp weather, I was excited about the day ahead. Regan picked me up at ten thirty. She looked like the all-American girl that morning, all scrubbed and fresh faced, without a trace of makeup, her hair pulled back into a sleek ponytail. As she drove she tapped the steering wheel with her hands to the rhythm of the music on the radio. She seemed so carefree and happy.

The Choice
Published by The Haworth Press, Inc., 2007. All rights reserved.
doi:10.1300/5791_06

"Here we are," Regan announced as she swung the Mustang into the parking lot of Xanadu. Xanadu was polished white marble on the outside with four huge pillars at the entrance. Double hung heavy oak doors graced the entrance. Walking through the grand doorway was like walking into a castle.

The receptionist, dressed in a black jumper and leggings was a painfully thin woman in her early fifties. Her sleek, steel-gray hair styled into a perfect pageboy set off her cornflower blue eyes. She stood up from behind her desk and greeted us in the lobby.

"Welcome to Xanadu. My name is Maggie. What can I do for you ladies today?" she asked.

"We have an appointment," Regan said. "Regan Martin and Mina Thomas."

"Oh yes, here you are," Maggie announced and checked our names off in the black leather reception book that lay open on top of her antique desk. "Yes, you are both here for our 'serenity package.'"

I looked over at Regan. She smiled and nodded confirmation. We paid Maggie for our packages. "I'll see if the staff is ready for you," Maggie said, and then she picked up the receiver of the antique French phone that sat on her desk. She listened for a moment, smiled, jotted down something on a white notepad with red feather pen, and then hung up the gold receiver. "The staff is ready. Please follow me," she said as she leisurely walked out from behind her elegant secretary desk and escorted us through two more polished oak doors taking us further into the spa. The heavy doors closed softly, shutting out everything behind us.

I blinked my eyes to adjust to the dim lighting. The air in the spa was warm and humid like a rainforest. Beethoven played softly in the background. *There is no way anyone could feel tense in this atmosphere,* I thought as Maggie led us further into a dressing room. The spa was carpeted wall to wall in thick white plush. I couldn't help thinking that it must be really hard to keep clean.

The dressing room was elegant, with its rich polished wood and gold fixtures. Two rows of polished oak bureaus stood back to back in the center of the room. Maggie opened one of the bureau doors, releasing a scent of lavender and roses. Inside were piles of thick white

Turkish bath towels, a pair of white terry cloth slippers, and a luxurious white terry cloth bathrobe.

"You can undress in here," Maggie said. "Take everything off and wrap yourself in one of the towels. You can then slip on the bathrobe and slippers. Someone will be in shortly to escort you to the sauna, which is the first part of your treatment. If you'd like to shower first, the shower room is over there behind that tiled wall," Maggie said, gesturing across the room. "Any questions?"

I looked at Regan. She shrugged her shoulders. "No, I don't think so," I said.

"Excellent. Have a wonderful time and I will see you when your treatment is complete." Maggie turned and floated out of the room with the grace of royalty.

I turned to Regan. "Boy, this is . . ." the words stuck caught in my throat. Regan stood with her back toward me, naked from the waist up. I froze. It was high school gym class all over again. I quickly turned around, pretending to be rummaging through the pile of towels like I lost something. I could feel my heart racing.

"Mina, are you okay?" Regan asked.

"Uh-huh." I answered, still rummaging in the bureau, trying not to look at her.

"What are you looking for?" Regan asked. I could feel her now standing next to me.

"Uh . . . my slipper, there seems to be only one slipper here." I tossed around some of the towels and folded one of the slippers up tight and stuffed it into the pocket of the bathrobe.

"Here, let me see," Regan said.

I diverted my gaze to white fluffy carpet and as Regan came closer and I noticed her toenails were painted a perfect coral pink. I stepped back from the bureau as Regan rummaged through the towels. She even took the bathrobe out and shook it. Still no slipper.

"Hmmm . . . wait here, I'll go get you another pair," she said, heading for the reception area.

"Thanks," I muttered, still to embarrassed to look at her.

Regan padded down the hallway we had just come down to get me a new pair of slippers. Thankfully she was now wrapped in the terry cloth robe. I sat down on the wooden bench in front of the bureau. My heart was pounding erratically. Suddenly, I jumped up, thinking I'd better get changed before she came back.

When I was growing up, locker room situations hadn't bothered me up until I got into high school. That's when things changed. Suddenly, I felt guilty being in there with the girls I had gone to school with all my life. They seemed so nonchalant about being in there half naked and I was extremely self-conscious about it. But more so, I felt ashamed because of what seeing them stirred up in me. Deep down I knew what I was feeling was wrong. At least that's what I had been taught by my parents, by my teachers, and by the Catholic Church: girls were attracted to boys not other girls. Anything that diverged from that was morally wrong. But how could feelings this strong be so wrong?

Being here with Regan brought those awkward feelings back again. I quickly undressed, wrapped one of the Turkish towels around me and pulled on the bathrobe, tying the belt tight around my waist. Regan returned.

"Here's another pair of slippers," she said setting them down on the carpet in front of me.

"Thanks, I really appreciate you going after them."

Just as I slipped them on, an Asian woman dressed in black stretch pants and a white T-shirt with the Xanadu logo embossed just above her left breast appeared in the doorway. "Regan and Mina," she said and gestured for us to follow her.

She introduced herself as Lu, and led us down another hallway to the sauna room. Once there, Lu instructed us on how to use the sauna. The heat and the smell of damp cedar were almost overwhelming as I half listened as Lu fiddled with the dials and gauges. "Towels are optional," she said before leaving us to bake in the dry heat.

I looked over at Regan. "I'm keeping mine," I said, clutching it to my chest and then climbed to the top of the sweltering booth. Regan laughed, "You crack me up sometimes," she said as she followed me to the top bench, still wrapped in her towel as well.

The heat engulfed my body, draining all the tension, all the fatigue, and all the toxins from my pores. I laid down across the wooden bench and closed my eyes, letting my mind drift with the heat and steam. Regan sat in the corner at my feet.

"My gosh, it's hot in here," Regan said, breaking my reverie. I opened my eyes and saw her fanning her flushed face with both hands. I watched curiously as she climbed down from the slotted cedar bench and walked over to the thermometer.

"One hundred and thirty degrees," she announced, as she examined the thermometer and the rocks where the heat was coming from. She reached for the ladle inside the wooden bucket of water next to the rocks. The ladle made a clunking noise as she dipped it into the bucket and filled it with water. "I wonder if I put water on the rocks if it will cool this down some,"

Before I could stop her, Regan poured the ladle-full of water over the rocks, causing a huge cloud of steam to emerge. Not only was the heat unbearable, now it was difficult to breathe because of all the steam. I sat up and immediately felt like I was going to pass out.

"I think I made it worse," Regan said sheepishly as she climbed back onto the bench beside me. "Sorry."

The sound of static and ringing in my ears was getting louder. I laid back down on the cedar bench, trying to hold on to consciousness. I was relieved when the timer dinged and a few minutes later Lu reappeared, carrying two large glasses of ice water. I gulped the icy water. Its coldness stung the back of my throat.

Slowly I got up on rubbery legs and staggered behind Regan as Lu escorted us out of the sauna and into the shower area to rinse off. I knew we were getting close to the shower area when the soft plush carpet under my feet disappeared and turned into a hard, cool, white marble floor.

In the center of the shower area was a huge marble pool. White granite statues of Roman Goddesses adorned the four corners of the pool. Eight carved marble steps descended from all four sides of the pool, leading down into crystal clear water. Pink and white rose petals floated on the water's surface. At the far end of the pool, a Jacuzzi swirled and bubbled. Several women, in different stages of undress, lounged in the water. It looked like a bath scene depicted in a Roman painting.

We finally reached the showers. The cool water felt so good on my hot skin, and I was able to regain my composure. And oh yes, thank God for shower curtains.

Regan and I emerged from the shower room all dewy and refreshed. Lu led us down another carpeted hallway and into the massage room. Two massage tables stood in the middle of the dimly lit room. Soothing music was piped in, and what looked like hundreds of aromatherapy candles were lit throughout the room. I sat on one of the tables. Regan sat on the other. Each table was covered in a three-hundred-count percale sheet. My body was still vibrating from the combination of the sauna and the shower. Regan's skin glowed pink in the candlelight.

"So, what do you think so far?" Regan asked, as she swung her silky long legs back and forth as she sat on the side of the massage table.

"I feel . . . exhilarated," I said. The ringing in my ears had finally stopped. "This was a great idea."

Regan smiled.

Our massage therapists entered the room. Both women were petite and fit and wore the uniform of Xanadu: black stretch pants and a white T-shirt. They instructed us to slip off our robes and to lie face-down on the table, wrapped in our towels. The massage therapists pulled the white towels out from underneath us, lowering them to cover our buttocks, but fully expose our backs. Expert hands kneaded every kink out of the tight muscles in my back and neck. I reveled in the exquisite feeling as the stress and tension melted away. *This is heaven,* I thought as I lay on the table facing Regan in the dim light. Her eyes were closed, and judging by the look on her face, she was in heaven, too.

"Turn over please," my masseuse whispered in my ear. She lifted my towel, holding it up to shield my nakedness from the other masseuse and Regan, who now was so relaxed she appeared to be in a coma. I lay down on my back and the masseuse covered me with the towel, but again, only from the waist down. My uneasiness showed through as I tugged the towel higher in effort to cover my exposed breasts.

"Don't be shy," she said softly. "We are all girls here. We all look the same."

I closed my eyes and tried to relax as the masseuse massaged my shoulders then moved to the muscles in my chest. My nipples hardened as she worked the pectoris muscles in my chest. I couldn't believe that just having my chest muscles massaged was arousing me. I was embarrassed, and thanked my fate for the dimness of the room.

Regan's masseuse instructed her to turn over as well. Panic shot through me. Regan would surely see me lying here half naked. I felt so exposed. What would she think? Did she feel the same awkward feelings I felt or would she, like most normal women, not think anything? I closed my eyes, trying to block out my nervousness. I even tried breathing in through my nose and out slowly through my mouth to calm down, but nothing seemed to help. I couldn't block the thoughts of Regan's naked body lying next to mine. What disturbed me most was the intensity of the desire I felt for her.

"You are so tense," my masseuse said as she rubbed more jasmine scented oil onto my neck and shoulders. Her strong fingers were digging into each muscle, trying to release the tension.

When our massages ended, the masseuses told us to take all the time we needed to relax and enjoy the effects of our massages and then quietly left the room.

So there we were, Regan and I, lying no more than a foot apart from each other, naked from the waist up. I couldn't move and I surely couldn't look at her, not with the thoughts that were going through my head. I lay there perfectly still, listening to Regan's gentle breathing. Finally I couldn't hold back any more. I turned my head and peeked over at Regan through half-open eyes.

Regan lay there, eyes closed, skin glowing in the candlelight. Her small, pert breasts *were* perfect. Just as I had imagined. She looked so enticing, lying there. My instinctive response to seeing her like this was overwhelming. I wanted to reach over and touch her, caress her skin, and feel her warm, soft body next to mine. What I wanted was to fulfill my deepest, darkest secret, to make love to her, and it scared me to death.

Regan stirred. I panicked. Afraid she would catch me looking at her and know what was going through my head. I jumped off the table, clutching the towel to my chest and made a hasty exit out of the massage room and into the hallway. I stumbled through the hall, backside exposed, looking for the locker room. Lu appeared from nowhere, fluffy white bathrobe in hand. She draped the robe over my shoulders and silently led me down the hall to the locker room.

"Thanks," I said as Lu turned to leave.

She nodded and smiled and disappeared as quietly as she appeared in the hall to save me.

A few minutes later a sleepy-eyed Regan emerged from the massage room.

"I must've fallen asleep," she said with a yawn. "That was wonderful."

"Yes," I answered now sitting in a fireside chair, fully clothed and feeling more secure.

Regan began to slip out of her robe to get dressed.

I bolted out of the chair and headed for the door. "I'll wait outside for you," I said and went down the hall to the reception area. Maggie was sitting at her desk as prim and proper as a schoolmarm.

"Did you enjoy your massage?" she asked.

"Yes, I did."

"Afterward, most people say they have never experienced anything like it," Maggie said.

"Yes, I guess you could say that." And I didn't mean the work on my muscles. It had indeed been nothing like I had ever felt before.

Chapter Seven

Regan and I spent the rest of that Saturday together and pretty much the next two weeks as well. We'd work day shift together then go out for dinner or catch a movie. Sometimes we'd just come back to my apartment, throw two Lean Cuisine dinners in the microwave, and veg out in front of the TV.

One day, after we'd both put in a grueling twelve-hour day shift, I made a reservation at the quaint new Victorian restaurant on the spillway of Mosquito Lake. It was a special treat. The place was packed, and even though we had a seven-o'clock reservation, we had to wait close to an hour for our table to be ready. Regan and I sat at the bar, where we both consumed a little too much wine on empty stomachs.

Finally, the hostess, a stunning brunette who could make any woman think twice about her sexual preference, rescued us from the bar. When we finally got seated, we ordered our food immediately. We were famished. As Regan sat across the table from me, sipping her third glass of wine, I couldn't stop thinking of how beautiful she was. The images of her lying half naked on the massage table sprawled in my mind. Even two weeks later, those images were very vivid, and they stirred me physically the more wine I drank.

"Mina, you seem preoccupied. Are you okay?" Regan asked.

"Hmmm? Oh, I'm sorry. Must be the wine," I said, lifting my wine glass and swirling the contents.

"Boy, I thought work today was never going to end," she said.

"I know. If we'd gotten one more admission I think I would have screamed."

"Yes, and if one more person had peed or pooped on me today, I think I would have screamed as well."

The Choice
Published by The Haworth Press, Inc., 2007. All rights reserved.
doi:10.1300/5791_07

We both laughed. She had had an unlucky day, as three of her patients did not make it to the bathroom in time.

When our dinner finally came, we both devoured our food like we hadn't eaten in a week. We passed on dessert and I probably should have passed on my third glass of wine as well, but it was going down so smoothly.

My face was hot and my legs felt rubbery. "What do you say we get out of here and get some air?" I suggested. "I think I'm drunk."

Regan laughed. "Okay, I'll get the check," she said as she signaled to get our waitress's attention. Apparently she was handling the wine better than I was tonight.

I slid the keys to the Corvette across the table to her. "Here, you drive."

Regan's face beamed. "Really?"

"Yes. As you can see, I'm in no shape to drive."

"Wow, I've never driven a Corvette before," Regan said.

She bolted out of the booth we were sitting in and paid the check. She came back to get me and tossed a five and two ones on the table for a tip. She guided me by my elbow as we made our way through the waiting crowd out into parking lot.

"How about a drive out to the lake?" Regan suggested as she opened the car door and helped me into the passenger's seat. "The fresh air will help you feel better."

"That sounds great," I answered. "Just don't make too many fast turns. I'd like to keep the meal I just ate, for a little while at least."

Regan laughed and we headed off to Mosquito Lake, tires spinning out, spraying gravel all over the restaurant parking lot.

"This is one of my favorite sections of the beach," Regan said as she pulled the car in to a deserted parking lot. "Not many people know this cove is here. It's quiet and secluded. I come out here sometimes just to walk along the shore and think."

We got out of the car and walked down to the water's edge. The fresh air felt good on my face, and I felt myself starting to sober up. We removed our shoes and rolled up our jeans to walk on the beach. The sand was cool and damp under our feet from an earlier rain shower. The air smelled clean and sweet as a soft warm breeze blew in off the lake. Small white caps crashed onto the shore, chasing us higher up onto the beach.

"What do you think about when you come out here?" I asked.

"A lot of things really. I think about my life, what the future holds . . ."

"What does it hold?"

"I'm not sure. I mean, I always thought I'd be married by now, but you know as well as I do the prospect of that for me is looking pretty dim."

"Why do you think your chances of getting married are so slim?" I asked.

"I'm just not very good at dating. I guess I don't have what it takes to be in a relationship," Regan said.

"Maybe you think that way, but I think you have a lot to offer someone. You're kind, you're considerate, and you're fun. I just think the right person hasn't come along yet," I said as we walked in the sand.

"Well, it's not like I don't put myself out there. And I've had a few guys ask me out. But it's always the same: We go out a few times, and then by the second or third date they want to . . ." She hesitated, as if searching for the right words.

"Get physical?" I said.

"Yes, get physical."

"And you don't want that?"

"It's not that I don't want that, it's just that it's the only thing they're interested in. Their feelings, if you can call them feelings, seem so superficial. There is no intimacy, no unconditional love. They don't seem to care about what I want or how I am feeling; it's all about what they can get. I know we are not living in the 1950s, but for me to be intimate and to give myself to someone in that way, there needs to be more there than just attraction or desire."

"I see. Is that what happened with Chris, the paramedic?"

"Uh-huh," she nodded and then looked up at me. "Mina, do you think that kind of love exists, or am I just looking for something that may never be?"

I hesitated. It was a question I had asked myself many times. The answer had always been evasive. Now was no exception.

"Yes . . . I think it exists, but I believe it's a hard thing to find." I hated being so vague. "Regan, you and I were brought up to believe that when we grew up, our goal in life was to hook a man, get married, and have a bunch of children, regardless of what our wants and needs are. That's what our mothers did and that is what's expected of us. But things have changed over the years since our mothers were our age. Women are becoming more independent. I think being able to be more independent makes us want and expect more from our lives."

"But does that mean our values have to change?" Regan asked.

"No. I'm not saying that at all. But what I'm saying is that women have more choices these days. They don't need men to take care of them anymore, and we don't need to settle for what everyone else expects from us. Even though that's what our mother's drummed in our heads, it's simply not true anymore," I said.

Regan nodded thoughtfully.

"Regan, I know you'll find someone who will be willing to wait for you, someone who will appreciate your values and will love you for you."

We walked further down the beach. I picked a few strands of beach grass and wove them between my fingers. "I can see it now, you'll have the American dream, the little house with the white picket fence, the two point two children, and the little furry dog named Scamp."

Regan laughed, "Yeah, right."

"Regan, you're too good of a person to spend your life alone. It'll happen for you, I know it will. It just takes time, and when you least expect it—BAM, there it is, right in front of you."

Right in front of you. The love of your life is right in front of you. My own words echoed in my mind. Thankfully Regan's next comment quickly banished that thought.

"See, that's another thing. I know this may sound terrible, but I really don't want the two point two kids. I don't want any kids," Regan said. "Do you think that's terrible of me, not to want kids?

"Oh my gosh, no. Regan, I don't want them either," I said, feeling liberated at just saying the words. "I thought I was the only woman on earth that felt that way. You are the first person I have come across who feels the same way too."

"Really? I always felt so ashamed about not wanting children. I never told anyone about this before," she said as if a heavy weight had been lifted off her shoulders. "The thought of being tied down to kids for the rest of my life . . . scares me to death."

"Me too!" I said.

"What about Sean? Does he feel the same way you do?" Regan asked.

Suddenly, my elation dimmed. "Well, when we got married, we both agreed to not start a family right away because we were so young. It wasn't easy, because we received a lot of pressure from his family as well as mine to start a family before it was too late."

"What did they consider too late?"

"Well, in my family, if you didn't have your first kid a year after you got married, they assumed that something was wrong with one or both of us and started dropping hints about infertility clinics."

Regan laughed and shook her head in disbelief.

"Sean's family wasn't as aggressive as mine, but with him being an only child after his brother died, they definitely were looking forward to a lot of heirs from us." I paused. "I still think waiting was the best thing we ever did. But I'm beginning to think his patience is running thin. He asked me recently when we were going to have a kid and I sort of blew him off. I really can't blame him. Both of our careers are pretty stable and I'm sure I could cut down to part time at the nursing home. But honestly, I'm not ready to give up my career yet."

"Have you talked to Sean about how you feel?" Regan asked.

"No. I've just been putting it off."

We walked along the shore and came across a dilapidated picnic table stuck into the side of a sand dune at the water's edge. Regan and I climbed up and sat down on the tabletop. We sat side by side, denim-covered thigh brushing denim-covered thigh as we watched a gaggle of mallards swoop down and gracefully land in the water in front of us.

"So, if you don't want kids, what do you want out of life?" Regan asked.

"What do I want out of life?" I said, tearing at the strands of beach grass and tossing the in the water. "Well, I love being a nurse, but I'd really like to go back to school someday. Maybe even take a shot at medical school."

I looked over at Regan to see her reaction. She was smiling.

"Taking care of the sick and elderly really gives my life a sense of purpose. I don't think you could get this feeling from working in an office or a store. I feel like I can make a difference in those people's lives and that is the best feeling in the world."

"I feel the same way," Regan said. "It's amazing how our patients touch our lives. Remember that day when Rosie in two eighteen arrested?"

"Yes. You did a great job that day."

"And I was scared to death. I didn't know anything. Thank God you were there, Mina," Regan said.

"You know, sometimes I feel like I have everything in life I could ever want, but then there are times when I get this ache deep inside my heart. It feels like something is missing."

"What do you think is missing?" Regan asked.

The question made me uncomfortable. How could I tell her what was missing when I had trouble admitting it to myself?

"I'm not sure," I lied. I knew all to well what it was. "It feels like something big and more intense. Like there's something out there that can make life even better."

"I think I know what you mean. Like there is something out there that can make your life more passionate, more intimate," Regan said.

"That's it. More intimate. That's a good way of putting it."

"You know, it's funny, but sometimes . . . sometimes I think that if I could experience the intimacy I've had with my female friends in a relationship with a guy, I'd really have something," Regan said.

The comment made my heart jump.

"What do you mean?" I asked.

"Well, sometimes I think that, well, let's take you and me for instance. We've known each other for a relatively short amount of time, but our relationship has evolved so intensely that it has a certain intimacy to it already. Don't you agree?"

I nodded mutely.

"So you see, if you were a man, this would be a perfect relationship for me."

My breath caught in my throat as Regan continued. "We care about each other, we look out for each other. We have a lot of the same interests . . . Heck, one of us even knows what the other one is thinking sometimes."

Regan shyly smiled when her eyes met mine. I felt her gaze probe gently into my very soul. Did she really know what I was thinking? How I really felt about her? That I was falling in love with her? *No, no way,* I thought. I looked away.

The breeze coming off the lake suddenly turned cold. "We better get back before it gets dark," Regan said. I looked up at her and her smile had dimmed as if she regretted everything she had said, afraid she had bared too much.

We walked back to the car in heavy silence. I'd had a golden opportunity to tell Regan how I felt about her and I blew it. My mind was a churning sea of thoughts and emotions: hope, regret, and disappointment all crashing into one another. A sense of urgency took over, and I was certain that if I didn't say something now I would never have another chance. My feelings for Regan had come to the boiling point and I couldn't contain them any longer.

"Regan, wait a minute," I said.

Regan stopped and turned toward me.

"What if I told you I have been thinking about the same thing . . . about you and me?"

Regan's eyes searched mine. My heart beat wildly in my chest. I didn't want to scare her away, sending her off running back to the nursing home and telling everyone what a pervert I was. But I wanted this, and something inside of me sensed that she wanted it too. That feeling gave me all the courage I needed.

"Wait a minute," Regan protested feebly. "You don't think I meant that you and I . . . I meant it in a hypothetical way; if one of us was a guy, this would be a perfect relationship. I'm not a lesbian, Mina, and neither are you. You have a husband, remember?"

Without a word, I leaned in toward her and gently kissed her full on the lips. The kiss was slow and thoughtful and nothing like I have ever experienced in my life. Her lips were warm and soft, with a faint taste of merlot. But that wasn't the best part. The best part was that Regan kissed me back.

Chapter Eight

Kissing Regan opened the floodgates on emotions and desires I had been trying to suppress for a long time.

In my heart, I had known from the first time I met Regan that there was something special about her. The harder I tried to ignore the truth, the more it persisted: I was falling in love with her. And now, it all seemed to be coming together.

Interestingly, my emotions swung from exuberance and liberation to heavy sadness and desperation. I felt that I had found what had been missing in my life, but I loved Sean too, and the last thing I wanted to do was hurt him. But how do you tell your husband that while he was away, you kissed a girl and now your life would change? Did it have to change? Couldn't I keep the two separate?

The ticking of the alarm clock on the nightstand echoed in the darkness. I lay in bed, too keyed up to sleep. That first kiss out at the lake was followed by many more. Behind an oak tree, in the shadows beneath the old rusty sliding board on the beach, in the Corvette, shielded by the shadows of night. Each kiss, deeper and more passionate than the first, sent spirals of ecstasy through my heart and tiny shock waves through my groin; I felt seventeen again.

When Regan pulled the Corvette into the parking lot of the apartment complex that night, we sat in silence, holding hands, afraid to let go. Regan's petite, silky soft hands felt so different than Sean's large, callused hands.

I wanted Regan to stay with me. I wanted to hold her in my arms all night long. But I couldn't bring myself to initiate it. I was afraid I'd scare her away, afraid that all this would come to an abrupt end. She was inexperienced as it was and I knew I had to move slowly. It was close to two in the morning when we finally broke away from

The Choice
Published by The Haworth Press, Inc., 2007. All rights reserved.
doi:10.1300/5791_08

each other, knowing it would only be a few hours until we saw each other again at work.

The cool night breeze caressed my body as it blew in from the open bedroom window. Butterflies fluttered in my stomach each time I recalled our kiss. Sleep came in short spurts. I was too excited to sleep, so after lying there for almost two hours I gave up and headed for the kitchen to make some coffee. The sun was making its slow ascent, the start of a glorious new day. Rose-tinted light filtered in through the mini blinds in the living room as I sat on the couch with a steaming mug of coffee, admiring the beautiful sunrise. Suddenly the buzzer rang. My heart nearly leapt out of my chest at the sound of it. I pulled my bathrobe tighter and pushed the intercom button.

"Who is it?" I asked through the speaker somewhat timidly.

"Mina, it's Regan. Can I come up?"

My mind and my heart were racing. What was she doing here at this hour? I hadn't even brushed my teeth. "Sure, come on up," I answered as calmly as I could muster and raced into the bathroom, throwing cold water on my face and digging the crusty sleep from the corners of my eyes. I brushed my teeth and ran a comb through my hair. The doorbell rang and I knew I wouldn't have time to change into anything other than my terry cloth bathrobe. This would have to do.

I opened the door and found Regan standing in the entryway, dressed in a clean, freshly pressed uniform dress, carrying a small brown paper bag.

"Here, I made these for you," she said thrusting the bag toward me.

I took the bag from her and opened it. From inside the bag wafted the smell of freshly baked blueberry muffins.

"I couldn't sleep when I got home last night, so I baked these," Regan said as she followed me into the living room. I closed the door behind us.

"They smell wonderful," I said, breathing in the delicious aroma. "I just made some coffee, would you like some?"

"Yes, that would be great," Regan said and sat down on the couch.

The neckline of my robe gaped open and I was acutely aware of my nakedness beneath it.

"I hope you don't mind me dropping over like this, so early in the morning," Regan said. "I just couldn't sleep when I got home. I couldn't stop thinking about . . ."

"I know, me too."

I took Regan's hand and stroked it lovingly, reassuring her that it was all right.

"Mina . . . I've never . . . felt like this before," Regan said.

"Me either."

"I don't understand. Everything I have been taught tells me this is wrong, but . . ."

"I know."

I took Regan into my arms and pulled her on top of me. Our bodies trembled as we lay together and kissed, slowly at first, then more hungrily. My head swooned and my body vibrated with longing. In an effort to make room for both of us on the narrow couch, I slid my knee between Regan's legs, hiking her dress halfway over her hips. As we kissed I felt the warm wetness of her excitement seep through the crotch of her panty hose and spread across my bare thigh. My heart swooned from the pleasure of it all.

The phone rang, startling us both. I bolted out from underneath Regan, practically dumping her on the floor and scrambled into the kitchen to answer it.

"Hello?" I said breathlessly into the receiver.

"Meen, it's me," Sean said. "Did I wake you?"

"No, I'm up, I'm up."

"You sound out of breath. Are you okay?

"Yes, fine . . . the phone ringing this early startled me, that's all. Is everything okay down there? "

"Yes, great. I wanted to catch you before you went to work. I need to run something important by you."

"Okay . . . what?"

"I've been asked to teach one of the specials units. It's the one on surveillance. The course means an additional two weeks down here, but they are offering to pay me five hundred dollars a week if I take it.

I wanted to run it by you to see how you felt about me being down here for another two weeks," Sean said.

"Sean, that's great," I said, my heart rate finally returning to a normal rate. "No, I don't mind at all. Sounds like a great opportunity, Sean. I wouldn't want you to miss it," I said glancing around the corner at Regan, excited about getting another two weeks to be with her.

"Thanks Meen. I knew you'd agree. So how are things going up there without me? Do you miss me yet?"

The question caught me off guard. "Of course," I said, careful of what I said as I was sure Regan was in earshot of this conversation.

"Hey, what do you think about coming down here next weekend? A couple of the other guys' wives are coming down. I could book a room at the Adam's Mark downtown and we could go out on the town in Columbus."

A feeling of apprehension swept through me. I didn't want to go. I didn't want to be away from Regan, but if I didn't go . . . It had already been weeks since Sean and I had seen each other. I felt I had no choice.

"That sounds great," I answered trying to hide my reluctance.

"Great. I'll make all the arrangements and call you back with—"

"I gotta get going," I said, cutting him off. "I haven't showered yet and I don't want to be late for work."

"Okay. Talk to you soon. I love you, Mina," Sean said.

The words caught in my throat. "I love you too," I whispered into the phone and then hung up.

I returned to the living room and found Regan, still lying on the couch, but now fast asleep. Our coffee, which sat on the end table, was now cold, and our blueberry muffins sat uneaten on the sunny yellow Fiesta Dinnerware plate. I picked up the mugs and plate and took them into the kitchen. I dumped the coffee in the sink, and carefully wrapped the muffins in Saran wrap for later and then headed for the shower.

It seemed so strangely erotic to be naked in the shower with Regan only one room, one closed door away. My body still pulsed with longing for her as the warmth of the water hit my chest and back. I wanted her here with me, both of us naked under the warm shower, our bodies melting together.

I got out of the shower, knees still weak from what had transpired earlier, toweled off, and got dressed. I emerged from the bedroom feeling fresh, awake, and alive. When I returned to the living room Regan was still asleep on the couch. She looked like a sleeping angel in her white uniform dress and white panty hose. I sat down on the couch next to her and stroked her hair.

"Regan . . ." I whispered.

She stirred, but did not wake up.

"Regan . . . we have to go to work," I said and gently kissed her forehead.

She opened her ice blue eyes, blinking the sleep away.

"Did I fall asleep?"

"Uh-huh." I nodded and brushed her bangs from her eyes.

"The last thing I remember was the phone ringing. Who was it?"

"It was Sean," I said unable to hide the hesitation in my voice.

"Oh," Regan said.

"He called to tell me he was chosen to teach one of the surveillance classes and that he would be down in Columbus an extra two weeks." I didn't have the heart to tell her he wanted me to come down there next weekend. I would deal with that later.

Awkward silence filled the room.

Regan stretched as she got off the couch. "I can't believe I fell asleep. What time is it?" she asked as she adjusted and smoothed out her uniform.

"Six thirty," I said as I slipped the uneaten blueberry muffins into my backpack.

"We better get moving," Regan said. "I need to use the bathroom first . . . to freshen up a little."

I smiled at Regan, acknowledging what she meant. She blushed.

"There's an extra toothbrush in the medicine cabinet and clean towels and washcloths in the cabinet next to the sink," I said following her into the bathroom.

Regan stepped into the bathroom and turned toward me. "I can take it from here," she said with a smile and then gently closed the bathroom door.

I smiled back, feeling totally love-struck and a little stupid smiling at a closed door.

Chapter Nine

Being at work together seemed to take on a whole new light. It was hard for me to concentrate. I screwed up the treatment sheet twice and forgot to schedule the nurse's aides' breaks and lunch times. I felt like a bumbling idiot.

Could the rest of the staff see what was going on between Regan and I, or was it just my imagination? I tried to be more self-conscious of my behavior toward Regan, but then all my composure would fall apart when Regan would brush against me or I would get a whiff of her hair. My feelings would fly into orbit and I'd get an irresistible urge to kiss her neck or something.

Regan seemed a little better at handling these situations. If the need came upon her, she'd take the secretive approach and sit down so close to me at the desk that our legs would be touching. When I'd look over at her, she'd smile, but would never look up from her work.

Regan finished the last chart of the day, just as I finished giving report to the afternoon shift. It was a typical Saturday afternoon; many of the residents were signed out with their families for a few hours, and the ones that remained napped in their rooms or in the TV lounge.

"What do you say we stay in tonight and order Chinese?" I asked Regan as we rode down in the elevator to punch out.

"That sounds good. I would've liked to take a drive out to the lake, but the air feels electric, you know, like a storm is on the way."

A gust of wind blew, ruffling Regan's hair around her face.

"Mmmm that breeze feels good," Regan said. "I need to stop at home before I come over. My uniform is sticking to my back. I'd like to shower and change clothes."

"I know. I can't believe this humidity. It's unbearable sometimes."

The Choice
Published by The Haworth Press, Inc., 2007. All rights reserved.
doi:10.1300/5791_09

"If you call our order into the Asian Moon, I'll pick it up on my way back to your place." Regan said.

"Okay. How 'bout I call and tell them to have it ready for five thirty?"

"That's fine."

I reached into my pocket and pulled out a twenty-dollar bill and handed it to Regan.

"I don't want your money," she said, snatching her hand away. "I can pay for dinner."

"Fine, I'll get the next one."

"Whatever," Regan said smugly, obviously content that she won the money struggle. That was another thing that was different about dating a woman. Who pays? When Sean and I dated, he usually did. But this was different. More like Regan and I were on equal ground. We seemed to be working it out as we went along.

Regan and I walked down the path that connected the nursing home parking lot with the apartment complex. I walked her over to her car.

"See you later," I said as Regan got into her car.

"Five thirty . . . I'll pick up some wine coolers too," Regan said closing the car door and then drove away.

I checked the answering machine as soon as I got into the apartment. There were two messages. One was from my mother wanting to know where the hell I had been for the past few weeks since Sean was out of town. The second one was from Sean with the details of our weekend in Columbus. He had booked us a room at the Adam's Mark downtown. He asked if I could leave work a little early on Friday to make the six thirty dinner reservation at the Columbus Club where we would be having dinner and drinks with three other police officers and their wives.

I erased both messages, not too anxious to respond to either one of them. The thought of spending my only weekend off this month down in Columbus, having to sit for hours and politely listen to the wives of the his colleagues drone on and on about potty training, breast-feeding, or their gifted child's latest accomplishments with the violin or in tap class, made my stomach tighten with anxiety.

I peeled off my sweat-stained uniform and took a long shower.

The doorbell rang at six o'clock, and without flipping on the intercom on to see who it was I hit the buzzer to let Regan in. She appeared at my door carrying a large white bag in one hand, and a beautiful bouquet of purple irises in the other.

"These are for you," Regan said, thrusting them toward me.

"Thank you . . . these are so beautiful," I said, awestruck. I had never received flowers, or anything else, for that matter, from anyone but Sean. Another milestone.

I took the bunch of irises from her and searched for a vase under the sink. I found a crystal vase I'd received as a wedding present and filled it with water from the tap.

"Regan, these are gorgeous," I said as I set the vase on the dining room table. "Thank you so much."

Regan blushed and smiled. Her smile was eager and alive with affection and delight.

"Let's eat," she said carrying several white cartons of moo goo gai pan, steamed rice, and vegetable lo mein by their wire handles into the living room, setting them down on the coffee table in front of the sofa.

A burst of wind blew through the open window in the living room.

"Feels like that storm is finally coming in," I said as I got up from the couch to close the window.

"I love summer storms. Don't you?" Regan asked as she wound her lo mein noodles around her fork.

"Um-hmm," I nodded, my mouth full of rice and Chinese vegetables. "As long as it's just a storm and not anything severe like a tornado."

Lightning flashed followed by the detonation of thunder. Then the downpour came.

"I love the sound of rain. It sounds like it's whispering. Like the rain is telling a secret," Regan said.

Lighting flashed again and suddenly the power went out. We both smiled, anxious and excited at the adventure.

"I guess we will have to finish our dinner by candlelight," I said as I rummaged through the junk drawer in the kitchen for a candle or two. I found two candle stubs that were once long white tapers. I lit them both and set them on the coffee table in front of us. The glow of the flames gave the room a warm and cozy feel.

"This is nice," Regan whispered. Her eyes were luminous in the candlelight.

"Yes, it is," I said.

My heart swelled with love for Regan, and at that moment I set down my carton of moo goo and took Regan's face into my hands. "You are so beautiful," I said, and then kissed her soft lips. Regan sat down her carton of lo mein, grabbed hold of the front of my T-shirt, and pulled me down on top of her. Lightning flashed and thunder crashed as the storm raged outside while our passion for each other raged inside, our kisses now more fervent than ever.

"This couch is killing my back, can we move to the floor?" Regan asked, breathlessly, struggling to get up to move onto the floor.

"Yes . . . yes . . . let's move," I said, and then took her hand as we both slid off the couch and onto the floor.

Soft tiny moans escaped her lips each time we parted. Regan lay on her back and I lay next to her on my side.

"Are you okay?" I asked.

Regan nodded.

I gazed down at her, her sun-streaked, caramel-colored hair swept around her face. Regan reached up to touch my face. Slowly with her fingertips she began to trace the outline of my profile as if she were trying to memorize it.

Lazily I stroked Regan's flat belly while she explored my face. She pulled me to her and we kissed again. I slid my hand up Regan's side, causing her to squeal with laughter.

"I'm a little ticklish there," she said.

I moved my hand back to her soft belly. "How's this?" I said, gazing down at her.

"Better," she said. Then she picked up my hand and laid it onto her right breast. "This is better, yet."

I couldn't contain the moan of ecstasy that escaped my lips. It felt like my entire insides were set on fire. I leaned down and kissed her hard as I fondled the small, supple globe, caressing it through her thin white T-shirt, feeling the nipple come to life under my palm. Regan arched her back and moaned at my touch I kissed her again, my tongue ravaging her soft warm mouth.

As amazing as all this was, I knew I had to restrain myself, and let whatever happened be under Regan's direction. I didn't want her to think that this was just about sex. That would make me no different than the guys she dated. I wanted her to know that I loved her and would wait for as long as it took. Still, a bigger hunger gnawed at me, wanting more, needing more, craving total abandon.

I slowly slid my hand from Regan's breast, down her belly to just above her jutting pubis. Her hand caught mine, before it could go any further. She pressed her hand against mine, holding it close against her. I was drowning in a haze of feelings and desires. Good feelings and bad desires. Guilt over my greediness finally took over.

"I'm sorry if I . . . went too fast," I said, suddenly feeling shy and unable to look at her.

"You didn't . . . I mean, it's okay . . . bad time of the month," she said with a shy smile.

Regan and I lay quietly on the floor as the storm outside subsided and all that remained was the silent calm. The candles on the coffee table had burned down to a wick and a puddle of wax. Regan snuggled up against me. "I feel so, so safe with you, Mina. You make everything seem alright."

I pulled her close, burying my face in her soft hair.

"Let's go away next weekend," Regan said. "We're both off. Let's just get into the car and drive and wherever we end up . . ."

I shuddered inwardly at the thought of what I had to tell her.

I broke our embrace. "Regan, I can't go away with you this weekend," I said, in an odd, but gentle tone.

Regan sat up cross legged and faced me.

"Oh. Why not?" she asked.

"Sean asked if I could come down to Columbus this weekend."

"Oh, I see." Regan said all enthusiasm deflated from her voice.

"Regan, I don't want to go. I want to be here with you."

"Then don't go."

Weighty silence filled the entire room. I felt ashamed because I couldn't tell her what she so desperately wanted to hear.

"I take that back," Regan said as she got to her feet. "I have no right to tell you what to do. Go Mina, you have to go, after all, he is your husband."

I couldn't look at her. Shame and anguish choked my heart.

"Anyway, the time apart will give us time to think if this is what we really want," Regan said somberly.

"Regan, I don't need time to think. I know this is what I want. I want to be here with you."

"But what about him? You know, you act like it's no big deal that you have a husband. Like this kind of thing happens all the time. Does it Mina? Have you done this before?"

"No . . . never," I said. Regan's remark stung. "I have never felt like this about any one but you," I said "What you and I have is different. It feels different than what I have with him."

"And what is that, Mina? What do we have?"

"Regan, what I feel for you is intimate and passionate and romantic, like nothing else I ever felt before."

"And what about him?"

"What I feel for him . . . is comfortable . . . like an old pair of slippers. But there's no spark, no fire, and there hasn't been for a long time."

"Doesn't this scare you?" Regan asked.

"Of course it does, but in my heart, it feels right."

"Aren't you afraid someone will find out about us? What if they find out at work? We could lose our jobs. Mina, everything about this . . . relationship . . . smacks of trouble."

Regan gathered her things and headed toward the door.

"Regan, what makes this so bad? Because what some religious doctrine dictates or that it's wrong because of someone else's opinion? How is loving someone wrong?"

"It's wrong when people get hurt."

"We aren't hurting anyone."

"What about Sean?" Regan said, with her hand on the doorknob. "Mina, don't you think this is going to hurt him?"

I couldn't answer her.

"You know Mina, someday you are going to have to make a choice. And that, my friend, is going to be very painful for a lot of people."

"Regan, don't go. We need to talk about this. Everything is happening so fast—"

"I have to go Mina. I need time to think, to put this in some kind of perspective. I'm sorry," Regan turned the doorknob and left. Her footsteps echoed in the stair well and then disappeared with the slam of the door.

Chapter Ten

Regan was right. People were going to get hurt. I could see it happening already. My head hurt. My heart hurt. And the potential for pain wasn't just what was happening between me, Sean, and Regan. I could see telling my mother, "Oh, by the way, I have fallen in love with someone else, and that person happens to be a woman." She would be appalled and devastated not to mention embarrassed and shamed. She'd excommunicate me from the family. She adored Sean and had told me time and time again that he was the best thing to ever happen to me. She would never understand what was going on inside of me. Catching a man was the ultimate goal in life, according to her. She would never understand my desire to be with a woman instead.

I got up the next morning feeling lonelier than ever. I packed up my things for work and headed over to the nursing home. My feelings oscillated between fear of seeing Regan and excitement about seeing Regan. I walked down the path and into the parking lot and looked for Regan's car. I checked my watch. It was six thirty and she hadn't arrived yet. It wasn't like Regan to be late. I waited until six fifty and then punched in and rode the elevator up to the second floor, thinking that maybe she just overslept; after all, we did have a late night the night before. I decided that once I got to the floor, I'd call her house and give her a wake-up call.

"Good morning," I said as I entered the dimly lit nurses' station. Brenda was sitting at the desk, finishing up her charts for the night.

"Oh, good morning," Brenda said, looking up from her paperwork.

I went back into the locker room, put my backpack into the locker, and changed into my clinic shoes.

The Choice
Published by The Haworth Press, Inc., 2007. All rights reserved.
doi:10.1300/5791_10

"How was your night?" I asked as I took a seat next to Brenda at the desk, still concerned where Regan was since it was already after seven.

"Good. No one died. Everyone is pretty stable right now."

"That's good."

"Hope your day is the same, working short and everything," Brenda said.

"Working short?" I asked, my heart racing.

"Regan called off this morning. You didn't know?" Brenda asked as she removed the bobby pins from her nurse's cap.

"No . . . no I didn't. I thought she was just running late this morning."

"Gee, I thought you two knew everything about each other. You two are so close."

"When did she call off?" I asked.

"About three thirty."

"Uh-huh."

"You seem pretty worried. Did something happen?" Brenda asked.

Something did happen, but I knew I couldn't tell Brenda or anyone else about it. The acute sense of loss I felt last night when Regan left my apartment returned.

"Uh . . . it's just that, well, Regan and I had dinner last night. Gosh, I hope the Chinese food we ate didn't make her sick," I said thinking quickly.

"Some people get a bad reaction to the MSG they put in Chinese food. Maybe that's what it was?" Brenda suggested.

"I don't know," I said, knowing full well it wasn't the food that kept Regan away.

Brenda finished report, but I only comprehended about one-fourth of what she said. She packed up her things and headed for the elevators.

"Oh, by the way," she yelled before getting on the elevator. "Brownie Troop 193 from Vienna is coming in this morning to visit with the residents. They are going floor to floor to sing and visit with them. I believe they are bringing Girl Scout cookies with them, so you might want to keep a close eye on the diabetics, especially, Otis. You know how charming he can be. He can talk anyone into or out of anything, especially a Brownie out of a box of her cookies."

"I'll keep an eye on him. Thanks Bren. See you tomorrow."

Brenda waved and stepped onto the elevator. Suddenly I felt very alone. I pulled the medication cart out into the nurses' station and tried to concentrate on pouring the first round of meds. I couldn't help thinking about Regan.

Most of the residents were up and dressed and at their places at the table in the solarium. Even Opal was up and dressed, although you could tell the difference between the days Opal dressed herself and the days Regan dressed her. Today Opal wore pink and green floral culottes and a brown wool ski sweater. On her feet she wore a blue tennis shoe on her right foot and a pink fuzzy slipper on her left.

"Opal, honey, lets go back to your room and get you a pair of shoes that match and another shirt. It's going to be eighty degrees today and I'm afraid you will swelter in that sweater," I said, gently taking Opal by the elbow and guiding her into her room. I helped Opal change her shoes and then I rummaged through Opal's dresser drawer and found a pretty white cotton blouse and helped her change into it. On top of Opal's dresser was a picture of Regan and Opal sitting outside in the courtyard.

"She's pretty," Opal said pointing to Regan in the picture.

"Yes, she is," I said. Obviously, Opal and I adored the same person. I walked Opal back out to the solarium and found a seat for her at the table next to several other residents watching the *Today* show on television.

I returned to my med cart, fighting the urge to call Regan at home to see what this was all about. As I poured the morning meds I saw a familiar black cowboy hat transverse the top of the desk of the nurses' station.

"Good morning Otis," I said as the hat stopped at the end of the desk.

"Good morning, ma'am," Otis said tipping his black Stetson toward me just like John Wayne in all those old black and white cowboy movies.

"My, you are all dressed up today. What's the occasion?"

"We're getting company after breakfast this morning. The Girl Scouts are coming to sing to us after breakfast."

"That sounds like a lot of fun."

"Yes. And I hope they bring some of those cookies, you know, the kind with chocolate on them. The mint kind," Otis said in a slow drawl. "I like those."

"I know you do, but Otis, you have to take it easy, you know your blood sugar has been a little high lately."

Otis looked down, dejected. "I know, but a couple of cookies aren't going to kill me," he said.

I thought about this for a moment. He was right. After all, what other pleasures did he have left? I had no right to take this simple joy away from him. "No, Otis, I don't think a couple of those cookies would cause much harm. Just a few though—not the entire box like last time."

I handed Otis his pills in a tiny paper soufflé cup. He took the cup from me and tossed his pills into the back of his throat, washing them down his gullet with a big gulp of prune juice. He took another swig of the prune juice, finishing it off, and then crushed the paper cup in his massive hands and tossed it into the trash can next to the desk. Otis then wheeled himself into line to be taken down to the dining room for breakfast.

By the time I finished the morning med pass, the desire to call Regan became absolutely unbearable. The only thing that held me back was that I didn't know what to say to her. My emotions were a jumbled mess. I was caught up in the high of Regan's warm body next to mine and then the crashing low of her leaving and not knowing if I'd ever see her again.

I pulled three charts out of the rack, hoping work would distract me from the turmoil inside. I flipped through the pages, initialing treatments and filling in the graphs with vital signs. Just as I finished the second chart, the oldest Brownie I had ever seen in my life appeared at the desk.

"Excuse me, I'm Nancy Wynyard and I'm here with Troop 193. We're here to sing to the residents this morning," she said as she stood before me, meaty forearms propped up on my desk. Fifteen little girls, all dressed in identical brown uniforms with chocolate brown beanies on their heads and cloth-badge-studded sashes angled across their prepubescent chests, milled around behind their leader.

Nancy was sturdy and robust, her Brownie troop leader uniform strained at its seams.

"Hello, I'm Mina," I said and extended my hand to the woman. She took it and shook it firmly.

"Where would you like us to set up?" The troop leader asked.

"How about over here by the window in the solarium. We can put the residents in a semicircle so they can see the girls better."

The little girls clamored into the solarium, patent leather Mary Jane's tapping on the linoleum.

Two of the nurse's aides came down from the third floor to help gather and seat the residents. I looked in Otis's room, but he wasn't back from breakfast yet. I asked one of the aides to make sure Otis made it back in time before the concert started. The Brownies were set up like a choir, backs against the large picture window in the solarium. Their leader blew into a tiny harmonica which emitted what I think was a B-flat note and then the troop broke out into song.

I went back to my charting and peeked over the top of the desk to see if Otis made it back yet. I didn't see the familiar cowboy hat and began to worry. I signaled Alberta, one of the nurse's aides over.

"Where's Otis?" I asked.

"He's still in the bathroom. I put him in right after breakfast and when I went to check on him a few minutes ago, he told me he wasn't done yet. I'll check on him in a few minutes," Alberta reassured me.

I opened another chart, wrote out my assessment, and initialed the vital sheet. I heard the toilet flush in Otis's room, and a few minutes later the black Stetson came cruising across the top of the nurses' station desk.

Suddenly there was an outburst of high pitched little girl screams. Chaos erupted as Troop 193 had stopped singing and were screaming and scattering. Some covered their eyes with their tiny, white-gloved hands while others just screamed and pointed. They were pointing in the direction of the black Stetson.

I nearly catapulted over the desk to see what was the matter. As I reached the solarium, there was Otis, sitting in his wheelchair, naked as a jaybird except for his cowboy hat and socks and shoes. The ear-piercing screams continued as wheelchairs were clanking together, tangled in a geriatric traffic jam in the solarium. No one could get in or out. I grabbed Otis's wheelchair with one hand and snatched the Stetson off his head with the other and plopped it into his lap to cover his nakedness and wheeled him into his room and closed the door behind us.

"Otis, what do you think you are doing?" I tried to be stern with him, but he was such a teddy bear of a guy, it was difficult.

"I wanted to see the kids sing," he said mournfully.

"But Otis, you're naked. You know you can't come out in the common area without any clothes. You scared the Brownie troop, and their leader too," I said.

"Well . . ." he started in his slow drawl. "I'm sorry . . . I didn't mean to scare the kids."

"I know you didn't Otis. Just try to remember next time. No streaking in the hallway," I joked.

"Okay, Nurse Mina," Otis said patting my hand with his. "Anyway . . . it's probably been a while since that leader has seen a naked man," Otis said and than laughed so hard that tears streamed down his cheeks.

I smiled, shaking my head, trying to hold back my own laughter: he was probably right.

"Otis, where are your clothes?" I asked.

"In the bathroom, ma'am. I had an accident during breakfast. It's that damn prune juice you give me every morning," Otis said.

"Oh, Otis, I'm sorry. Here, let me help you get cleaned up."

I helped him get dressed into a clean pair of pants and a button-down shirt. I removed the soiled clothes from the bathroom floor and threw them in the laundry shoot down the hall. By the time we returned to the solarium there was no sign of Troop 193 or their leader, Ms. Wynyard. I would have some explaining to do when Jacobs found out about this.

I returned to the desk and sat down with my head in my hands. My head was pounding. Suddenly, Alberta appeared at the desk.

"Mina, I'm sorry about Otis, I was in changing Giselle Webber's bedclothes and didn't get back to him in time to help him get dressed," Alberta said apologetically.

"Otis is fine. I guess we better lay off the prune juice for a while. I'll make a note in his chart to let the other shifts know," I said.

"Can you come and check Giselle? When I turned her she seemed to be having a hard time breathing."

I grabbed my stethoscope off the med cart and followed Alberta to Mrs. Webber's room. Giselle Webber was ninety-eight years old and had been in a vegetative state for the past two years. She never spoke, only cried out when she was wet, or in pain. I put my stethoscope to Giselle's chest. Her breaths were few and far between, and very moist.

"Alberta, lets give her a little oxygen. Get me one of the small oxygen cylinders and a mask. Oh, and bring one of the small suction machines," I ordered.

Alberta left the room to retrieve the oxygen and the suction machine. I knew that Giselle was a DNR, which meant that if she stopped breathing or if her heart stopped, we could not perform any lifesaving techniques such as CPR or administer any cardiac meds. But that didn't mean I had to let Giselle drown in her own secretions.

Alberta returned to the room with everything I had requested. I assembled the oxygen tubing and mask and attached them to the oxygen tank. I let Giselle breathe in the oxygen for a few minutes until I put together the suction machine and attached the tubing.

"Okay, Giselle, this might feel a little uncomfortable, but only for a minute," I shouted over the vibrating suction machine motor.

Giselle didn't respond, but then again she hadn't responded to anything in the past two years. I lifted the oxygen mask from her face and slid the suction catheter into the side of Giselle's mouth. I slid the catheter deeper into Giselle's lungs, sucking out copious amounts of thick yellow mucus.

"Wow, she's loaded," Alberta said as she stood by in case I needed any more supplies.

Giselle bucked and gagged with the insertion of the suction catheter into her lungs. She flailed her arms, trying to knock the catheter
away. Not only does the suction clean the mucus out of her lungs,
sometimes it takes her air too.

"It's okay, Giselle," Alberta said, holding Giselle's gnarled hands,
trying to comfort the old woman.

Giselle's color had turned from pale to ashen blue. I pulled the
catheter out of Giselle's lungs to check her breathing. I laid my
stethoscope on Giselle's frail chest, but did not hear any air exchange
in her lungs. I placed the oxygen mask over Giselle's nose and mouth
and waited a few seconds to see if the oxygen would stimulate her
breathing. It did not.

I turned the oxygen up, from two liters to four liters. Still nothing,
only the gurgling sounds of a person near death.

"Alberta, quick, go get me the Ambu bag," I ordered.

"But she's a DNR," Alberta said. "You can't—"

"Alberta, I can't just let her suffocate. If this was your mother lying
here, gasping for air, what would you do?"

Alberta sprinted out of the room and returned with the Ambu bag.
I inserted a white plastic oral airway and attached the Ambu bag to it.
I had to alternate the pressured breaths the Ambu bag gave Giselle
with intermittent suction clear out the thick mucus that was blocking
her airway. Finally, Giselle started to pink up.

"Whew, that was close," I said to Alberta. "I thought I was going
to lose her."

"I know, but look how much easier she's breathing," Alberta said.
"You made the right call, Mina."

"Thanks," I said, feeling weary.

I just wanted this day to end. I wanted to go somewhere where
I didn't have to think. I wanted to crawl away from the world and
just be.

I looked at the clock in the solarium and couldn't believe that it was
already eleven forty-five. I returned to the desk and pulled the med
cart to pass the lunchtime meds. The aides were lining up the residents to go down to the dining room for lunch, so I scrambled to get
their medications to them before they went down. Once they were

medicated, I started down the hall to take care of the residents that were too weak or too sick to leave their rooms. I checked on Giselle again and found her breathing much more easily. I made a mental note to change the mask to a nasal cannula as soon as possible; they seemed to fit better and were more comfortable for the patient. I also needed to replace the small oxygen tank with a larger one.

At one o'clock the meds had been passed and I was able to return to the desk to catch up on the charting. My stomach growled with hunger, but I didn't have the time or the energy to unpack the peanut butter and jelly sandwich I had packed this morning. *I'll eat when I get home,* I thought and trudged on with the charting. The phone rang. By the way it rang, I could tell it was an outside call. My heart jumped. Maybe it was Regan. Eagerly I grabbed the receiver.

"Second floor, Thomas, RN," I said into the receiver.

"Mina. It's Miss Jacobs."

My heart sank.

"Yes, Miss Jacobs."

"Mina, you are getting an admission this afternoon. I know we usually don't admit on the weekend, but the hospital isn't giving us much choice."

"Yes, ma'am," I said into the receiver calmly. I wasn't about to mention the incident with the Brownie troop. Jacobs would find out about that soon enough.

"Mina, this new patient is very ill. She has multiple medical problems, and from the report I got from the hospital, her condition seems pretty unstable. There is nothing more they can do for her at the hospital, so they are basically sending her to us to die."

"Any idea what her ETA will be?" I asked, rubbing my aching forehead. I hated these cases. It's like everyone has given up on them and then they dump them on us. The idea of dealing with an unstable patient seemed too much today.

"She's en route now. She'll probably make it to the nursing home within the hour."

"Is there anything I need to know before she gets here?"

"She's got an IV and she finished her last round of chemo this morning. And I believe her daughter is with her."

"What's the patient's name?" I asked.

I heard Jacobs shuffle papers on the other end of the receiver. "Rosetti, Teresa Rosetti," she said. "She's eighty-three with terminal lung cancer."

Rosetti? I heard that name before, but couldn't quite place it.

"Okay, we'll be ready for her," I told Miss. Jacobs, then hung up the phone.

Suddenly, it dawned on me. Rosetti was the name of Sean's new partner. Well, whether I was ready or not, today I would meet her.

Teresa Rosetti arrived by ambulance at two fifteen in the afternoon. A younger woman with short black hair accompanied her. The woman wore a police officer's uniform and had a nine-millimeter duty gun strapped to her hip. This had to be Sean's partner. Now it made sense that she moved. She had done so to take care of her sick mother.

I met the Rosettis at the elevator and helped the paramedics get Teresa comfortable.

"Hello, my name is Mina Thomas," I said to her. "Once we get you settled, I have a few questions to ask you and then I'm going to listen to your heart and lungs."

Teresa Rosetti nodded weakly.

"Maybe I can help you with the questions. I'm her daughter," the woman in the police officer's uniform said and extended her hand to me.

"I'm Mina, I'll be taking care of your mom until the next shift comes on," I said shaking her hand.

"I'm Rosemary. Rosemary Rosetti," she said with a smile, exposing even, white teeth that contrasted pleasingly with her dark complexion. "I came straight from work."

"I can see that, officer." I answered more brusquely than I wanted too. "Let's get started. Do you have her medication list?"

"Yes." Rosemary fished into the breast pocket of her blue uniform shirt and pulled out a well-worn piece of paper.

I copied the meds down and went on to the next section of the admission form.

"Are you her next of kin?"

"Yes."

"I need your address and phone number and work number for the chart, in case of emergency."

Rosemary rattled off the information I requested. "I'm staying at her house for now. I just moved back home from Cleveland.

"I thought your name sounded familiar. You work with my husband, Sean."

"Excuse me?" Rosemary said.

"On the drug task force . . . Sean Thomas, isn't he one of the guys you work with?"

"Yes . . . how did you know that?"

"I'm Sean's wife, Mina."

"Oh my . . . I didn't . . . Sean never . . . I mean, we've only worked together for a couple of weeks. Well, it's nice to meet you," Rosemary said, her face flushed.

"Sean never even mentioned my name?" I asked, hurt and incredulous.

"Like I said, we've only worked together a few times. I've been stuck alone on a surveillance project. The times we did work together, I'm not sure Sean was so thrilled with having a female partner," Rosetti said.

"Really? What makes you think so?" I asked.

"He just seemed uncomfortable. It's not like I haven't seen this before. A lot of guys have trouble working with a female officer at first, especially one that outranks them. He seemed like a nice guy, and a good officer as well," Rosetti said.

Somehow, meeting Rosetti calmed my fears of my husband having an affair with her. She definitely was not Sean's type. The stranger thing was that there was something about her that stirred something in me. I admired her for pulling up stakes and coming back home to care for her ailing mother, but it went deeper than that.

I received the report from the paramedic and went into Teresa's room to get her admitted and settled. She was a tiny woman with huge brown eyes and banana yellow skin that told me her liver had already given up its fight. I finished the admission questionnaire and physical exam just as afternoon turn came onto the unit. Sandy, the afternoon charge nurse, and not one of my favorite people, sat waiting patiently for me to count narcotics and give report. It's not that Sandy wasn't a nice person; it's just that she could be so cynical at times. She always managed to find the negative in any given situation.

"Looks like you were busy today," Sandy said.

"Yes, and I worked short today too. Regan called in sick."

"What's wrong with her?" Sandy asked.

"I'm not sure. The flu I think. I was going to call her earlier, but no time. On top of everything else, I got an admission from the hospital this afternoon."

"Admission? But it's the weekend."

"I know, but there was a problem at the hospital . . . we had no choice." I had wanted to continue my complaints when Rosemary came up to the nurses' station.

"Excuse me, Mina. Can you check to see when my mother last had her pain medication? She seems terribly uncomfortable."

"Sure, I'll check and bring her something in a few minutes," I answered.

Just as soon as Rosetti had turned her back to us Sandy whispered, "Who's the dyke?"

"What?"

"That woman?" Sandy asked, gesturing with her eyes in Rosetti's direction.

"That's the new admission's daughter. She's very nice . . . seems to care a lot about her mother's well-being. She's a police officer."

"I kinda got that by the way she was dressed."

"Actually, she works on the force with my husband, Sean."

"Well then I guess you'll never have to worry about him cheating on you with her," Sandy said.

"What kind of thing is that to say?" I asked, trying to sound nonchalant.

"I don't think she plays on our team," Sandy said with a wink.

I knew what she was getting at, but I wanted to hear her say the words. Suddenly I was in a mood to challenge her, challenge everybody—the world.

"What do you mean, 'our team'?"

"She's a lesbian. No straight woman looks like that. And look at how she walks. No straight woman walks like that either."

"Just because a person walks a certain way doesn't mean . . . I mean you can't tell a person's sexual preference by the way they walk, can you?" I hoped my insecurity would not show.

"Sure you can. I'll bet she carries a wallet in her back pocket and doesn't wear a stitch of makeup."

"I don't wear makeup, does that make me a lesbian?" I said, my heart pounding so hard I was afraid Sandy would hear it.

"No, of course not, silly, you're married," Sandy said with a snicker.

Sandy's comments made me angry, but flipped a light on inside of me. A light I wasn't sure I wanted to see. Would people view me as a pervert or freak because I chose to love a woman?

I shook the thoughts from my head and checked Teresa's medication sheet. Rosemary was sitting at her mother's bedside but stood up when I entered the room carrying some liquid Dilaudid to ease her mother's pain.

"Thanks for taking care of this so quickly," Rosemary said.

"It's no problem," I said and administered the cherry red elixir to her mom.

Teresa made a face at its bitterness. "How about a sip of water?" I asked Teresa.

She nodded.

"Excuse me," I said coming face to face with Rosetti as I turned in the cramped space between the bed and the bathroom to get Teresa a cup of water. It was true, Rosemary didn't wear makeup, but then again she didn't need any. Her olive skin was flawless and her dark, Italian looks radiated natural beauty.

I helped Teresa take a few sips of water. She was so weak, I practically had to hold her up with one arm and tilt the paper cup for her with the other.

"Enough?" I asked Teresa.

She nodded. I laid her back down and I helped her get comfortable in her bed. I felt Rosetti's gaze on my back. It made me nervous.

"My shift is over, but I'll be back in the morning. If you need anything, Sandy, the afternoon charge nurse, can help you," I said and turned to leave.

"Thank you for everything. And tell Sean I said hello. I'm supposed to join him down in Columbus next week, but if Mom's condition doesn't improve, I won't be able to make it."

"I'll be sure to tell him that we met," I said leaving the room, wondering if what Sandy said was true: Could you really tell a person's sexual preference by the way they dressed or walked? *Nah,* I said to myself as I thought of how feminine Regan dressed and how well she applied all that makeup. There was no way you could tell by just looking at someone. What next? Would people start developing radar to pick gay folks out of a crowd?

Chapter Eleven

I checked the answering machine as soon as I got home. No messages. I felt edgy, caged in. I couldn't stand to be alone in the apartment, so I changed into shorts and a T-shirt and headed outside for a long walk. I hoped that the fresh air and sunshine would clear my head.

Many of the residents were sitting outside enjoying the afternoon shade under the oak trees. I stopped to tie my shoelace and waved hello to two of my neighbors, Mabel and Delores, who sat on one of the wooden porch swings. I could hear them chitchattering. They were so hard of hearing, it was impossible not to eavesdrop.

"There goes that girl that lives in one-A," Mabel shouted to Delores. "You know, her husband, the good-looking policeman has been away for quite some time."

"Is that so," Delores responded in the same tone. "You know, I see a fancy red car parked in their space at all hours sometimes. I hope she's not keeping company with some other man while he's away," Delores said.

"Don't be ridiculous," Mabel said. "That car belongs to that pretty little nurse from the nursing home. You know . . . Rita . . . Rena . . . Regan."

"Regan? Like the president?"

"Yes, like the president," Mabel answered.

"Well, that's a strange name for a pretty girl like that. I wonder if her parents were hippies or something." Delores asks.

Mabel shakes her head, not bothering to answer her friend of over fifty years.

"So how do you know that's whose car it is?" Delores asked.

The Choice
Published by The Haworth Press, Inc., 2007. All rights reserved.
doi:10.1300/5791_11

"I'm up every hour, you know, because of that damn water pill I gotta take for my blood pressure. I saw her leave one morning in her uniform," Mabel said.

"Oh. Good thing. I'd hate to think that she was cheating on her husband while he was away. They seem like such a nice young married couple." Delores said.

Their voices faded as I walked along the gravel path and down the hill to the cemetery. *If they only knew,* I thought.

I used to go to the cemetery a lot, but it had been a long time since. As I passed each marble headstone I began to realize that I had taken care of many of the people buried there. The cemetery was well kept; its grass was mowed and trees were trimmed. The grounds were dotted with purple rhododendrons and white and pink peonies the size of cabbages.

I headed directly for my father's gravesite. It used to be such a comfort to be there, near him. Now, I was lucky to make it there on his birthday, Christmas, and Father's Day.

As I looked at the black granite headstone I couldn't believe how many years had gone by since his death. I felt an ache in my heart. I missed him so much. I said the Our Father in my head and silently wondered what he would think of my life now. Sadness crept over me as I sensed that although he wasn't a big fan of Sean, he would never approve of my relationship with Regan. Never.

I pulled a couple of weeds from the base of his headstone and moved on, walking between the headstones and up onto the gravel path. Up ahead I saw a familiar car parked alongside the road. The wavy heat coming off the gravel driveway made the golden color of the car shimmer in the sunlight. A few feet away was a woman in a floppy brimmed straw hat, crouched down on her hands and knees, planting flowers in front of a very elegant marble headstone. It was Vivian's friend, Martha, tending to her friends grave.

"Martha, how are you?" I asked, hoping I didn't startle her.

Martha shielded her eyes with her gardening gloved hand. "Mina? Is that you?"

"Yes. I'm glad you remembered. Martha, it's good to see you. How have you been?"

Martha shook off her gardening gloves. They were caked with top-soil and mulch. She got to her feet with a grunt and hugged me tight. "I'm well, Mina. Lonely, but well," Martha answered.

Pale green grass shoots emerged over Vivian's burial plot. I couldn't believe that Vivian had been gone long enough for grass to grow. A fresh bouquet of white roses and lavender sat in the permanent bronze vase in front of the headstone. I smiled, knowing they were probably from Martha. Vivian's headstone definitely suited her: Italian rose granite with a picture of the Blessed Mother etched in the stone on the right side, Vivian's dates on the left. Vivian. Always dressed to the nines, even in the afterlife.

"What brings you out here?" Martha asked.

"I come out here sometimes to walk . . . and think," I said. "My father's grave is here."

"You look troubled honey. Problems at home? " Martha asked.

I sighed. "I guess you could say that."

Martha's eyes met mine. "Whatever it is honey, let it go. Life is too short to let little things bother you," Martha said.

"I'm not sure it's a little thing."

Martha looked at me for a long time, trying to decide whether she should pry into my life.

"It's hard to believe that almost two months have gone by since Vivian's passing," she said gently, as if to remind me that life and death belong together like right and left, day and night, good and bad.

"It seems like yesterday to me," she continued. "I still get up in the morning and think, 'I need to stop at the library to get something new to read to her,' but then I catch myself."

"I know what you mean. I think about her every day when I take care of Mrs. Laird. She has Vivian's old room now. Her family placed her in the nursing home so her care would not interrupt their daily lives."

"It's a shame how some folks treat their loved ones. Like they are disposable or something. Awful . . . just awful," Martha said, shaking her head. Looking at her, you'd never know that she was eighty-four years old. She was so vibrant.

Martha bent down, picked up her gardening gloves, and shook them again. Clumps of dirt and mulch fell to the ground.

"Whatever it is that has you troubled, honey, go with your heart. You only get one chance to live your life. Why shouldn't it be to the fullest? You never know what tomorrow is going to put in your path, so live today, with no regrets."

"Do you have any regrets?" I asked.

"My only regret in life is that I wasn't with Vivian that night when she passed away. I feel like I let her down."

A gust of wind blew the floppy brim of Martha's hat up and tousled Martha's steel-gray hair as she stared down at the clumps of dirt that had fallen off her gloves

"Martha, can I ask you something?"

"Sure, honey. What is it?"

"Martha . . . you and Vivian were close, right?"

"Well, yes dear, I've known Vivian longer than anyone in my entire life. She was a special person—strong, funny, kind, and considerate. She was the one person in my life I knew I could count on, no matter what."

Martha looked down at the new growth of grass and whispered, "She was the love of my life."

When Martha looked up at me, I finally understood. I smiled.

"Oh, Martha, I am so sorry for your loss," I said and I hugged her tight.

"Thank you honey," Martha said brushing her tears away with the back of her hand.

"Oh, Martha, I knew, I mean, I always had a feeling that there was something more between you . . . something deeper."

"Isn't that something? You could pick that up when most people would never give our friendship a second thought?" Martha said. "You know, Vivian always told me that there was something special about you. She liked you very much."

"I miss her so much. Going to work just isn't the same now that she's not there anymore."

"What I wouldn't give to have just one more day with Vivian. Just one more day to sit in the sunshine, to laugh and to read to her and to tell her how much I love her," Martha said, sadly.

"Martha, can I tell you something?"

"Sure, honey, what is it?

"I've found a love like yours and Vivian's and it's tearing me apart." My voice was trembling.

"Oh, honey, love is never easy, but true love is never wrong. If it's truly love and you are meant to be with this woman, then it will work out." She paused. "Love with all your might, because love is the only thing that matters in life."

"But I don't know where I'm supposed to be. I'm in love with this woman, but I am married too."

Martha looked at me for a moment. "I see. I guess you'll have to decide who holds the biggest place in your heart."

"I can't. I love them both."

"There is no easy answer. All you can do is what feels right and go with your heart. Someday you will know that this rough time, like everything else, was but a stepping-stone to where your life is supposed to be. No matter how wrong it seems if you look at it from your head," she said and pointed to her heart, "it's what's in there that really matters."

"Is that what you did? With Vivian?"

"You betcha. It took a long time for both of us to feel comfortable in our feelings for each other. Everything about our relationship was wrong. But in my heart and I know in Vivian's heart, it was right."

"I imagine back in your day, being gay was not easy."

"No. Even though neither Vivian nor I had a husband to deal with, we still had to be secretive. Not only was being a homosexual thought of as a mental illness, it was a crime too. A crime against nature, as they used to say," Martha said. "Vivian and I loved each other very much. We were both schoolteachers. Can you imagine what would have happened if a child's parent or the school board found out about us? We would have lost our jobs and been lynched for sure. But it didn't matter. I would have paid any price to be with her."

"It's a shame the prejudices you have to endure just because the person you love has the same chromosomal pattern as you"

Martha laughed. "I guess you could put it that way."

Although my "coming out" to Martha should have relieved some of my anxieties, it didn't. Actually it made me look at the difficulties of lesbian relationships more closely. It scared me more than I wanted to admit. I wasn't as brave as Martha. And I didn't know whether I was as committed either.

"The sun's going down. I better head home before it gets dark. My doctor says I shouldn't be driving at night so much. Age, ya know?" Martha smiled.

I helped her load the gardening tools into the trunk of her car.

"It was nice seeing you again, Mina. Maybe we could get together some time for lunch or something. I have some old friends you might be interested in meeting someday."

"I'd like that very much."

We hugged. Martha eased herself into the Oldsmobile and started the engine. I watched as she slowly drove away, gravel crunching under her worn tires.

The sky was streaked with pink feathery clouds when I headed back to the apartment. I walked along the gravel path, silently reading the names on the headstones as I passed them: Priore, Watkins, Bernard, and Webber. They all seemed familiar. Webber . . . Webber? Giselle Webber—the oxygen. I suddenly realized that I had forgotten to change the oxygen tank.

I sprinted through the cemetery and through the empty courtyard and bounded up three flights of steps. I burst into my apartment and frantically dialed the phone.

"Second floor, this is Sandy, can I help you?"

"Sandy, it's Mina," I said huffing and puffing. "Sandy, I forgot to change Giselle's oxygen tank over from the portable unit to—"

"I know," Sandy interrupted. "I changed it over when I did four o'clock rounds. She was practically on 'E' and the oxygen mask was up around her eyes. I changed the tubing and switched her over to a nasal cannula."

Thank God, I thought. "Thank you, Sandy," I said, my heart finally returning to a more normal rate. "I owe you."

"No problem. I knew you had a tough day, working short and all. Giselle is fine. Don't worry about it," Sandy said.

But I did worry about it. What was I doing? The thing with Regan had gotten me so messed up I couldn't even think straight. Now it was affecting my work. I had to do something about it and I had to do it now. I dialed Regan's number.

"Hello."

"Regan?"

"Yes."

"Regan, it's Mina. What's going on? Are you alright?"

There was nothing but silence on the other end for an excruciatingly long second or two.

"Yes, of course I'm alright."

"I was worried."

"I'm fine, really. I just needed a mental health day, that's all."

"Regan, I feel like I am going crazy . . . the way we left things last night . . . I was afraid, afraid that I have ruined everything, afraid you didn't want to see me again."

"Mina . . . it's just that this is all so confusing."

"It does feel confusing and strange and wonderful. You know how much I care about you, Regan, don't you? I can't imagine not having you in my life."

"Yes, I know, but everything I have been taught says that what we are doing is wrong."

"How can it be wrong when it feels this wonderful?" I pleaded. "I know I sound like a cliché, but c'mon, Regan. I know you feel it too."

"I'm not sure how I feel." She seemed so distanced. I had to find a way to close the distance between us.

"Can't we get together tonight and talk about this? I'll cook dinner for you here. Whatever you want, I'll try and make it."

"I don't know Mina, I really need some time to think this through."

I had to leave in a few days for Columbus and I didn't want to leave things like this.

"Please Regan, I want to make things right between us before I have to leave for Columbus." I could feel her hostility before she answered.

"And what am I supposed to do while you're gone?"

"Regan, believe me if this wasn't something I had to do, I wouldn't do it."

"Mina, you're leaving me here to tend to your more socially accepted life with Sean. Do you know how that makes me feel?"

I didn't know what to say. I knew she was right.

"You can't have it all, Mina. Nobody has it all."

"I don't know what else to do. This is important to him and his career. He needs me there."

"So you leave me here to go down to Columbus and play the good wife?" Regan said.

"I just feel so obligated to Sean . . . and so guilty for leaving you. I'm sorry, Regan, I don't want to hurt you. I don't want to hurt anybody, I just don't know what else to do," I said.

"You really don't know what to do, do you?" she paused. When she continued I could sense that she already knew the answer to her own question. "I believe you when you say you don't want to hurt anyone, but in this situation, that seems impossible, now doesn't it?"

A heaviness centered in my chest. I knew she was right.

"So what are you going to do?"

"I have to go. I have no choice. If I don't go, he will become suspicious that something is going on up here and come home. I'm not ready for that, are you?"

"But something *is* going on. Don't you think he's going to find out eventually? And when he does find out, then what? Don't you think it's better if you tell him yourself than for him to find out from someone else?" Regan asked.

"Yes, yes, you're right, but I'm just not ready to tell him. Not yet anyway."

"But you do intend to tell him, don't you?"

"Yes. Yes, I do. But I need to find the right time."

"So if you're not willing to tell him about us now, then promise me one thing before you go?"

"Anything," I said.

"Promise me you won't sleep with him. Save that for us."

"I promise," I said feeling grateful, happy, confused, and scared all at the same time. But I knew that her making me promise to be with her was a gift, a dedication of love, and a commitment. I cherished that thought and let it rock me to sleep that night.

When I saw Regan the next morning at work she had brought Opal another brightly colored polo shirt and was leading her by the hand to the solarium for breakfast.

"Good morning."

"Good morning," Regan smiled at me warmly.

The morning sun in her hair made her look angelic. I loved watching her patiently help Opal get ready for breakfast. She was so gentle and kind; how could I not have fallen in love with her? Somehow I needed to make this relationship work. Martha was right. I needed to go with my heart. At this point, my heart was overflowing with love, with love for Regan. I couldn't wait to be alone with her again, to show her and tell her how much I loved her. I walked over to where she and Opal were sitting in the solarium.

"Do you want to come over tonight? Maybe we could catch a movie or something?" I asked, hoping she'd agree to see me that night.

"I don't know. There really isn't anything good on. How about if we rent a movie?" she said as if things were all back to normal.

"Great. Why don't you stop at the video store and I'll go to the grocery store to find us something for dinner."

"You're gonna cook?" Regan asked, surprised.

"Yes. What's the matter with that?"

"Well, for as long as I've known you, you've never cooked anything other than Lean Cuisine. A monkey can do that," Regan said.

"So, what are you saying?"

"Nothing, don't get so defensive, It's just that I'm surprised, that's all."

"You'll see. I am half Italian, you know."

"What does that have to do with anything?" Regan asked, with a chuckle.

"You just be at my apartment at six o'clock. You're in for a real treat."

Regan rolled her eyes and we both laughed. It felt good to laugh again.

By the time Regan arrived that night I had marinara sauce simmering on the stove next to a big pot of boiling water, just waiting for the cheese tortellini I had bought at the Italian market down the street.

"Mmm, something smells good," Regan said as she came into the kitchen. She set down the bag of videotapes and lifted the lid on the saucepan. "Wow, you made this?"

"Yes, I did."

"Are you sure that's not Ragú or something?" Regan asked, looking around the kitchen for an empty jar as evidence.

"No, it's not Ragú," I was insulted. "What kind of Italian do you think I am?"

"I'm just kidding you," she said. "I'm actually impressed with your culinary skills," she said, replacing the metal lid on the pot.

I finished cutting up cucumbers for the salad and wiped my hands on the dishtowel I had tucked into the waistband of my cutoffs. "What movies did you get us for tonight?"

"I picked up a couple, because I couldn't decide," she said and dumped the contents of the plastic bag onto the dining room table. "*Risky Business, Yentl,* and *Personal Best* . . . any of these sound good?" she asked.

"*Risky Business* is a good one, although I've seen it three times already. *Yentl* I've seen twice, and *Personal Best* I've never even heard of."

Regan picked up the tape and turned it over. "'Penetrating, heartfelt, and thrilling. One sweet explosion,'" Regan read the back of the tape. "There are actual Olympic athletes in this movie, as well as Mariel Hemingway."

"Sounds riveting," I teased. "Let's eat first, and then we can settle into the living room, have dessert, and watch the movie."

I lit the candles on the dining room table, opened a bottle of merlot, and poured each of us a glass. Regan helped by cutting the crusty loaf of Italian bread and putting the thick slices into a wicker basket. I ladled the marinara sauce over the tortellini and brought the large bowl to the table.

"Ta-dah! And you said I couldn't cook," I said to Regan as we took our seats at the table.

"I never said you couldn't cook. It's just that, well, it was always a mystery. But I have to say I am very impressed."

"Thank you," I said, and then ladled a large portion of tortellini onto Regan's plate. "There's a lot of things about me you don't know."

"I'm sure there are," Regan laughed. "I'm sure there are."

We finished dinner and did the dishes. I washed and Regan dried. I took the cheesecake from the refrigerator along with the quart of fresh strawberries I had cleaned earlier. I set the cheesecake, strawberries, and the half-empty bottle of wine along with our two glasses on the coffee table in the living room while Regan slid *Personal Best* into the VCR.

I sliced and plated two hefty pieces of cheesecake and covered each piece with the strawberries. Regan and I both moaned after our first bite. The cheesecake melted in our mouths, sweet, silky, and cool.

"This is incredible," Regan's mouth was still full of the cheesecake. I noticed that she had a smear of cheesecake and graham cracker crumb crust on her lower lip. I reached up and wiped it away with my finger and licked it off.

Regan and I sat close on the couch. It felt so wonderful to be close to her again. The movie started, with a track meet where Chris Cahill, Mariel's character, loses her race. Regan and I commented on how thin and fit the women in the movie were.

"My body will never look like that, no matter how much Jane Fonda I do," I said.

"Mine either," Regan commented. Then we both looked down at the half-eaten pieces of cheesecake on our plates and burst out laughing.

The movie played on. It wasn't an Academy Award winner, but it was entertaining, and then all of the sudden Mariel and Patrice Donnelly, who played Tory Skinner, a track star who qualified for the boycotted Olympics in 1980, kiss after an arm wrestling match.

Heavy silence filled the room. I could not believe what I was seeing, and, by the look on Regan's face, neither could she. Regan's gaze was glued to the screen and I think she even stopped breathing. What was playing out on the screen was exactly what we were going through. I could barely breathe myself during the next scene. The two young women were naked and making love by the muted light of a life-size plastic swan nightlight.

Regan burrowed closer to me, laying her head on my shoulder as we watched. The Boz Scaggs song played and by the time Chris Cahill blows out her knee attempting to do the high jump, Regan was lying on top of me, with her hands up my shirt.

"Regan, I . . ." I said, squirming beneath her.

She stifled my words with more kisses.

I broke our kiss again. "Regan, I, uh . . ."

Regan kissed me again and we slid onto the floor. I took her in my arms and laid her down on her back on the floor. I gazed down at her.

She smiled and pulled me to her, kissing me again and again. She tugged at my T-shirt, pulling it over my head and off in one efficient motion. Regan looked at me as if she was photographing me with her eyes. The sensuality of her gaze sent chills throughout my entire being. If I had known she would've reacted this way to this type of movie I would have rented it weeks ago.

I removed Regan's shirt as well and gazed at her lace-covered breasts.

"You are so beautiful," I whispered as I stroked her taut nipple through the pink lace cup. When I lowered my mouth to her breast, feeling the rough lace against my lips and tongue, Regan arched her back and let out a soft, sweet moan. My hands explored the soft skin of her belly, her hips, and her back, feeling so lucky and so grateful to have her back in my arms again.

Regan reached up and unhooked the plastic clasp that was nestled between her breasts. I pushed the lacy cups to the side, my heart hammered in my ears as I lowered my mouth to her naked breast.

Regan buried her hands in my hair, guiding me from her right breast and then to her left and then pulled me up to her, kissing me hard and sliding her sweet tongue into my mouth. I reached around my back, unhooked my bra, and tossed it next to my discarded T-shirt. Naked breast touched naked breast. I thought I was going to come right then and there.

Regan's hands explored my back as I slid down her body, tasting her neck, collarbone, and beautiful breasts. It was wonderful—an ecstasy so deep and so meaningful, I had never experienced anything like this before. I kissed my way down her taut belly to the top of her Levi's 501s. *It's now or never,* I thought as I slid one finger into the waistband, teasing her. Slowly I unbuttoned the first button and then the second. I glanced up at Regan for a sign as to whether I should continue or stop. She held my gaze as I unbuttoned the third button. No resistance, so I continued onto the fourth and finally the fifth. I tugged on the jeans and Regan raised her hips off the floor so I could slide them off.

She wore pink lace panties that matched the lace bra, which still hung by satin straps from her shoulders. I inhaled deeply, savoring her musky scent, a true aphrodisiac. I rubbed my face against her belly and silky inner thighs, savoring it all, the sight, the scent, and the sensations all of this evoked in me.

Regan was wet, soaking wet. Her excitement seeped clean through her panties onto her inner thighs. Slowly I slid her panties over her hips, down her long, tan legs, and tossed them aside. I looked down at her and for the first time in my life saw a naked woman lying before me, waiting for me to make love to her. I lay down between her legs, her crotch now only inches from my face. I stared into her secret place, as fragrant, dark, and lush as I had imagined. My own underwear were soaked clean through my cutoffs, the seam of which teased my swollen clitoris with each movement. The sensation was exquisite.

I couldn't hold back any more. I lowered my mouth to her and blew a soft stream of air over her swollen sex. Regan arched her back, practically shoving her crotch in my face. Her tormented groan was a heady invitation to go further. Closing my eyes, I kissed her there as if I were kissing her full on the mouth. I savored the salty sweet taste of her, the feel of her warm wetness on my mouth and tongue. My heart exploded with joy and ecstasy as I made love to Regan for the first time. This was it. I finally found it. This was what it was all about.

Regan writhed on my face as my tongue dipped into her tight, wet opening and then lightly traced the length of her swollen, erect clit. Her moans grew louder now and I began to wonder if the neighbors could hear. All of the sudden, Regan's body stiffened and she bolted upright, drawing her knees to her chest.

"Mina . . . I can't do this," she said, gasping for breath. Regan staggered to her feet and collected her discarded clothes from the floor. She pulled on her jeans and T-shirt and stuffed her panties into her back pocket.

My head was spinning and my groin ached. "Regan." I got to my feet. "Regan, what's the matter?"

"Mina, I can't do this . . . it's not right. It's not normal."

"Regan, we love each other. How could it be wrong?"

"Because we're both girls. It's not the way things are supposed to be."

"Regan, please. Please don't go."

"Mina, we can't tell anyone this ever happened, you hear me— never. And don't ever touch me that way again," Regan said shaking her finger in my face. She quickly turned around and left the apartment, slamming the door behind her.

I heard the pounding of her footsteps echo in the stairwell. I hung my head in despair as I heard the door leading out to the parking lot slam shut. I didn't have the strength to get up and go over to the window to watch her speed away. My whole life had just run out that door and I feared I would never be happy again. I lay down on the floor, curled up in the fetal position, and cried myself into oblivion.

A few hours later, I awoke with a start to the harsh sound of the door buzzer. The room was dark and the digital clock on the microwave oven blinked one fifteen. The buzzer sounded again, indicating that whoever it was at the door was very impatient. Apprehensively, I pressed the intercom button to see who it was.

"Mina, it's Regan. Can I come up?"

I pushed the button releasing the lock on the front door. When I heard her approach the last flight of steps to my apartment, I opened the door, then sat down on the couch, not bothering to turn on any lights.

Regan appeared at the door, much meeker than when she left. She came over to the couch and sat down next to me and took my hand in hers.

"Mina, I am so sorry for running out on you like that," Regan said. "I freaked out. I never felt that way before and it scared me. All that kept going through my head was that it was unnatural for two women to feel this way about each other and to be doing what we were doing."

"Regan, if it's so wrong, then why did you come back?"

"Because as hard as it is for me to admit it, I do love you," she said and my heart immediately perked up.

"Regan, I love you too. That's why this can't be wrong."

Regan pulled me into her arms and held me tight. For a long time we just sat there on the couch in the dark. Regan finally broke our embrace. I felt an eager affection radiate from her as she gazed into my eyes.

A mischievous smile slowly crept across her full lips. "So . . . what do you think about finishing what we started?"

I grabbed her by the hand and led her into the bedroom where we made love until the morning light creeped in through the blinds.

Chapter Twelve

I felt like two people with two different personalities. With Sean, I was quiet and reserved and not at all enthused about sex. With Regan, I couldn't get enough of it. Her slow, drugging kisses, the way her soft curves molded into mine, and the scent of her skin evoked responses in me I never knew were possible. Making love with her seemed so natural, so real. There was no thinking about it, no working at getting aroused. It just happened and it happened a lot.

Regan had spent the night at my apartment for the third time this week. The only time she went home was to pick up a clean uniform for the next day and to give her mother some lame excuse about working back-to-back shifts and how much easier it was just to stay at my place because it was so close to work. I didn't care what she told her mother, I was just happy to have her by my side every night. Unfortunately, that streak of luck would have to come to an end. It was Friday morning, and I would be leaving to join Sean for the weekend.

The alarm went off at five o'clock. I climbed out of bed and headed for the kitchen to put on the coffee and then get in the shower before I had to wake Regan at five thirty. As the steaming hot water hit me, expectations of the next few days ran through my head. How am I going to pull this off with out hurting anyone? Is Sean going to know there is something different about me? What about Regan? Will things be the same when I come back? I toweled off, unable to shake off the feeling of dread these thoughts produced. I slipped on my bathrobe to go in and wake Regan.

I tiptoed back into the bedroom. Regan was still sound asleep. It was strangely exciting to see her lying there in my bed, a bed I had only ever shared with my husband. Regan stirred as I sat down next to her.

The Choice
Published by The Haworth Press, Inc., 2007. All rights reserved.
doi:10.1300/5791_12

"Regan, it's five thirty. Time to get up," I said, smoothing out her tousled hair.

"Morning," she said and smiled lazily.

"Good morning. How'd you sleep?"

"Like a rock," Regan answered, stretching out her long limbs.

"Good. Me too. I guess having three orgasms before bedtime really helps."

Regan laughed and then sat up in bed. The rumpled white sheet that covered her naked body had fallen to her waist. A tidal wave of passion flowed through me. My groin tingled. It was amazing what the mere sight of her did to me.

I bent down and kissed her. Neither one of us had brushed our teeth yet, but that didn't seem to matter. Regan kissed me back in a way that left no doubt that she felt the same way. We made love for the fourth time in eight hours and then both headed off to shower quickly and dress for work. I poured coffee into a thermos and tossed a couple of Twinkies into my backpack for later. If we hurried, we'd only be ten minutes late.

We got to the floor at seven fifteen. Brenda was standing at the nurse's station, phone in hand.

"I was beginning to think no one was coming," Brenda said, putting the phone back in the cradle.

"Sorry, we're late," I said, trying to conceal my embarrassment. I secretly wondered how Brenda would react if she knew that the reason Regan and I were late was because we had just had sex. Regan slipped past by me into the locker room to change her shoes and retrieve her notebook for report.

"How was your night?" I asked Brenda.

"Long. The laxatives the afternoon turn hands out like candy all took effect around midnight. We ended up having to change three beds last night. Otis was up most of the night insisting that we get him up into his wheelchair. We finally gave in around two. He roamed the halls all night long, calling out for Cora, keeping everyone else up as well. There were so many call lights on that the hallway looked like Broadway."

"I'm sorry to hear you had a rough night. I'm sorry, too, for being late," I said.

Regan slipped into the chair next to me at the desk.

"How come you were both late?" Brenda asked.

I froze. Now what do I say? We got stuck in traffic? Brenda knew I walked to work. I looked over at Regan, who stared down at the blank page of her notebook, not offering any explanation.

"Uh, Regan stopped by at my apartment this morning. We got to talking and lost track of time," I said.

"Oh. You both look like you just woke up. I thought that maybe you were having a slumber party or something." Brenda said.

"No, nothing like that," I said with a nervous chuckle.

Brenda continued with report. When she finished, she gathered up her things and headed back to the locker room.

"Oh my God. I thought we were busted," Regan whispered.

"That was close," I said, trying to look busy in order to avoid any further questioning from Brenda.

"Well, have a good day and a nice weekend," Brenda said as she got on the elevator. Relief filled the air as the elevator doors closed behind her.

Regan stood at the med cart, pouring the morning's medications. The expression on her face held a touch of sadness.

"You okay?" I asked.

"Uh-huh." Regan nodded.

I got up from the desk, took Regan by the hand, and pulled her into the bathroom for some privacy.

"Talk to me," I said.

"Mina . . . what if someone finds out?"

"No one is going to find out."

"How can you be so sure?"

"Because on the outside, we appear to be two women who are close friends. There is nothing suspicious about that, now is there?"

"No, I guess not. But why do you think Brenda said the things she did, about having a slumber party?"

"I don't know. Maybe she's fishing for information. Maybe she's just jealous," I said. "Hey, but let her get her own girl. You're mine," I said and pulled Regan close to me.

Regan's body stiffened. "No Mina, not here." She pushed me away. "Mina, I'm sorry, this is all so new to me and so scary. Aren't you scared?"

I hesitated. "Sure, I'm scared. But when I'm with you, that's all that matters. The rest of the world can go—"

There was an abrupt knock on the door. "Mina? Regan? Is either one of you in there?" Alberta's muffled voice came through the door. "There's a family member at the desk that wants to speak to a nurse."

"I'll be out in a minute," I answered, and then waited until I heard Alberta walk away. Slowly, I opened the bathroom door and crept out. Regan was close behind me.

"Mina, hello," Rosemary Rosetti said. I stopped dead in my tracks, causing Regan to run right smack into my back.

I blushed. Rosemary Rosetti's face split into a wide grin.

"Well, hello," Rosetti said to Regan. Once again in a compromising situation, I feared Regan might faint, right then and there.

"Regan, this is Rosemary Rosetti, Teresa Rosetti's daughter."

"Hello, it's nice to meet you," Regan said with deceptive calm.

"Hi. I don't know if Mina told you, but I also work with her husband, Sean, at the police department."

"No, Mina didn't tell me," Regan fixed her gaze on me.

"So, what can we do for you?" I asked, desperately trying to change the subject.

"Could you come down and check my mom, she seems to be having more trouble breathing than usual."

"Sure, I'll be right down. Let me get my stethoscope out of my locker and I'll meet you in her room."

Rosetti headed back to her mom's room and I scrambled into the locker room.

"Jesus," I said. "This place is turning into a minefield."

Regan dropped down on one of the wooden benches in the locker room.

"Did you see how she looked at us?" Regan said. "It's like she knew."

"I think she knows because she's one too."

"What?"

"I think she's a lesbian too."

"Mina, we are not lesbians," Regan whispered with determination.

"Then what are we?"

"We are two people who love and care about each other who happen to be women."

"Regan, you just gave a perfect description of lesbians."

"No sir."

I didn't have the time or the energy to argue with her. I pulled my stethoscope off the top shelf of my locker and headed toward room 216. Regan didn't follow. She stayed in the nurses' station, pouring the rest of the morning medications. When I finally got to room 216, Teresa Rosetti was definitely in trouble.

"I'll replace her nasal cannula with an oxygen mask and turn up her oxygen to six liters per minute." I placed my stethoscope on her frail chest and found that both lungs were filled with fluid. She was working very hard to breathe. "I need to call her doctor for some Lasix to take the water off her lungs."

Rosemary nodded. "Is she going to be okay?"

"She should turn around after the Lasix, but with someone as sick as Teresa, it's hard to tell."

"Can you sit with her until I come back?"

"Yes. I'll be right here," Rosetti said.

I dialed Dr. Sullivan's number and got the answering service. "This is Mina Thomas at St. Mike's. Could you page Dr. Sullivan for me? One of our patients is in respiratory distress and I need an order for Lasix."

The receptionist assured me that the doctor would call back with in the half hour. In the meantime I went in to check on Teresa again. The oxygen seemed to help a little, but her breathing didn't sound that good. She really needed the Lasix.

Regan appeared in Teresa's doorway. "Mina, Doctor Sullivan is on line one," she said.

"Great. Regan, can you stay with her while I take the call?"

"Sure," Regan said reluctantly, but stayed and checked Teresa's vital signs and breath sounds like I had taught her only a few months ago.

I got the order for forty milligrams of Lasix IV. Regan ran down to the pharmacy to get it while I suctioned Teresa, trying to open her airway. Regan returned with the vial of Lasix. I pushed the plunger of the Lasix injection slowly into the IV tubing, until the entire amount of medication was dispensed.

"Now, we just wait and see what happens," I said to Rosemary Rosetti, who had never left her mother's bedside during the whole ordeal.

I returned to the nurses' station, where Regan was just finishing up morning med pass. "Thanks for taking over."

Regan smiled. "You're welcome. We're a team, right?"

"Yes, we are a team."

By two thirty Teresa Rosetti put out 1,500 ccs of urine, in spite of her kidney failure. Her respiratory distress eased to the point where we could replace the mask with the cannula again and turn the flow rate back down to two liters per minute.

"I want to thank you for taking such good care of my mother," Rosemary said.

"I'm glad everything turned out okay," I said, closing the last chart of the day.

"What you did in there was amazing. You knew exactly what to do for her."

"That's what we're trained to do," I said.

"I'd like to do something for you, buy you lunch or dinner or something," Rosemary Rosetti said.

"That won't be necessary. We're not allowed to accept gifts. But thank you, anyway."

"Well, thank you. Thank you both," Rosetti said.

Regan, surprised to be included in the congratulations, looked up from her charting.

"You're welcome," I said.

"Yes, you're welcome," Regan chimed in.

Rosetti returned to her mother's room.

"I think that woman has a thing for you," Regan said.

"What are you talking about?"

"Did you notice the way she looks at you?"

"What way?"

"Like she wants you."

"Don't be ridiculous," I said. "And anyway, she knows I'm married to Sean."

As soon as the words left my mouth, I regretted saying them.

"Yes, we can't forget that now, can we?" Regan said as she shot me a hurtful look and slowly rose and went into the locker room. She emerged a few minutes later, cap case in hand, and brushed by me as she headed toward the elevator.

I walked over to the elevator. "Regan, I'm sorry. I didn't mean it to sound like—"

The elevator doors opened, Regan got on and never looked back, practically knocking over Sandy, as she exited the elevator.

"Wow, what's wrong with her?" Sandy said as she entered the nurses' station.

"She's mad at me. I said something that upset her," I said.

"My goodness. You know, you two act like you're an old married couple sometimes," Sandy said, her voice heavy with sarcasm.

"Shut up, Sandy. This is none of your business."

Sandy appeared too startled to offer any objection or retort. I finished report in ten minutes flat and then gathered up my things and headed out without saying another word to anyone. The elevator seemed to be taking forever, so I took the stairs, two at a time. I needed to get the hell out of there. I was angry and sad and I was not looking forward to the long drive to Columbus ahead of me. And I certainly wasn't looking forward to a weekend with Sean.

Chapter Thirteen

The drive to Columbus took three hours on boring Interstate 71. Nothing to do except think and wallow in self-pity. Things with Regan were uncertain at best, my marriage was in trouble, and I had a splitting headache. At least it wasn't raining. I hated driving in the rain.

Thoughts of Regan kept going through my head. Where was she? Was she alone, or would she seek comfort with someone else while I was gone? Would things be the same when I got back? The pounding in my head got louder and louder as I approached the Columbus city limits.

I arrived in Columbus around five thirty, right on schedule. The directions Sean gave me were pretty accurate, and I made it to the Adam's Mark hotel in good time. It was a beautiful hotel, white marble entryway, gold fixtures, and plush maroon velvet carpeting.

Sean arrived just as I finished checking in.

"Well, aren't you a sight for sore eyes," Sean said, as he joined me at the registration counter. He pulled me into a big bear hug, crushing me to his chest. I couldn't help thinking, how strange this felt. He seemed so . . . so big, so solid, so flat—a definite contrast to Regan's petite softness.

"Hello, yourself," was all I could manage with a forced smile.

"Mina, you look great. What have you been doing since I've been away?"

"Uh, Jane Fonda workout tapes. I get a great workout from them." I said for lack of a better answer. I knew the truth would kill him.

"Well, they seem to be doing a great job. You look great," Sean said again, as his gaze raked over my body from head to toe.

"Hey, do I have time to freshen up before we go to dinner?" I asked, trying to avoid any confrontation.

The Choice
Published by The Haworth Press, Inc., 2007. All rights reserved.
doi:10.1300/5791_13

"Okay. But we better hurry or we will miss our reservation."

Our room was on the seventeenth floor and just as elegant as the lobby. A huge king-size bed filled most of the room. A cherry writing desk sat in one corner, and a hunter green fireside chair and a small sleeper sofa occupied the other. Sean sat on the king-size bed while I freshened up and changed clothes in the bathroom.

I emerged from the bathroom feeling a little better.

"I've really missed you, Meen," Sean said as he got up from the bed and drew me into his strong arms.

I felt my body stiffen; the promise I had made to Regan rang loudly in my ears. "I've missed you too," I answered. I laid my head on his firm chest and listened to the gentle lub-dud of his heart. It seemed like I didn't recognize its beat. This man was my husband, yet he felt like a stranger to me.

Sean held me close and kissed me on the top of the head.

"We better get going or we'll be late," I said breaking our embrace.

"Yes, I guess so," Sean answered. A hint of disappointment lingered in his voice.

The Columbus Club was a busy place. Sean's staff commander, Lieutenant Ken Roberts was a member at the exclusive club. Since Sean agreed to take on the guest teaching position, the Lieutenant and his wife invited us to join them and some of the other teaching officers for dinner. It was a good thing we had a reservation, because otherwise we'd be waiting for a table all night. The tuxedo-clad host guided us to our table. Three couples, none of which I knew, were already seated.

"Hello, everyone. This is my wife, Mina," Sean introduced me to his colleagues and their wives.

Everyone at the table smiled and nodded their hellos. I smiled back shyly, wishing I was anywhere but there.

Sean pulled a chair out for me as we took our place at the table. The conversation centered on police work, of course. There was a lot of testosterone in the air, because these guys were the best of the best of their departments.

The first course was brought to the table. A huge antipasto salad with dark green lettuce covered in silvery, slimy, anchovies. The waiter set a large platter at either end of the table. Sean dug in, taking a large portion for himself, and then offered to dish some out for me.

"Just a little, thanks," I said handing him one of the three bone China plates that were stacked before me.

I poked my fork into the lettuce, careful to avoid the slimy anchovies. The lettuce glistened with olive oil and tasted salty. I took only a few bites, and then put my fork down.

"Not hungry?" the woman sitting next to me asked.

"Not really," I answered. "I had a late lunch," I lied.

She introduced herself as Shirley, the staff commander's wife. She was an attractive woman in her late forties, with all the life experience to go with it. Being married to a cop had its advantages and disadvantages. The guys that joined the force back in the sixties and seventies were a different breed than the guys coming on now. It was no secret that things could get really tough sometimes.

"So, Mina, do you and Sean have any children?" Shirley asked.

"No, it's just the two of us right now."

"Are you planning on having a family?"

"Yes, I guess, eventually," I said, evasively. Why does the conversation always turn to children anyway? Doesn't anybody want anything else out of life other than to procreate?

"Ken and I have five children: three boys and two girls. Our oldest will be heading off to Ohio State in the fall. She got accepted into the premed program."

"That's wonderful. I'll bet you are very proud."

"Yes, we are. She worked really hard to get to where she is."

"Medical school? How exciting that must be for her. Boy, if I had the chance to do things different," I said.

"Yes, I know what you mean. Kids today seem to have a lot more advantages than we did growing up," Shirley said, pulling a gold-plated Zippo lighter from her purse, flicking its wheel to light an Eve cigarette.

She took a long drag on the cigarette and blew a plume of smoke straight up in the air.

"So, do you work?" Shirley inquired, taking another drag on her cigarette.

"Yes, I'm a nurse. I work at St. Michael the Archangel Nursing Home."

"I bet that can be very depressing, working with sick, elderly patients every day," Shirley said.

"Actually, I enjoy it. My job has many rewards. Not only monetary, but spiritually and intellectually as well. I love talking to the residents. Some of them have overcome some horrific experiences. And they are so grateful for every little thing you do for them. They're from a whole different generation."

The main course was being served: Beef medallions covered in horseradish sauce with green beans on the side. The table fell silent as everyone ate. I cut the beef up into tiny bite-sized pieces, eating only a few bites. My heart was so heavy from missing Regan it seemed to be pushing on my stomach, leaving no room for food. I moved the beef bits around my plate, hiding a few under a pile of almond-studded green beans.

"Hey, if you're not going to eat that, can I have it?" Sean asked eyeing my plate.

"Be my guest," I said and traded his clean plate for my full one.

After dinner we all went across the street to an Irish pub called McDougal's. It was loud and smoky. I excused myself from the table to use the restroom. A payphone hung on the wall in the cramped alcove between the ladies' and men's restroom. I couldn't resist the temptation and I dropped a quarter in the slot and dialed Regan's number.

The operator came on the line. "You must deposit seventy-five cents in order to complete this call. I fished around in my pockets for two more quarters. I plopped them into the coin slot, causing the phone to ding with every drop of a quarter. Finally, the phone on the other end began to ring and ring . . . and ring. No answer.

I hung up the receiver and my seventy-five cents came crashing down into the change return like a slot machine giving up a jackpot. I pushed open the heavy wooden door to the ladies room. The line was ten women long. Obviously a lot of beer was consumed and expelled in this place. I waited patiently. I was in no hurry to get back to the table.

When I finally did get back, three of the guys were downing shots of Jack Daniel's and stacking the shot glasses in the middle of the table creating a pyramid. I took my seat next to Sean.

"Jesus, Meen, where've you been?"

"The restroom," I said. "The line was almost a mile long."

"Who did you call on the pay phone?" Sean asked, more curious than accusing.

"My mother," I lied, trying to hide my shock that he even saw me use the payphone. Another disadvantage to being married to a cop: they don't miss anything that's going on in their surroundings.

"Your mother?"

"Yes, she wasn't feeling well when I left, so I called to check on her."

"Oh," Sean said. "So, how's she doin'?"

"I . . . I don't know. She wasn't home."

Sean turned back to his friends. They hooted and hollered well into the night. I was exhausted from all the drama and just wanted to go back to the room to sleep.

Finally, the guys seemed to be winding down. They had all had a lot to drink, including Sean. Around two fifteen everyone at the table got up to leave. "I'll drive," I said and slipped my hand into his front pants pocket to retrieve the car keys.

"Oh, I like a woman that takes charge," Sean said, trapping my hand in his front pocket where I could feel the edge of his erection.

His buddies burst out in laughter.

My face turned crimson red. I withdrew my hand from his pocket as if it were on fire. "Jesus, Sean," I said annoyed at his brazenness.

"Ah, come on Meen . . . I'm only jokin'. Hey, it's been a long time," Sean said pulling me close to him. "Don't you miss me?"

My heart pounded with anger. "Sure I do, but let's save it for when we're alone," I answered with all the resolve I could muster.

We said our good-byes as the others dispersed to their cars. Sean reached over and took my hand.

"Meen, I'm sorry about that back there," he said. "I was acting like a jerk."

We rode back to the hotel in silence.

Sean lay sprawled across the bed, hands folded behind his head, eyes closed, as I started to unpack my suitcase.

"I'm gonna take a shower," I said.

Sean nodded without opening his eyes.

I locked the bathroom door behind me. I turned on the shower full force and then stepped under the hot stream. The hot water pounded my back as tears ran down my cheeks. How did things get so fucked up?

I emerged from the bathroom, ready to confront Sean and armed with at least three excuses why we couldn't have sex tonight. I had to keep my promise to Regan. To my surprise I didn't need any of them. Sean was already fast asleep. I pulled the heavy comforter back and slid in between the cool percale sheets. Then I flicked off the light and settled in. One day down, two more to go.

Chapter Fourteen

At first I thought I was dreaming, dreaming of Regan and the last time we were together, but when I finally became awake, I realized my nightgown was bunched up around my neck and Sean lay on top of me, pinning me to the bed. His firm erection pressed into me as his warm mouth covered my left breast, sucking, licking, and biting at the nipple. The feeling was intense and I felt my insides burn, slowly and deliciously. Then I realized what was going on. I struggled beneath Sean, trying to get free. Sean, probably mistaking my squirming as passion, held me tighter as his strong hand swept down across my belly, into my underpants, where his thick fingers raked through my pubic hair. He slipped a finger inside me and my vagina contracted around it. Sean's kiss stifled my protests along with a whimper of pleasure as his tongue sent shivers of desire through my body. He climbed further on top of me, his weight crushing me, his stiff penis stabbing at my thigh. Panic erupted in my heart. This couldn't be happening.

"What are you doing?" I said, finally shoving him off of me.

"Making love to my wife," Sean said, wounded, sitting in the center of the bed, his penis jutting up over his thighs, pointing toward the ceiling.

"Couldn't you have waited until I was conscious?"

"You looked so beautiful, lying there, I couldn't resist," Sean said.

He moved toward me to kiss me. I pulled away.

"Meen, what's the matter?"

I tugged my nightgown down and hugged my knees into my chest. "Nothing," I whispered.

"Are you still mad about last night? I said I was sorry."

"No, that's not it," I said.

The Choice
Published by The Haworth Press, Inc., 2007. All rights reserved.
doi:10.1300/5791_14

"Mina, I miss you. It's been a long time since we've been together. What's wrong?"

I couldn't answer him.

"I used to wake you like that all the time when we first got married. You used to love it, remember?" he said, inching closer to me on the bed.

I nodded. I did remember. It was wonderful. But things were different now. He didn't know about the different part, not yet anyway.

"Sean, I'm sorry. I've just been going through some . . . stuff lately."

"What kind of stuff?"

"I can't talk about it just yet. I need more time to work on it," I said.

Sean got out of bed. His penis, limp now, appeared to be staring sadly at the floor. He went into the bathroom and closed the door behind him. I felt bad. None of this was his fault. When I heard him turn on the shower I got up and quickly dressed, feeling lucky that I dodged another bullet and was able to keep my promise to Regan. I made a note in my mind that tonight I would sleep on the little sleeper sofa next to the desk.

Sean emerged from the bathroom twenty minutes later, naked, hair wet, and skin glowing pink. He caught me looking at him. His boyish smile warmed my heart from across the room.

"Mina, I am really sorry. I've been acting like a Neanderthal since you came down here," Sean said.

A pang of desire rippled through me as Sean came closer, so close I could smell the Dial soap on his skin. I thought about Regan and the promise I made to her, but this time only half listened to my conscience. Sean pulled me to him. The warmth of his skin was intoxicating. He pressed his lips to mine, caressing them more than kissing them. This was different. This was more like the old days and I felt the hard shell that I so carefully built around me crack into a million pieces.

My mind told me to resist, but my body wasn't cooperating. I didn't protest when his hands sought the buttons of my shirt. His eyes closed in complete surrender as I cupped his testicles in my hand and gently fondled them. His penis twitched as I stroked it gently, mar-veling at the silky smooth skin and spongy head. The look on his face was pure pleasure.

Afterward, we lay in bed, our bodies damp with sweat from our lovemaking. Sean was sound asleep. My head rested on his shoulder as I listened to his soft breathing. That's when the panic attack hit.

I couldn't breathe. An elephant seemed to be sitting on my chest. I felt dizzy, even though I was lying down. My hands and feet felt cold and numb. I pulled myself out of bed and staggered into the bath-room, seeking refuge, locking the door behind me. I curled up on the gray and white tile floor. The cool tile felt good against my face. What have I done? Not only did I break my promise to Regan, but also, in the heat of it all, I didn't use any protection. What if I got pregnant? The thought made me sick to my stomach. I retched and got up just in time to vomit into the bathroom sink. I laid back down on the bathroom floor and curled up in the fetal position.

"Meen, you in there?" Sean called from the bedroom.

I didn't answer.

"Mina, are you alright?" Sean shouted through the door. Panic in his voice.

"Yes, I'm fine," I answered.

"Well, open up," Sean said. "I gotta pee."

I reached up and unlocked the door. Sean pushed his way in. He lifted the lid on the toilet and began to pee.

"What are you doing on the floor?" he asked as he flushed the toi-let.

"I don't feel so good," I said.

Sean washed his hands and then crouched down and sat on the floor next to me and stroked my sweaty, matted hair.

"Mina, what's going on?"

I started to cry.

Sean picked me up and drew me into his arms. "Meen, whatever it is, it can't be that bad." He kissed my forehead and gently rocked me in his arms.

This made me cry harder. I didn't want him to understand, I wanted him to be a prick. I wanted to be angry with him so I could walk away and not feel guilty.

"Jesus, Meen, what's the matter?" Sean asked as he held me tight against his smooth, bare chest. My body trembled.

Finally, I sat up and wiped the tears from my face with the back of my hand. Sean brushed the damp hair out of my eyes. "Now tell me what's going on."

In my heart I knew I had no choice. It wasn't fair to him to keep him in the dark and it wasn't fair to Regan. If my relationship with Regan, if there was one when I got back, was going to work, I needed to legitimize it. I had just broken the one and only promise I'd ever made to her, and I needed to stick up for her, for myself, for us, even if it meant hurting Sean.

I told him everything. It came pouring out with the torrential force of a hurricane and, by the look on his face, it caused just as much damage. The light in his eyes had gone dim and his boyish smile had vanished.

"Sean, I am so sorry. I never meant to hurt you."

He didn't speak at first. He couldn't. My heart ached for him. In the ten years we had known each other I had never seen him cry. That day I did. I reached up and brushed the tears away.

"Mina, I don't believe this," he choked out between sobs. "How . . . how could this happen?"

I held his face close to mine, inhaling his clean scent, sad that it may be for the last time.

"Maybe your feelings will pass. Maybe it's just a phase," Sean said.

"Maybe," I said, but in my heart I knew it wasn't.

Sean pulled me close and held me tight. We both cried, hanging on to the shreds of our marriage while sitting on the cold, tile bathroom floor of the Adam's Mark hotel.

It was almost noon by the time we got up the strength to leave the hotel room. My eyes burned and my head ached from crying. My chest felt empty where my heart used to be. Sean didn't look any better than I did. We spent the rest of Saturday on our own in spite of the multiple invitations for lunch and dinner out with his colleagues from the police academy. It just didn't seem right to go to these things as a couple anymore. There was so much to talk about, but neither one of us knew where to begin. We stopped for lunch at one of the cafés in German Village, but neither one of us was hungry. I picked at my Cobb salad and Sean ate only half of his bacon cheeseburger.

"Mina, I don't want to lose you," Sean said, as he blankly stared out the front window of the restaurant.

"I don't want to lose you either," I said. "I love you so much, but things have changed, I don't know how we can go on."

"We can't just give up, Meen. What about counseling or something?" Sean offered.

I didn't know what to say. In my heart I knew the effort was futile. But I knew I'd do it, I'd do it for him. Maybe it would help, not so much with patching our marriage together but with the transition to whatever would be ahead. I had caused him enough pain. It was the least I could do.

"Okay, when I get back home I'll do some investigating. I'll find someone to work with us," I said.

"I'll come home right now if I have to," Sean said. "I'm sure I can get a day or two leave from my classes."

"Finish up your work here. I know it's important to you and you owe it to the academy. We'll work things out when you come home," I said, trying to buy some time—the time I would need to explain things to Regan.

We took in a movie, hoping that sitting in the dark for a few hours that afternoon would provide some escape from our predicament. It didn't. I couldn't stop thinking about Regan and how we left things back home and how I betrayed her here. Being here with Sean under these circumstances, I felt more closed in than ever, finding it more and more difficult to fight the urge to just get up and run.

After the movie we came back to the hotel. I tried to bury myself in a book while Sean took a nap. I so desperately needed to call Regan, but couldn't muster up the courage. Now that Sean knew about our affair, it put things in a whole different light.

Sean and I had an early dinner downstairs in the Capitol Grille. Our appetites hadn't improved much since lunch.

"So, are you going to see her when you get back?" Sean asked.

His directness caught me by surprise. "I don't know. We had an argument before I left, so I don't know what to expect."

"How long have you felt this way . . . about women?" Sean asked, stabbing a piece of the well-done steak he had ordered.

"I think I have felt this way forever. I mean, I thought everyone felt this way. I thought it was part of growing up. My mother used to make me go to slumber parties when I was a kid, and I remember feeling like I didn't belong there. I felt so embarrassed when everyone started changing clothes for bed that I'd usually run and hide in the bathroom."

"If you always felt this way, why did you marry me?"

"I fell in love with you. After I met you, I didn't think much about it anymore."

"Did you ever do anything about it? I mean, act on it before?"

"No, never," I said.

"Then why now? Is it because of me? I mean, is it something I did or didn't do?"

I reached across the table and covered Sean's hand with mine. "No Sean, that's not it at all. It has nothing to do with you. It's me. It's what's going on inside of me."

I knew this was hard for him. Hard for him to even grasp what was happening. We finished the rest of our dinner in silence. When we got back to the room, Sean sat on the side of the bed, tears streaming down his cheeks. I walked over to him and gently held him in my arms.

"Everything will work out," I said. "I promise."

"How can you say that?" Sean asked. "It's not every day your wife tells you she's having an affair with another woman."

It seemed like the whole world was spinning out of control. I held Sean close as we lay on top of the bed. My affair with Regan made me realize who I am: a woman who loves another woman. I was torn between being true to my husband and being true to myself. I was stuck between staying with Sean, whom I did love truly and deeply, and thus deny who I truly was, and leaving Sean to be who I really was, risking everything I had, hurting everyone I knew. Which was the higher price to pay?

Chapter Fifteen

A clap of thunder awakened me from a deep and dreamless sleep. The room was dim and rain plummeted the windows. I squinted at the digital alarm clock on the nightstand. Its red numbers flashed 6:45. I slid out of bed, careful not to wake Sean. We both must have fallen asleep from emotional exhaustion as we were still dressed in our street clothes. I slipped into the bathroom, dragging my small suitcase behind me. I had to get back to Regan and straighten this whole mess out. I quickly showered and dressed, and when I emerged from the bathroom fifteen minutes later, Sean was still asleep. I pulled out a sheet of stationary from the middle drawer of the cherry desk and wrote him a note:

> *Dear Sean, I am so sorry I hurt you. God knows that was never my intention. Please believe me when I tell you that none of this is your fault. You have always been a wonderful husband to me. I love you Sean, and I always will. Love, Mina*

I folded the note in half and tented it on the nightstand next to Sean's side of the bed so he would see it when he woke up. I picked up my suitcase and tiptoed out into the hallway, closing the door softly behind me.

Tears streamed down my face as I rode down in the elevator. I hurried through the lobby so no one would see me crying. I handed my valet ticket to the parking attendant, a gray-haired African-American gentleman, who retrieved my car for me. I slipped him a five-dollar bill and managed a weak smile. He smiled back and touched the brim of his Cincinnati Reds baseball cap.

The rain was still coming down pretty hard and I could barely see, even with the windshield wipers on high. I stopped in German Vil-

The Choice
Published by The Haworth Press, Inc., 2007. All rights reserved.
doi:10.1300/5791_15

lage, at Der Kaffe Haus on Thurman Avenue to wait out the rain for a little while and for a cup of coffee. As I waited in line to pay for my coffee I noticed a newspaper on the counter next to the cash register called the *Gay People's Chronicle*. I picked up the paper and began to read the front page.

"That will be a dollar twenty for the coffee," the clerk said from behind the counter. He was about my age, with lavender spiked hair and a tiny silver nose ring.

"How much for this?" I asked holding up the newspaper.

"Oh, those are free," he said, as if it were nothing.

I stood by the window in the crowded coffee shop and sipped my coffee. This was the very first time in my entire life that I had admitted in public that I was gay. Not in words, but through my actions. I wondered if anyone noticed.

It didn't look like the rain was going to let up, so I folded the newspaper under my arm and headed back out into the rain. Once I was back in my car, I opened the newspaper. I was amazed at what I read. There was an entire section of where gay people could go to meet other gay people. There were listings for gay coffeehouses, gay bookstores, gay churches, and gay restaurants. There was also a listing for gay counselors—just what I had been looking for.

I searched the pages for information on a counselor close to home. The closest one was a Dr. Karen Metcalf, whose office was in Akron. I tore the address and phone number out of the paper and slid it into the front pocket of my Levi's. I also found that there was a "women friendly" gay bar that was right in downtown Youngstown.

I hated driving in the rain. Actually, it scared me to death. It was difficult to see the road and I felt I couldn't see if hazards lay up ahead. Much like my life. I could pull over and sit in the middle of the storm waiting for it to pass, or keep going no matter how scary and pray that I would make it out on the other side in one piece.

I kept going. The further east I drove, the darker the skies became. I couldn't help but think this was some type of omen or something: that things back home weren't good and this was God's way of telling me. The wind picked up and hail began to fall. The sound it made as it hit the roof on my car was deafening. Corvettes are not the best car to be driving in a torrential downpour. They have a tendency to hydro-plane. I was positive I'd end up flipped over in a ditch somewhere. My stomach clenched tight as I clutched the steering wheel with both hands and drove on. Finally, just as I passed the Mansfield exit, the hail stopped and the rain let up. The sky in the distance was brightening to a watercolor blue and it looked like it might turn out to be a pretty nice day after all.

Maybe things will work out, I thought as I drove the rest of the way home on glistening streets and under sunny skies. Maybe the key was to ride out the tough times no matter how bad they got. I hoped Regan saw things the same way. I hoped she understood the things I was going through and was willing to wait it out. After all, I did tell Sean about her and I. That was a big step, and a painful one at that.

As soon as I got home, I checked the answering machine. A red 3 blinked in the message window.

I pushed the play button. The first message was from my mother, letting me know that one of my father's cousins had passed away. "You know the one with the fingers missing," she said into the answering machine just as if I were on the phone with her. She said that the calling hours were Saturday evening at Morelli's and that she would meet me there. Since it was already Sunday afternoon, I would surely be in the doghouse, again.

The second message was a hang up. I had no idea who it was from; in my heart, I hoped it was Regan. The third message was the nursing home wanting to know if I was available to work the day shift on Sunday morning. If I did they needed me to call back before midnight, Saturday night. I erased the messages, not intending to respond to any of them.

I unpacked my suitcase and changed into a pair of sweatpants and a T-shirt. I gathered the week's laundry from the hamper and a roll of quarters and headed down to the laundry room on the first floor.

The air in the laundry room was muggy and thick with the smell of heated cotton and spray starch. As I was putting clothes in the front load washer I spotted Regan's car pulling into the parking lot. My heart leapt. I dumped a cup full of Cheer into the washer, closed the

140   THE CHOICE

lid, and slammed four quarters into the change slot. I raced up the
three flights of stairs so I could catch the buzzer.

I didn't want Regan to see me looking out the window, so I low
crawled on the floor to the dining room window to see if she had gotten out of her car yet. I nearly jumped out of the window when the intercom buzzer rang.

"Who is it?" I asked, like I didn't know.

"Mina, it's Regan. Can I come up?"

I pushed the door release to let her in. I opened the door of the
apartment, not even waiting for her to knock.

"Hi," Regan said sheepishly.

"Hi."

Regan closed the door behind her.

I pretended to be busy, going through the mail.

"How was your trip?" she asked.

"Okay, I guess."

"I bet Sean was happy to see you."

"I guess," I said. Guilt overcame me and I couldn't look her in the
eye. I had broken my promise to her and felt horribly ashamed.

"Mina, I'm sorry for running out like that on Friday. It was stupid
and immature."

"I'm sorry, too," I said. "I didn't even think about what I was saying. I never wanted to hurt you."

Regan stepped toward me and slid her arms around my waist. "I've
missed you," she whispered, as she nuzzled her face into neck.

I held her tight. "I've missed you, too." I said and stroked her hair. I
closed my eyes, getting lost in the sensation of her body next to mine,
but also preparing myself for what I had to tell her.

"Regan, I told him about us."

"You what?" Regan said, stepping back and out of my arms.

"I told Sean about us. I couldn't keep it a secret any longer."

"Oh my God, Mina," Regan said slowly lowering herself to the
couch. "What did he say?"

"He didn't know what to say. It hit him like a ton of bricks. He was
very sad. Practically devastated."

"I can't believe you told him," Regan said.

"I felt I didn't have a choice. He kept asking me what was wrong. He wouldn't let up, so I told him."

I joined Regan on the couch. Anxiety hung in the air.

"So, what's going to happen?"

"Well, he wants us to get counseling."

"Counseling?"

"Yes, he thinks with counseling I can change."

"What do you think?" Regan asked, looking down at her shoes.

I turned toward her and took her hand. "Regan, this is not a phase. The first time we made love, fireworks exploded in my head. It was the biggest 'a-ha' I had ever had in my life. It felt so right and more natural than anything I had ever felt before."

Regan pulled me to her and held me tight. Guilt stabbed my heart. My betrayal of her loomed larger than ever in my mind. Since we were getting everything out, the fact that Sean and I had had sex while I was in Columbus needed to come out too.

"Regan . . ." I began. But I chickened out. If I told her now, I would lose her *and* Sean.

"What?"

"Never mind," I said.

Regan sat up straight. "What? What is it?"

"Regan, I want to . . . I want us to get out and meet other people like us."

"Mina, what are you talking about?"

"I want to find other women who are like us. I want to see what their lives are like."

"What brought this on?" Regan asked.

"Well, now that Sean knows about us, I want to move forward, you know, see what life out there is like."

Regan grimaced. "I don't know, Mina," Regan said. "Where do you suppose we do that?"

"I stopped to get coffee this morning before I left Columbus and I came across this newspaper." I handed it to her.

"*Gay People's Chronicle*. What's this?"

"A paper that tells people where to meet other gay people."

"But we're not gay," Regan said.

I looked at her. "Regan, we are two women who love each other . . . who make love to each other. If we aren't gay then what are we?"

Regan's face clouded with uneasiness as she searched for an answer.

"We're not lesbians. Look at us, we don't look like lesbians, we don't dress like lesbians." Regan thrust out her hands. "See, I wear nail polish, pink nail polish. How many lesbians do you know wear pink nail polish?"

"That's the thing—I don't know any lesbians. Regan, there is more to people than the way they look or dress. I want to look beyond the stereotypes, beyond the jokes. I want to learn more."

"But isn't what two people share between each other private?" Regan asked.

"Yes. But don't you want to see how other women handle this type of lifestyle? There have to be women out there who have been together for years and have coped with the prejudices, coped with the looks, and coped with not being accepted in society. Don't you want to see how they get through all that?"

"Not particularly. You know, if you're trying to entice me into that kind of lifestyle, you're not doing a very good job."

Feeling the sting of Regan's response, I took a deep breath, scrounging up the nerve to ask my next question. "Regan, there's a gay bar in Youngstown. Let's go see for ourselves. This really means a lot to me. Please?"

"Oh no. I'm not going to a gay bar," Regan protested. "Mina, what if someone sees us?"

"Who's gonna see us? Anyway, if they do, well, they are in a gay bar, too . . . so what's the big deal?"

Regan let out a sigh. "But I'm content with the way things are now."

"Regan, we can't hide out in this apartment forever."

"But what if we do run into someone we know? Once word got out we could lose our jobs. God, I hate to think what my family would do. I don't know Mina. It's too risky."

"If it gets too weird I promise we'll leave. You just give the word and we're out of there."

I took Regan in my arms and planted tiny kisses on her neck. "C'mon Regan, where's your sense of adventure?" I teased.

Reluctantly, Regan gave in. "Oh alright. So when do you want to start this big adventure?"

"How about tonight?"

"Tonight? It's Sunday. They probably aren't even open."

I pulled the paper out. "They're open, see?" I said practically shoving the newspaper in her face. "See, ladies two-for-one night. All drinks for the ladies are two for the price of one."

"Wonderful," Regan sighed.

It was nine o'clock and still light out when we cruised down Market Street looking for the "The Other Side Lounge." Regan read the passing addresses out loud as we crept along in the right-hand lane. I hadn't been on this side of town in years and neither had much else. Most of the stores, like many of the businesses in the rust belt, had folded, there once enticing storefronts now boarded over with plywood and spray painted with graffiti and gang signs.

"Oh my God, is that a prostitute?" Regan said, craning her neck as we passed a tall and anorexic black woman in a red and white striped tube top and black leather miniskirt, smoking a cigarette in the doorway of an abandoned pawnshop. Regan continued to gawk at the woman as we pulled up to a red light. The woman crushed out her cigarette with the heel of her thigh-high boot and started to approach our car.

"Is your door locked?" I asked.

Before she could answer me, I blew through the red light. My heart pounded in my chest from the adrenaline rush in my head. I had visions of Regan and me appearing on the evening news. "Two local women mutilated by deranged prostitute on Youngstown's east side. Film at eleven."

"Mina, be careful. The last thing we need is to get stopped by the cops for running a red light," Regan said.

"Well, if you weren't so fascinated with the local vice . . ."

"I didn't think that there were prostitutes in Ohio, let alone so close to home," she said.

"I don't believe you sometimes," I said. "You're supposed to be checking for addresses and instead you're . . . never mind. Where is two seven seven eight?"

"It should be coming up here in the next block. The Rexall drugstore is two seven seven six and the hardware store is two seven eight zero. That's funny, no two seven seven eight," Regan said.

We circled the block and came to a parking lot jammed full with cars. In the back of the Rexall building was another entrance. Above the entrance was a weathered green canopy with the numbers 2778 painted in white block numerals.

"Here it is," Regan exclaimed. "That's weird, why would the entrance be back here?"

"Discretion, maybe?"

"But how can we be sure this is the right place? There isn't even a sign."

"I guess we take our chances."

"This entire thing seems like a big chance to me," Regan muttered uneasily. "Mina, aren't you scared? What if we get mugged?"

"We're not going to get mugged." The truth of it was that I was terrified, but I wasn't going to admit that to her. "Look at all the cars here. It can't be that bad, can it?"

"Whatever," Regan said as she slumped down in her seat.

I pulled the car into a space alongside a rusted chain-link fence, the only open parking space left in the lot.

"Ready?" I asked, looking over at Regan, who was gripping the door handle.

"I don't know why I let you talk me into this," Regan said.

"Because you can't resist my captivating charm?"

"No, that's not it," she teased. We both laughed.

"I promise. If it gets too weird, we are outta there."

"Let's get this over with," Regan said and opened her door.

We walked quickly through the parking lot. As we approached the entrance, I pulled open the heavy steel door. The sour stench of urine and beer greeted us.

"After you," Regan wrinkled her nose and gestured for me to go ahead of her.

We stepped into the cramped, dreary entrance. A short, stocky, bald man sporting a full face of makeup, including false eyelashes that looked like someone glued two tarantulas to his eyelids, sat on a bar stool with a cigar box and rubber stamp. The place reminded me of an entrance to a freak show at the circus instead of a night club.

"I need to see some ID please, dear?" he lisped, batting his tarantulas at me. I handed him my license and tried not to stare but couldn't help it. Where else could you see a Danny DeVito look-alike fresh from a Mary Kay makeover dressed in a dingy white T-shirt with the words "It's raining men . . . Hallelujah!" splayed across his barrel chest?

Regan stood behind me and hesitantly produced her driver's license.

"Five dollar cover tonight," he said, after barely glancing at our licenses.

"Five bucks!" I heard Regan complain from behind me.

"The Miz Ohio pageant finals are tonight," he said.

I handed the guy a ten, thinking to myself that this was a weird place to have a beauty pageant. I extended my hand to the guy so he could stamp it.

"No sweetheart, the other way," he said. He turned my hand over and stamped the inside of my wrist. I looked at him puzzled.

"First time in a gay club?" he asked.

I nodded.

He smiled and then stamped Regan's wrist as well. Regan stared at the stamp on her wrist like it was going to leave a scar. The guy hit a button on the wall next to his bar stool, which sounded a buzzer letting us into the club. When I opened the door, the entrance became flooded with white light. Lights flashed all around us, strobe lights bounced off a large disco ball that hung over the platform dance floor. The club was packed and it was difficult to move. Gloria Gaynor was belting out "I Will Survive" over the sound system. The dance floor was crammed with people bumping, grinding, and gyrating to the music.

Regan had a death grip on my arm, so we couldn't be separated. We found a free bar stool at one of the two bars in the place. I let

Regan take the stool, and I stood next to her. The décor of the club made it look more like a cathouse than a dance club. Lime green carriage lanterns hung on the walls covered in blood-red velvet wallpaper. The bar was beer-soaked mahogany edged in tattered black vinyl.

"I can't believe this place," I said as I looked around the room. "I never knew that there were this many gay people in the state, let alone here in town."

"Me either," Regan replied as she scanned the bar.

"Do you want something to drink?" I asked.

When she didn't answer, I turned toward her and suddenly noticed she was no longer sitting on the bar stool. I turned around to see if she was standing behind me, but she wasn't. She was nowhere in sight.

The guy sitting on the bar stool next to me noticed my plight. He was bare-chested, dressed only in black leather chaps and a little black leather cap. He tapped me on the shoulder and then pointed toward the floor, under the bar.

There was Regan, crouched on the floor, back against the torn vinyl, clutching her knees to her chest.

I extended my hand to her to help her up. "What are you doing down there?" I yelled over the music.

"Oh my God! My roommate from Moreland College is here. I don't want her to see me in a place like this," she said.

"Regan, if she's here, she's either gay or gay friendly, don't you think?"

"I don't know . . . but I don't want her to see me here. What if she gets the wrong idea about me?"

"What idea would that be?" I asked.

"That I'm like these people."

"Regan, we are like these people," I said.

"No, we're not," Regan insisted.

The guy dressed in leather tapped me on the shoulder again.

"Maybe you would be more comfortable over there," he said pointing across the room to the other bar. "That's the women's side."

"Oh, we're not gay," Regan said, cutting the guy off.

Leather guy shrugged his shoulders and returned to his martini and his date, a boy of no more than eighteen years old, sitting on the bar stool next to him sporting a red plastic dog collar and false eyelashes.

I let the comment go. I didn't know if she was lying to herself, or to me. Did she really love me, or was this just an experiment to her?

"Stand here in front of me where no one will see you." I told Regan. She squeezed between me and the bar. I could feel her body trembling. "How about something to drink?" I said and signaled to the bartender.

"What'll it be?" the bartender asked.

"I need something to calm my nerves. I'll have a seven and seven," Regan ordered.

"I'll have a Diet Coke," I said.

Our drinks arrived: Two seven and sevens and two Diet Cokes—it was two-for-one ladies night after all. Regan took a big swallow, downing almost half of the first one. At this rate she'd be trashed in ten minutes.

Regan downed her second drink as well. "I need another drink," she ordered. The room was hazy; blue cigarette smoke hung in the air. I pushed Regan's empty glasses to the edge of the bar and the bartender appeared.

"Another seven and seven please. And light on the alcoholic seven," I said.

He looked at me like I was speaking a language he'd never heard before and then took the glasses. I slid a five-dollar bill toward him. "Keep the change," I said. That he did understand.

Regan downed these drinks as well, and then two-fistedly slid her glasses to the edge of the bar, signaling the bartender for a refill. She was now standing on the metal rung of the bar stool waving a five-dollar bill, trying to get his attention.

"Hey! Bartender, over here," she shouted over the music.

"Sit down!" I said, and pulled her down from the chair rung. "You're gonna hurt yourself."

Regan peered at me through her drunken haze. "What's the matter? It was your idea to come here in the first place," she said. "All I want is another drink."

"You better take it easy," I said as I watched her take a gulp of her fifth and sixth drink. "You don't want to get sick, do you?"

"I love it when you take care of me," she said and threw both arms around my neck. "Mina Thomas, you are so good to me. I just wish . . ." Regan studied my face with glassy eyes.

"Just wish what?" I asked.

"You're . . . just . . . the best . . . the best friend anyone ever had. I am so lucky to have you in my life," Regan said and then pulled me to her.

The cigarette smoke stung my eyes and I had to blink to clear my vision. I was feeling weary and ready to end our little adventure when I spotted her.

Rosemary Rosetti was leaning against the women's bar. She was dressed in jeans, a white T-shirt, and a black blazer. Her gold duty badge hung around her neck on a silver chain.

"C'mon, Regan, we have to get out of here."

"What's the matter," Regan asked.

"Don't look now, but Teresa Rosetti's daughter is over there at the other bar."

"Oh God," Regan said. "Where?"

"Over there next to the women's bar by to the dance floor." Regan glanced over in the direction of the dance floor.

"Oh, God, she's looking right at us," Regan said. "Let's get out of here."

Regan grabbed my hand and we headed for the door. The room was crowded and we had to dodge and weave our way through a gaggle of drag queens and a line of stone butches who were guarding the women's restroom.

"Not staying for the pageant?" Rosemary Rosetti said just as we reached the exit.

"Ah . . . no," I answered, smiling, trying to conceal my nervousness.

"I never thought I'd run into you two here," Rosetti said.

My face felt hot. "I didn't think we'd run into anyone here either," I said.

"I work security here on Sunday nights," Rosetti said. She leaned in, her gold police badge swung toward me. "Your secret is safe with me," she said with a wink.

"Mina, we better get going," Regan said, tugging on my arm.

"Sorry," I apologized to Rosetti.

"That's okay. See you at the nursing home."

Regan grabbed my hand and pulled me through the rest of the crowd and out the door. By the time we reached the exit it was starting to rain. Big fat raindrops fell from the night sky, their coolness refreshing on my face. We walked fast to the car for safety reasons as well as trying to keep dry. I unlocked Regan's door and opened it for her. She slid into the passenger's seat safe and sound. I made it around to the driver's side as the deluge hit. The rain sounded like a million tiny pebbles being dumped in the car.

"I'm not sure I like that woman," Regan shouted over the noise as I started the engine. I couldn't see a foot in front of me, so I let the car idle a while, waiting for the rain to slow down.

"Who? Rosetti? Why not?"

"I can't put my finger on it but, there is something there."

"What are you afraid of? That she might steal me away from you or something?"

"Just what this relationship needs, another person in it," Regan said.

Regan and I looked at each other and both laughed.

"You know you're the only girl for me," I said, covering Regan's hand with mine.

Regan squeezed my hand. "This is really what you want, isn't it?" Regan asked.

"Yes, it is. I've finally found what was missing for all these years. I love you, Regan. Don't ever doubt my feelings for you."

Regan leaned toward me, practically pinning me to the car door. "I love you too, Mina," Regan whispered and then kissed me hard. Her kiss sent new spirals of ecstasy through my body. I slid my arms around her slim waist and held her tight. I loved the way her body felt pressed into mine.

"Take me to bed, or lose me forever," Regan said, quoting Meg Ryan's character in *Top Gun*. She lifted my hand and pressed it to her face, kissing the inside of my palm, gently stoking the fire already growing inside of me. I stroked her soft cheek, admiring how beautiful she was and how lucky I was to have found her. Lucky to love her. And lucky that she loved me back.

We headed home. Our little adventure to explore the gay community was a bust, but that was okay. We didn't need other gay people; we had each other and for right now, that was enough.

The rain never let up and the windows were fogged from our heavy breathing. We kissed at red lights, held hands, and fondled each other all the way home, shielded by the rain and mist. The ache to be together was exquisite and we were so hot for each other that we never even saw Sean's car in the parking lot.

"Shush . . . you'll wake the neighbors," I whispered as we stumbled up the stairs onto the landing in front of the apartment door. We were drenched from the downpour, our skin cool and slippery from the rain. Regan's wet hair was plastered to her head and her T-shirt was almost transparent against her chest.

"You look so beautiful right now," I said, tucking a strand of wet hair behind her ear.

Regan smiled, shyly. Her face glowed.

Regan slid behind me on the narrow doorstep as I put the key into the deadbolt and unlocked the apartment door. She lifted my shirt up, yanked up her wet T-shirt and lacy bra, and then pressed her rain-soaked body into to mine. Her hard nipples brushed against my back, taunting me, teasing me. The sensation sent a thrill through me and I couldn't wait to get her inside and peel off those wet clothes. Playfully she slid her hands around my waist, tickling me, and we both burst out laughing as I pushed the door to the apartment open and then fumbled for the light switch.

Our laughter came to an abrupt halt when Sean greeted us from the couch in living room.

"Hello Mina. I was beginning to think you were never coming home," Sean said. His voice was so absolutely emotionless it chilled me.

All the blood drained from my face. Regan pulled her shirt down and self-consciously crossed her arms across her chest. She looked so scared. I thought she was going to faint dead away.

Panic welled up in my throat. "Sean . . . what are you doing home?"

"I told the academy I needed to leave because of a family emergency. I couldn't stay down there Mina. Not knowing what—" Anger and resentment drowned out his words. He sized up Regan and then turned toward me.

"Mina, what the hell is going on?"

"I better get going," Regan said, her voice trembling. "I'll leave you two alone so you can work this out."

"You're not going anywhere," Sean said to Regan. He got up from the couch and walked toward us.

Regan and I swallowed hard. As Sean approached us, his off-duty gun, which rested in a leather holster on his hip, came into sight. Sean had carried the five-shot, snub-nosed revolver most of our married life. I had never been afraid of it until this moment.

I felt Regan shiver as he came closer. Regan closed her eyes as Sean slowly reached over her head and pushed the door closed. The click of the lock catching was the only sound in the room.

"We have a lot to talk about," Sean said, his face now only inches from Regan's.

"Sean, leave her alone. This is between you and me," My voice quivered.

"Shut up, Mina. Stop trying to protect your girlfriend." Sean shot back. He glared at me with utter disgust. His eyes were red and swollen.

"I tried to explain it to you in Columbus. I started this, I wanted it. This is not her fault—"

"Shut up Mina. Shut up!" Sean's anger was palpable.

Regan and I were backed against the door as Sean paced back and forth in front of us. I glanced over at Regan. She seemed frozen in terror.

"Mina, do you know what this will do to me if it gets out that my wife is a *dyke*?" He spat out the dreaded slur as if it was poison.

"We're not lesbians, we're just friends," Regan blurted out.

"Shut up you stupid bitch. If it wasn't for you, things wouldn't be so fucked up."

Regan backed up against the door. All color had drained from her face.

"Do you know what the guys on the force will think? They'll think I'm not man enough to keep my wife satisfied. And what do you think this will do to my reputation? I can tell you, it's not going to help me gain any respect in their eyes. I'm gonna look like a fool, a loser. Did you think about any of this before you slept with this cunt?"

"Sean, stop it!" I screamed.

"Mina, we've been through so much. What happened that you had to resort to this? What changed? Was I gone too long? Was I too involved with work? What Mina? Tell me what," Sean begged.

"Sean, it's not you. I'm the one who's changed. I tried to ignore these feelings for a long time, I just couldn't do it anymore. Regan fills a part of my life that you can't—that no one can." I knew what I said would hurt him, but he needed to know the truth.

Sean hung his head. "Do you know what kinds of things have been going through my head?" Sean said, his voice rough with anxiety.

"All I can think about is you and her together. What the hell, Mina. Why now? We've finally got our lives were we want them. We were going to start a family. Jesus, Mina, do you want to throw all that away for a fling?"

"It's not a fling." I said. I looked over at Regan. Fear, stark and vivid, flash in her eyes. "I care about her. There is much more to this than you will ever know."

Sean looked like someone had just punched him in the face. His eyes darkened with pain.

"Well if you care about her so much what were you doing with me this weekend? Huh, Mina? We haven't made love like that in a long time," Sean said, spitting the words out, knowing the damage they would do.

The force of his seething admission shocked and shamed me.

"She can't do anything for you that I can't do. I can take care of you. I love you. Isn't that enough?" Sean raged. His bloodshot eyes bore into me.

I felt defeated, empty, and drained.

Sean turned away. His anger was subsiding into grief. He collapsed onto the couch holding his head in his hands.

I turned to Regan. "Regan, I am so sorry," I whispered and reached for her hand. She pulled away from me.

"Don't," she said with tear filled her eyes. "I gotta go," she whispered and pulled on the doorknob twice before the latch released and the door opened. Her footsteps thundered in the stairwell. I followed close behind.

"Regan, please. Don't go."

"Mina, I can't do this anymore . . . leave me alone," she said, not looking back.

"Regan, I love you. I want to be with you," I said, finally catching up to her on the landing.

"I don't believe you," she said, turning to face me now. "As a matter of fact, I don't know what to believe anymore."

"I know. I'm sorry Regan, I am so sorry for breaking my promise. I was going to—" Regan put her hand up to stop me.

"Don't, Mina. Don't make excuses," Regan said. I could see the pain and sorrow of betrayal lingering in her eyes. She dropped her lashes quickly to hide the hurt, but tears streamed down her cheeks. "I have to go," she said, her voice hoarse with frustration.

"No, Regan, wait." I stepped in front of her, blocking the doorway.

"Mina . . . ," she said through gritted teeth and tried to push past me. I wasn't budging.

I pulled her into my arms. She fought to get free, but I held her tighter.

"You promised, Mina," she said, frustrated. "You promised you wouldn't be with him and I believed you," she said. She was crying hard now. Her body heaved against mine.

"Regan, I'm so sorry. Being with Sean in Columbus . . . it just happened. It didn't mean anything. I never meant to hurt you or anybody. You know all this is new to me too. Some days I don't know whether I'm coming or going. But in my heart I know I love you and want to be with you. I'm sorry Regan. I am so sorry," I said stroking her still damp hair.

I knew what she was thinking. Gone was the ease and simplicity of our love. The loss was so overwhelming, so intense, and so deep, could it ever be repaired?

"Mina, I can't do this anymore," Regan said as she broke our embrace. Taking a deep unsteady breath, she stepped back. "I'm sorry, Mina."

She pulled open the door and walked out into the misty cool night air. I followed her out into the parking lot to her car.

"Regan, I'm afraid if you leave now I will never see you again," I blurted out, grabbing her arm and spinning her around to face me.

"Let me go with you," I begged. "We can get a place of our own—"

"We can't Mina. It's not right. You need to work things out with him, and I need to go."

"But I don't want to work things out with him. Regan, I know how I feel. I want to make a life with you."

"Mina, I'm sorry. I don't know what you want me to say."

"Say that we can work this out. Say that you'll at least try."

Regan leaned against her car, arms crossed in front of her chest, head hung in despair. She let out a deep sigh. "Mina, it's late. Can we talk about it tomorrow?" Regan said, her voice weary.

"Okay," I whispered, drained from the fight but exhilarated from the spark of hope her words gave me. I opened Regan's car door for her and she slid into the seat. I bent down and gently kissed her cheek.

"I love you Regan," I said.

Regan looked down. "I love you too," she whispered as she turned on the ignition. I pushed down the door lock and closed her door to keep her safe. I stood in the parking lot and watched as she drove away, wishing it was morning already and we could begin to patch this whole mess up. But the night wasn't over yet. I still had Sean to deal with.

I trudged up the three flights of stairs back to the apartment. Sean sat on the couch staring into a half empty bottle of Budweiser.

"I saw you standing out there talking to her. I hope you were telling her to get lost," Sean said taking a long pull from the amber bottle.

I shook my head.

"Mina, you have to stop this. You're destroying my life, your life, and even her life. You can't tell me what you have with her is worth throwing everything away that we've spent years building."

Sean took another pull of his beer, finishing it off. "I can't live like this, Mina. It's killing me," Sean whispered. "I've got to know, what's it gonna be, me or her?"

No matter who I'd choose, I'd lose. In a way, I loved them both, but I knew I was hurting them both too. I closed my eyes, reliving the scene of this awful night. I couldn't hold back the tears any more.

"Sean, I'm sorry. I tried to keep my feelings buried, but I couldn't Sean. I really couldn't. Do you think this is easy for me? Well, it's not. It's probably the hardest thing I have ever had to do. I don't want to lose you, but I don't know if I can make this work anymore. I'm a different person, Sean. I'm not the girl you married."

Sean got up from the couch and pulled me into his arms. I felt the cold, hard revolver poke me in the side when I put my arms around his waist. "What's gonna happen to us?" Sean whispered.

"I don't know," I said. But deep down inside, I did know. My life with Sean was ending. I just didn't have the strength to tell him.

Almost as if he could read my mind, Sean held me tighter.

"Mina, we have to try to work this out. I can't imagine my life without you," Sean said, his voice choked with sadness.

I couldn't believe that after everything that had happened that night, he still wanted to try and save our marriage. Sean and I sat on the couch where he clung to me, his head nestled on my shoulder, where he eventually fell asleep. Anger at Sean burned inside of me as I sat in the shadowy living room, unable to sleep, thinking about Regan and hoping she could find a way to forgive me for what I had done. Soul-searching, troubling hours ticked by slowly until the dark night faded into gray.

Chapter Sixteen

Sean was curled up at the end of the couch, his blond head poking out from underneath the afghan, still asleep, when I left for work. I quietly slipped out of the apartment into the thick morning fog that shrouded the parking lot at the nursing home like a scene from a Bela Lugosi movie. Regan's car wasn't in its usual spot, so I waited. And waited. I desperately needed to see her and to put my arms around her again. I watched from the shadows as my co-workers filed into work. Panic set in at 6:55 a.m. when she still had not arrived.

I couldn't wait any longer and finally punched in at 7:01. I took the elevator up to the second floor, my hands sweaty and heart palpitating. Maybe she just needed some time to think and called off this morning. Couldn't say I blamed her. *Things got pretty rough last night,* I thought to myself as the elevator doors yawned open. As soon as I stepped off the elevator I could hear muffled conversation coming from a group of nurses and aides gathered around the nurse's station.

"Hey, Mina. What's up with Regan?" Brenda asked as I came around the desk and retrieved my coffee mug.

"What do you mean? Did she call off for today?"

"Call off? She called off permanently," Brenda said

"What are you talking about?"

"She quit," Brenda said.

"Where did you hear that?" I asked. She must have been mistaken.

"She called Jacobs this morning and turned in her resignation effective immediately. No notice. No nothing."

The shock of the news had kicked my legs out from under me. I dropped down into one of the desk chairs.

"Are you sure she quit and didn't just call off for today?" I asked Brenda.

The Choice
Published by The Haworth Press, Inc., 2007. All rights reserved.
doi:10.1300/5791_16

"Jacobs called here this morning around five and told me to take her off the schedule."

Brenda removed the clipboard from the wall behind the desk and showed me where Regan's schedule had been yellowed out.

"Mina, I would think that if anyone knew about her leaving, it would be you."

My mouth was cotton dry. "She never said a word." My words were barely audible. But inside I knew the truth. She hadn't said a word, no. But it had been clear that the entire relationship was too much for her to handle. The confrontation with Sean and my betrayal had been the final push over the edge. Things were tough right now, but I didn't think they were hopeless. I had so hoped she'd see it that way, too.

I felt Brenda's heavy gaze upon me.

"Mina, you okay?" Brenda asked.

"Give me a minute," I said and then got up and went into the restroom. I stared into the mirror above the sink. The woman looking back at me looked ten years older. Face puffy from crying and lack of sleep, my once vibrant complexion, now sallow and drawn, liquid brown eyes now flat with despair. I splashed cold water on my face in effort to revive the woman I once was, but with little effect. It was going to take a lot more that a little cold water to get rid of a hurt this deep.

I left the sanctuary of the restroom and returned to the desk for report. The group had dispersed, and Brenda sat alone at the desk waiting patiently for my return.

"Sorry," I said.

Brenda looked at me. "You really didn't know about her leaving?" she asked.

I shook my head. "I had no idea," I said.

Brenda just nodded.

"Staffing couldn't get you a replacement for today, but Sandy from afternoons agreed to come in at one o'clock. That will give you some help," Brenda said.

I nodded.

"Mina, for what it's worth, I'm sorry. I know you and Regan were close."

"Thanks," I said.

Brenda left. I was alone. In desperation I picked up the phone and dialed nine for an outside line. I had to find Regan. Against my better judgment, I dialed her number. After three rings her mother answered.

"Hello?"

"I'm sorry to have called so early, Mrs. Martin, but is Regan there?"

"Who is this?" Regan's mother snapped into the receiver.

"Mina Thomas, from work."

"You! You have no business with my daughter. If it weren't for you, my daughter . . .You stay away from her and don't ever call here again," she said and slammed down the receiver.

The sick feeling in my stomach intensified and I felt like I was going to throw up. I ran back into the restroom, but the feeling passed. I sat on the toilet seat with my head in my hands.

"Mina, call on line one," came over the intercom.

My heart pounded with excitement. I scurried to the desk to take the call.

"Hello?" I said desperately into the phone.

"Mina, it's me," Sean said.

My heart sank. "Oh. Hi."

"I wanted to see if you were okay," Sean said.

"I'm fine," I said calmly into the receiver.

"Good. Mina, I'm sorry about last night . . . about blindsiding you like that. I was wrong and I'm sorry."

I didn't know what to say. The damage had already been done. I was still angry with him for that. His apology seemed like too little too late.

"Mina, we have to do something. I'm afraid if we don't our marriage will be over. We talked about getting counseling when we were down in Columbus. What do you think?"

Deep down I didn't think it would make a difference at all. Yes, our marriage was over. My mind was made up, but something in his voice convinced me to give it a try. "I found a therapist in Akron who specializes in this type of situation. Maybe she would see us."

"Akron? Why so far away?" Sean asked.

"I guess there is more of this type of situation in the bigger cities," I said, thinking surely I didn't know of anyone else in our situation. Also, the distance was comforting because it reduced the chance of anyone finding out.

"Well, I'm willing to give it a try if you are," Sean said. His enthusiasm made me sad.

"I have the number in my backpack. Hold on while I go get it," I said and put the receiver down. I went back into the locker room and retrieved the *Gay People's Chronicle* from my backpack.

"Here it is. Dr. Karen Metcalf, PhD. 216-555-8790," I said into the receiver.

"Okay. I'll call and get us an appointment. Hopefully, they can get us in today or tomorrow," he said.

"Whatever, just don't make it before four in the afternoon. We are working short and there isn't anybody to replace me if I call off," I said.

I didn't know if he understood that Regan was supposed to be here with me, and that now she was gone. I'm sure he would be happy knowing that she left. That thought made me angry at him all over again. "I gotta go," I said. "Did you need anything else?"

"No . . . I guess I'll see you when you get home."

The sadness in his voice softened me a bit. He probably didn't think about Regan at all, but only about me and what was happening to our marriage.

The day seemed to drag on. When lunchtime rolled around, the thought of eating didn't appeal to me at all, so I helped the nurse's aides pass lunch trays and feed a couple of the residents who needed help. Opal was one of those residents. She didn't so much need to be fed as she did with being reminded to stay on task. She would take a bite of something, then get up and wander around the room if no one was there to remind her that she needed to eat. I sat with Opal as she munched on a celery stick, wondering if she noticed that Regan was gone.

Today Opal was wearing a lavender polo shirt, which was a gift from Regan, a red and green plaid wool skirt, and her roommate's blue fuzzy slippers. Didn't Regan know Opal needed her, just like I needed her? How could she just leave us like that, without any warning?

After lunch I redressed Opal and I decided that from here on, I'd take care of Opal each morning, getting her dressed and keeping her fed, at least until Regan returned.

Sandy arrived at one o'clock as promised. She wasn't one of my favorite people, but today, I was glad to see her.

"So what happened to your partner in crime?" Sandy said as she pulled her stethoscope out of her tattered and stained denim purse.

Her whiney voice was like fingernails on a chalkboard to me, but I wasn't going to let her get to me. "I don't know Sandy, you know just as much as I do at this point."

"You mean you didn't know she was planning on leaving?"

"No."

"Well, something must have happened," Sandy said. "Maybe she eloped or something?

"I don't think so."

"Well, have you tried to reach her?" Sandy asked.

"Yes, I called her house this morning. There was no answer," I lied. She didn't need to know all the details.

"Oh well. I guess we'll see what pans out," Sandy said.

I brought her up to speed on the patients. I was grateful that she offered to take the remaining treatments and the two o'clock med pass so I could catch up on my charting.

"I'm going downstairs for a minute to get a Diet Coke," I shouted down the hall to her. She waved and I pushed the button for the elevator.

As the doors of the elevator slid open, Rosemary Rosetti appeared. "Well, hello," she said, "Going down?"

I nodded and pushed my way past her to get on the elevator.

Rosetti held the elevator door open. "Glad to see you made it home alright last night. Where's Regan?"

I burst into tears.

"Oh God, I'm sorry. I didn't mean anything," she said and stepped back on the elevator.

The doors closed behind her.

"What happened? Bad day at work?"

I shook my head.

"Uh-oh," Rosetti said, suddenly realizing what the problem might be. "Sean stopped by the police station this morning. I wondered why he was back from Columbus so soon. He found out about you and Regan, didn't he?"

I nodded and wiped my nose with the back of my hand.

"Hey, it'll be alright," Rosetti said, putting a strong arm around my shoulder.

I shook my head. "No it won't. Everything is ruined," I blubbered. "Regan's gone."

"Oh, Mina. I am so sorry," Rosetti said and held me closer. Her breath was sweet, like Juicy Fruit gum, and the warmth of her strong body was comforting. "Gone? What happened?"

I broke our embrace and fished into the front pocket of my uniform for a Kleenex. I dabbed at my tears and my runny nose.

"I'm sorry . . . I'm so embarrassed. I don't even know you."

"It's okay. Tell me what happened," Rosetti said.

"Sean was waiting for Regan and I when we got home last night. When I flipped on the lights in the apartment, he was sitting there on the couch. By the look on his face, I thought he was going to kill both of us."

"Oooh . . . sounds like a pretty bad scene."

"Not only was last night devastating, I get to work this morning and find out Regan put in her resignation. She's gone and I don't know where she is," my voice was shaky.

The elevator doors opened, depositing us in the lobby. Rosetti took my hand and led me over to one of the leather couches in the center of the main lobby. "Here, sit here for a minute. Can I get you anything?"

"Diet Coke."

"You got it." Rosetti said and disappeared into the cafeteria.

I felt stupid sitting in the middle of the lobby, my face tear stained and bloated.

Rosetti returned with a box of Kleenex and a Diet Coke.

"Have you tried contacting Regan?"

"Yes. I called her house this morning right after report. Her mother answered the phone."

"Was she there?"

"I don't know. When her mother realized it was me, she told me never to call there again and hung up."

"That was rude. If she was there, she could have at least let you speak to her."

I nodded and took a sip of my Diet Coke. It was sweet and cold and felt good on my dry, parched throat.

"It sounds like Regan's scared. Living an alternative lifestyle is tough. I mean, it can be exciting, all the secretiveness and stealing precious moments to be together, but I am sure getting caught definitely put a damper on things."

"I need to get her back. What can I do to get her back? At least to talk to me?"

"I wish I knew," Rosetti said. "The only thing you can do right now is wait her out. She's probably confused, probably embarrassed or just plain scared . . . it could be any one of those things. Maybe she just needs some time to think things through."

The afternoon shift nurse's aides were beginning to arrive at work. A few of them gawked at Rosetti and me as they passed through the lobby on their way to the time clock. I realized that I had been off the floor for too long. I pulled two Kleenex's from the box Rosetti had brought over and blew my nose.

"I have to get back to the floor to finish up," I said and stood up on wobbly legs.

"I'll ride up with you," Rosetti took me by the elbow and guided me toward the elevator.

Once in the elevator, she pulled out her business card from the front pocket of her blue uniform shirt and scribbled something on the back. She handed me the card. "Here, this is my work extension and on the back is my home number. If you ever need to talk, give me a call," she said.

I took the smooth white linen card from her and ran my fingertips over the raised black lettering. "Thank you." I managed a weak smile. The elevator doors opened and we both stepped out. Rosetti went on to her mother's room. I could hear her greet her cheerily. I sat down at the desk to undertake the mound of charting that had piled up during the day. It looked like I was going to be late after all, but didn't have the energy to call Sean to let him know.

It was almost four o'clock by the time I finished the last chart. Thank God I didn't have to give Sandy shift report or I would have been set back another half hour. I packed up my backpack and quietly left the floor. The sinking feeling in the pit of my stomach seemed to get worse the closer I got to home. I scanned the parking lot for any sign of Regan, but came up empty. I secretly wished she'd be waiting for me, maybe hidden in the woods to sweep me away from all this. But deep down, I knew that would never happen, not with Regan.

As I walked up the cement walk to my front door I couldn't go in. I didn't have the strength to deal with Sean right then, and, more important, I had to find Regan.

I ran to the car and drove to the south side of town, creeping down her tree-lined side street, trying to see if her car was in the garage, but the door was down. From the road I could tell someone was home, only I couldn't tell who. I had to take my chances and hope and pray it was Regan and that she was alone.

I parked my car under the huge elm tree in front of Regan's house and tiptoed over to the side of the house where Regan's bedroom was, hoping the window was open and she'd be there. No such luck. The window was closed, and I couldn't hear any voices or movement from inside, so I mustered up all my courage and walked over to the back door. I knocked several times on the rusted screen door and waited for what seemed like an eternity. Just as I was about to walk away, Regan's mother appeared at the door.

"I thought I told you to leave us alone," she spat out.

"I'm sorry, but I need to speak to Regan. It's very important," I said, my voice quivered.

"She's not here!"

"Well can you tell me where she is? Please, I need to talk to her," I begged.

"No! Don't you think you've done enough damage to our family? You're the reason my daughter had to leave," she said her voice shaking with anger. "You should be ashamed of yourself, passing yourself off as being her friend. I know what you did to her and . . . and . . . you're a sick, perverse human being. Now get out of here before I call the police."

I hurried down Regan's driveway my heart pounding with fear and humiliation. I slammed the car door shut, threw the car into gear, and sped away. Tears of frustration blurred my vision as I drove aimlessly through town. I didn't want to go home, but I didn't have anywhere else to go. I could go out to the lake, but being there without Regan would be too painful right now.

When I got back to the apartment, Sean was waiting for me.

"Where have you been?" Sean asked. "I called work, but they said you had already left. I was beginning to worry something happened."

"I went for a drive," I said and set my backpack and keys on the dining room table.

"Where?" Sean asked as he followed me into the bedroom.

"Nowhere in particular. I just needed to get away for a little while."

Sean looked sullen. I felt a twinge of grief for him but then my heart immediately went protectively numb. "We have a seven o'clock appointment with Dr. Metcalf," he said, following me into the bedroom.

"Tonight?" I asked wearily

"Yes, they are working us in."

I sighed. "I need to shower and change before we go."

"Okay," he said then turned to leave the bedroom. "Meen?"

"Huh?" I answered, not bothering to look up at him.

"Meen . . . I'm sorry. I'm really sorry," Sean said, his voice steeped in sadness.

"I am too," I whispered.

I relished the solitude in the bathroom. I took my time showering and dressing. Actually, it seemed futile to me to even be going to the therapist. Regan was gone. Problem solved, right?

"Meen, we better get moving," Sean said through the closed bathroom door. I ran my fingers through my damp hair and joined him in the living room. "Ready?" he asked.

"Yes. Let's go," I said.

We spent the forty-five minute drive to Akron in silence. Not the comfortable silence that two people share who know each other so well that words don't need to be spoken, but a heavy, awkward silence. Sort of like the calm before something terrible happens.

We pulled into the parking lot of Dr. Metcalf's office. It was more of a home than an office, a majestic white colonial with black shuddered windows. It seemed like a welcoming place. I wondered how many people had walked through these doors trying to deal with the same predicament. I also wondered how it worked out for them.

Sean signed us in and then sat next to me on one of the black leather couches that lined the waiting room walls. We must have been the last appointment of the day as we were the only people in the waiting room. I picked up a copy of *Psychology Today* and thumbed through it. A few minutes later a woman in her mid-forties with a face that reminded me of a plump, ripe, peach appeared at the office door dressed in a flowing black and orange African print skirt, black T-shirt, and Birkenstock sandals.

"Mr. and Mrs. Thomas?"

Sean and I stood up and followed the woman into the back office.

"Welcome. I'm Karen Metcalf," she said and extended her hand to both of us. "Please make yourselves comfortable."

Dr. Metcalf's office was spacious and richly decorated in polished woods and calming earth tones. Natural light bathed the room through a large picture window that looked out onto a serene pond. One wall was a floor-to-ceiling oak bookcase that housed books titled *The History of Sexuality,* volumes one, two, and three; *Society and the Healthy Homosexual;* and *Lesbian Images,* which told me at least we were in the right place. The other walls displayed several degrees, diplomas, and awards, a framed and autographed Playbill from the Broadway play *Cats,* a reproduction of Monet's "Water Lilies," and a silk rainbow flag. Kleenex boxes adorned the two oak end tables that flanked the tweed love seat where Sean and I were seated, giving away that this room had witnessed a lot of heartache and tears.

Dr. Metcalf sat opposite us in a leather butternut yellow Tullsta armchair from Ikea. Her sturdy legs tucked beneath her skirt as if she were at home in her living room relaxing with friends.

"So, what brings you here today?" Dr. Metcalf asked.

Sean looked over at me and I looked back at him, neither one of us anxious to answer the question. Finally, Sean spoke up. "Mina has had an . . . affair . . . with a woman," Sean said.

"I see. Mina, is that true?" Dr. Metcalf asked.

I nodded.

"How long have you been having this affair?"

"A couple of months," I said.

"Is this the first time or have you had affairs with women in the past?"

"This is the first time."

"Did you have romantic feelings for women before meeting this woman?" Dr. Metcalf asked.

"I had crushes on women off and on for a while," I said.

"A while meaning a week? A month? Ten years?"

"I guess off and on since high school."

"And you never acted on your feelings until now?" Dr. Metcalf continued.

"Yes, that's correct," I answered, feeling like I was being interrogated over some crime.

"Tell me why this time was different."

I wasn't sure why this time was different. I had had crushes on many girls, but I guess I was too scared admit those feelings to myself, let alone to act on them. With Regan, even though I knew I was taking a big chance, especially since she was so naive about a lot of things, in my heart I knew she felt the same way and that it would be all right.

"It felt safe," I said.

"Safe? That's interesting. Safe, meaning that you knew she wouldn't physically harm you? Safe in that you knew she would keep your relationship a secret? What made you feel pursuing a relationship with this woman was safe?"

"I knew that the attraction between us was mutual. It felt safe because neither Regan—that's her name, Regan—nor I had done anything like this before. It seemed almost innocent, like we were exploring something new together. No judgments to fear and no expectations to live up to. Safe."

"I see. Does your relationship with Regan still feel safe today or has that changed?" Dr. Metcalf asked.

"Today . . . I don't know."

"You don't know?" Dr. Metcalf asked the question, but I know Sean was more curious about the answer.

"Regan left and I've lost contact with her."

"She left without telling you where she was going or why she was leaving?"

I nodded.

"That must have been quite painful. Did you try to contact her?"

I nodded, and quickly recounted the phone call and my visit to Regan's house. Sean listened silently but I could feel his resentment building for not telling him exactly where I had been after work this afternoon.

"When was the last time you saw Regan?"

"Last night."

"Tell me about that."

I looked over at Sean. Part of me wanted to hurt him and tell Dr. Metcalf everything that transpired last night, but then part of me felt sorry for him. It couldn't be easy listening to me talk about my feelings for someone else. I opted for the merciful version. "Regan and I went to a gay bar in Youngstown."

"The Other Side?" Dr. Metcalf asked.

"Yes," I said, surprised that she, or anyone else for that matter, had ever heard of the place.

"I've been there a few times. Not a bad place. It can get pretty crowded on the weekends. Go on, I didn't mean to interrupt."

"Anyway, we went to the bar to see if there were other people—women—like us. It was more my idea than hers. She really didn't want to go."

"Why is that?"

"Because she doesn't think either one of us is gay."

"That's interesting," Dr. Metcalf said and then unfolded her legs out from underneath her skirt. "Did Regan date men as well?" she asked.

"Only one that I knew about."

"What can you tell me about it?" Dr. Metcalf asked.

"He was a paramedic she met through work. He came on a call at the nursing home where we work. That's how they met. But it didn't last very long, a few weeks maybe."

"What happened?"

"Regan said the first few dates were great, but then things got . . . sexual. She was very adamant about saving herself for marriage. She said it didn't feel right and that she felt that the only thing that guys wanted was sex. So she basically shut him down. After that the relationship slowly died off."

"Is that true, Sean? That the only thing men want from women is sex?" Dr. Metcalf asked, catching Sean off guard.

"No . . . no, that's not all we want," Sean answered, straightening himself in his seat, his discomfort with this whole situation seeping through.

Dr. Metcalf smiled.

"So, Mina, help me with this. Regan's relationship with the paramedic didn't work out. She begins a relationship with you, sexual, I'm assuming here, but doesn't think either one of you are gay? So how did she perceive your relationship?"

"Regan thought our situation was special, because it was she and I, also she used to say we just did what we did because we didn't have any decent men in our lives. I told her I didn't think so, because I had a decent man in my life, yet I wanted to be with her." I realized that I said this in front of Sean. I couldn't look at him. I didn't want to see the pain the comment might have caused.

"So Regan viewed your relationship as more of a temporary thing, like her relationship with you was okay until the right man came along?" Dr. Metcalf asked tentatively as if testing the assumption.

For the first time I understood the meaning of those words. It made me angry that Regan felt that way about our relationship. Like it was a consolation prize or something. Is that why she was able to leave so easily?

I shrugged in an attempt to hide the hurt.

"Mina, let me ask you something. On a scale of one to ten, ten being one hundred percent homosexual and one being one hundred percent straight, where do you see yourself on that spectrum?"

I hesitated for a moment, wishing Sean wasn't there. I felt his heavy gaze upon me waiting for an answer.

"Seven. I'd say about a seven."

"That's pretty significant," Dr. Metcalf said.

Sean shifted on the love seat. I still couldn't look at him. Even though it hurt, I had to be honest. Otherwise, this was pointless.

"Sean, how do you feel about what Mina has just said?"

"I don't believe her. How could she and I be together for so long if she were that way?"

"That's the point of my question. Most people are not one hundred percent gay or straight. Mina sees herself as a seven. That's pretty high up on the scale, but it's not so high that a relationship with a man would be impossible. The question of sexual identity and how it is formed is not well understood. We have often simplistically assume that people have attractions to persons of one or the other sex, but not both. One's sexual identity is not always predictable on the basis of one's sexual behavior. However, it appears to be that sexual feelings and activities change; they can become fluid and dynamic."

Sean looked bewildered.

"I know this is a lot of information to digest in one session. Let me put it this way: Sean, Mina obviously loves you or the two of you would not have been together this long, nor would you be here this evening. The reality is that sexual feelings, identities, and activities may not at all times be congruent; for example, her loving feelings for you and her sexual feelings for Regan. Do you see what I am saying?" Dr. Metcalf asked.

Sean nodded.

"The most frequent reason couples seek my help is because a spouse has experimented with homosexual behavior. They come to me because they want me to change or 'fix' the spouse that has engaged in the behavior. I need to be quite frank with you. I can't change some-one who is homosexual into a heterosexual. No one can."

"But I thought it was a learned behavior. And if it's learned, it can be unlearned. Can't it?" Sean asked.

"A portion of it is learned, but the majority of it is genetic."

"So what you're saying is that we are wasting our time here," Sean said.

"No, I'm not saying that at all. I'm saying if you are coming here for me to 'exorcize' Mina of her homosexual feelings you'll be disap-pointed. What I can do is help you cope with what is happening in your marriage. What I'm saying is that nothing we do here in this of-fice will stop Mina from being attracted to women. Dealing with that fact in your marriage is something I can help you with. It will take a lot of work and a lot of compromise for both of you."

Dr. Metcalf paused for a moment and then turned to me.

"Mina, how do you feel about being married to Sean?"

I shrugged my shoulders. "I don't know what to feel." I said almost inaudibly. "I love Sean and I can't imagine not having him in my life. Our life together has been good, but it also feels like something is missing."

"What's missing?" Dr. Metcalf asked.

This was another loaded question. I had to choose my words care-fully as not to hurt Sean.

"Mina, what's missing?" Dr. Metcalf repeated.

"Intimacy," I said.

"Intimacy!" Sean blurted out. "That's a bunch of crap." Sean shifted in his seat turning his back toward me. "We're intimate. We couldn't be more intimate. What about just a few days ago in Colum-bus? That was pretty fucking intimate."

I stared out the picture window behind Dr. Metcalf's chair and watched as a chevron of mallards gracefully landed on the pond, wish-ing I were out there instead of in here. I had had enough of this and just wanted to leave.

Sensing we had hit a wall, Dr. Metcalf asked to speak with each of us alone. "Sean, would you mind stepping out in the waiting room for a few minutes while I talk to Mina alone?"

Sean got up from the love seat and walked over to the door. Dr. Metcalf followed him.

"I'll come get you as soon as we are through. I think there is still some coffee left in the waiting room," she said.

Sean declined the coffee. Dr. Metcalf returned, closing the door quietly behind her.

"Okay, Mina. I know this is difficult, but the only way I can help you is if you tell me honestly what's going on," Dr. Metcalf said as she settled herself back into her chair.

So I did. I told her everything about how Regan and I met, how we seemed to click immediately. I told her about the first time Regan and I made love and how everything seemed to fall into place for me. I told her, too, that I betrayed Regan, had broken the promise I'd made to her and how much I regretted it and that I was scared—terrified, actually, because my life was changing at the speed of light and everything felt so out of control.

I told her I was afraid I would lose my job or my family if anyone found out I was gay. I told her I couldn't imagine going to my mother and telling her I was leaving Sean and, oh, by the way, I'm a lesbian. I didn't think she even knew what a lesbian was.

I told Dr. Metcalf that I felt my future with Regan was bleakly uncertain. And I also told her that I didn't want to lose Sean either, that I loved him dearly and couldn't imagine a life without him, but that at this point, I found it hard to imagine a future with him.

A half a box of Kleenex later, it was Sean's turn. I sat in the empty waiting room trying to imagine what she and Sean were talking about. Twenty minutes later Dr. Metcalf emerged from her office to retrieve me.

When I returned to the office, Sean's eyes were red and swollen. He clutched a wad of Kleenex in his right hand. I sat down next to him and placed my hand on his leg. I wanted to reach out to him so badly.

"Mina and Sean, I have spoken to you both together and individually. There is no doubt in my mind that you truly love each other, but I have to tell you, it's going to take a lot more than love and understanding to keep your marriage together. It's going to take a strong commitment from both of you to make this marriage work, if that is what you want."

I looked down at my hands in my lap. Suddenly, I felt ill equipped to take on such a task to reach a goal I wasn't sure I wanted.

"Mina, for you it may mean giving up your relationship with Regan or any other woman that you may meet and become attracted to. Sean, for you it may mean turning away and allowing Mina to live that part of her life. That would mean sharing her with someone else. You need to go home and think about these things and decide if it is something you both can agree on."

Uncertainty crept into Sean's expression. My mind was congested with dread, doubt, and fear.

"I'd like to see you both again in two weeks. Does this time slot work out for you?" Dr. Metcalf asked as she flipped open a black leather appointment book.

Sean and I nodded. All I could think about was whether he'd return to Columbus. I desperately needed some time alone to sort things out.

"Okay, I'll see you both on Monday, the twenty-fourth. In the meantime, if you need anything, here is my card. I have a twenty-four hour answering service. Please feel free to call at anytime."

We left Dr. Metcalf's office and stopped at the Bob Evans just before Interstate 77 for dinner.

"Doesn't seem like there is much hope for us, does it?" I asked poking with my fork at a slab of meatloaf.

"We can do this, Meen," Sean said reaching over and taking my hand in his. "We've been through tough stuff before. We can get through this, too. We just have to stick together."

Sean's enthusiasm filled me with resentment and sadness. He was wishing for one thing and I was wishing for another. I think I had hoped he would punish me with his anger for wrecking his life. Instead, he showered me with his love and understanding. My sense of guilt and frustration was growing by the minute.

Chapter Seventeen

It had been almost two weeks since Regan had left, and I still had not heard a word from her. Each morning on my way to work I'd scan the parking lot and side street for any sign of her. After work, whether I was in the grocery store or just driving around, I'd always be on the lookout for her.

Sean resigned his position in Columbus. He returned to the city police department and eventually reunited on a work detail with Rosemary Rosetti.

I promised Dr. Metcalf I'd be open and honest with Sean and didn't want to keep anything from him. So I told Sean I met Rosetti at the nursing home and had been taking care of her mom. I didn't know if he knew that Rosetti was a lesbian and I didn't want him thinking there was something going on between us other than friendship. I really enjoyed my friendship with her and didn't want Sean to get the wrong idea and force me to end it.

As the days went on they seemed to get harder to endure. Sean was home every evening, and I was suffocating. It was like he was watching me all the time. I couldn't walk downstairs to the mailbox without feeling guilty. So I volunteered to work as much overtime as I could. It got me out of the apartment, and I knew it was the one place Regan might call to contact me. Peggy had just returned from her two-week vacation. She and I worked a lot together and I was tempted to confide in her. But I didn't.

My relationship with Regan was acceptable in my mind, but I wasn't so sure about anyone else's. Would they think I was some kind of sexual deviant? A pervert whom you would be afraid to be alone with? I couldn't stand the thought of them feeling that way toward me, so I kept my mouth shut, revealing only the sketchy details of Regan's abrupt disappearance.

The Choice
Published by The Haworth Press, Inc., 2007. All rights reserved.
doi:10.1300/5791_17

The only person I could talk to was Rosemary Rosetti. I saw her almost every afternoon. She'd come straight from work to visit her mom. I'd wait until she'd arrive to take my lunch break, so we could go downstairs for a Diet Coke and a private conversation. She seemed to enjoy our time together as much as I did. Each day she'd ask me if I'd heard from Regan. Then we would talk about her day at work. Sometimes we'd talk about how she and Sean were getting along. She said when they were out on patrol, Sean didn't say much. If she asked him a question, he'd give her one- or two-word answers, and never shared any personal information with her, even when she'd ask him how I was doing or what I was up to.

I asked her if it was hard to work under those conditions. Apparently she was used to it. Most guys didn't know what to do with her or how to treat her, especially since she outranked most of them. She didn't think the problem was that she was gay; it was more that she was a woman and that the male officers had to take orders from her. But once they saw what a competent police officer she was, the prejudices came down and most of them came around.

The weekend was approaching. I was dreading it. I was scheduled off, but offered to work Saturday night for Brenda. It was her and Charlie's fifteenth wedding anniversary and he had made big plans. I secretly wondered if Sean and I would make it to our next anniversary.

Rosetti and I kept our usual one thirty lunch date.

"Any word from Regan?" was her usual opener.

"No, not a word."

"This isn't over yet. She'll contact you," she said, taking a swig of her Diet Coke.

"You really think so?" I asked. "I feel like she has written me off."

"How could she Mina, after what you two shared?"

"I don't think what we had meant the same thing to her as it did to me. Anyway, I betrayed her. That alone is enough to keep her away."

"How are things at home?" Rosetti asked.

"Not good. I feel like a caged animal. Any time I go anywhere it's forty questions from Sean. It's so bad that on my weekends off I offer to work for anybody who wants time off. This Saturday night I am working midnight turn for Brenda. It's her anniversary and her husband is taking her out."

Rosetti seemed to understand everything I felt. She was so easy to talk to; I felt I could tell her anything.

At three o'clock, I stuck my head into Teresa Rosetti's room before leaving for the day. Teresa was sound asleep and Rosetti was sitting at her bedside reading a worn-out paperback version of *The Choirboys*. She looked up from her book as I entered the room. "I'm taking off now," I whispered in order not wake up her mother.

Rosetti flashed me a smile, "Hang in there," she whispered back and then waved good-bye.

When I reached the parking lot, there was no sign of Regan. Again. When I crossed through the small thicket of woods between the nursing home and the apartment complex, I noticed there was no sign of Sean, either. *The warden has left the building.* My heart felt a little lighter as I looked forward to spending some time alone at home.

I stopped in the hallway and retrieved the mail from the mailbox: Sean's August edition of *Guns and Ammo,* the electric bill, and a pink envelope that looked like a birthday card tumbled into my arms as I unlocked the tiny metal door. I pulled the card out from the pile of mail and inhaled deeply. On the card's surface was the faint scent of Avon Soft Musk cologne—Regan's perfume.

My heart stalled in my chest. The envelope was addressed to me, written in Regan's loopy feminine handwriting with no return address, postmarked Wheeling, West Virginia. My hand shook as I sliced open the envelope with my thumbnail and removed the card. The front of the card was a beautiful watercolor picture of a bright yellow shooting star. Under the star were the words: "For what you did and for who you are." I opened the card. It read,

> *I am so sorry I had to leave without saying good-bye. I couldn't stay any longer and be who you wanted me to be. You deserve more. More than I could ever give you. Just remember that I will always hold a special place for you in my heart and that I will never forget you. Love R.*

Closure. There it was. Right in front of me. She really was gone, and by the sound of things, gone forever. I slid the card back into the envelope and carried it upstairs, clutching it to my chest. The apartment was serenely quiet. Dust motes floated in the late afternoon sun that spilled through the shears on the dining room window. On the table was a note from Sean:

Took the car in for an oil change and run some errands. Be back soon. Made a six-o'clock reservation for us at that new Victorian restaurant by Mosquito Lake. Be ready by 5:30. Love, Sean

I hid Regan's card in my backpack, a place I knew Sean would never touch, a place where I hid everything that was near and dear to my heart. I felt numb. Regan was gone for good and tonight I had to play the good wife. This was more than I could handle. It would take every ounce of energy I had to get through dinner. The voice inside of my heart told me to run, because I couldn't change who I was, but the voice inside my head told me to stay because I owed it to Sean and myself to try and work this out.

Suddenly, it was difficult to breathe and my throat felt as if it were going to swell shut. The walls of the apartment seemed to close in on me. I had to leave. I changed into jeans and a T-shirt, grabbed my backpack, and left. I drove and drove until I realized I was headed out to the lake. I found the secluded spot between the ancient weeping willow trees and a bank of Azalea bushes where Regan and I spent many hot summer nights, our rendezvous concealed by the tree branches and bushes. I sat there for a long time, hyperventilating and staring out over the water, waiting for the panic attack to subside.

I pulled Regan's card from the safety of my backpack and inhaled its scent. My heart ached at the thought that I would never see her again. I held the card in my hands and stared at the postmark: Wheeling, West Virginia. That wasn't so far away. If I left now I could be there by late evening. But Regan left no forwarding address, a gesture that looked painfully deliberate. She didn't want me to find her, and it was quite evident she never wanted to see me again.

I thought about Sean and what might happen to our marriage. I thought, too, how angry he would be when he got home this evening and find me not there. Then, suddenly, Rosetti crossed my mind. I took her business card out of my wallet and thought about walking up to the ranger station to the pay phone and calling her.

I searched my pockets, my backpack, and the console in the car for a quarter, but came up empty. Then decided that was the universe's way of telling me that calling her was a bad idea. It really wasn't fair of me to drag her any further into all this. After all, she did work with Sean, and our relationship at the nursing home was strictly professional. It was supposed to be anyway.

I sat for a while longer watching a family with two small children pack up from their day on the beach. The kids were cute, a boy and girl, neither one of them over the age of five. They squealed and frolicked in the sand while their parents lugged a huge green Coleman cooler, wicker picnic basket, beach bag, umbrella, and a blown-up Mickey Mouse inner tube across the white sand. The mother and father both looked exhausted. I didn't envy them in the least.

There were so many reasons for me not to stay with Sean besides my attraction to women. The fact that Sean wanted to start a family and I didn't was a big one. Maybe if I left he would find someone who wanted children.

That thought sent an icy chill through me: Seeing Sean with someone else. Although we weren't getting along to well right then, I truly did love him. Seeing him with someone else would be difficult. Looking at it that way made me realize deep down inside how he must have felt about seeing me and Regan together. It must have hurt him terribly, but the amazing thing was he still wanted to make our marriage work. I grasped the steering wheel with both hands and pressed my head against its cool hardness. I felt bad for hurting Sean. He was one of the good guys and didn't deserve the crap I'd been putting him through.

I needed to look at things realistically now. Regan was gone. She wasn't coming back. I was married to a man who loved me dearly, so why couldn't I just grow up and make this marriage work? There had to be other women in the same position who did. Sex was just a small

part of marriage anyway. Maybe Sean was right, we just needed to
stick together and everything would fall into place.

Feeling stronger and with a renewed outlook on the situation, I
started the engine and headed home. Sean would be back soon and if
I beat him there, he would never know I'd left.

I was in the shower when Sean returned. I slipped on my terry cloth
robe and towel dried my hair. Sean knocked on the bathroom door.
"Meen, you almost ready?"

"I'll be out in a minute," I said.

I emerged from the bathroom and headed to the bedroom to get
dressed. Sean met me at the bedroom door. He was dressed in beige
linen dress pants and a white cotton shirt, both of which I had never
seen before. He was carrying a huge bouquet of pink roses. "These are
for you," he said, presenting them to me as if I had just won a beauty
pageant.

"They're beautiful," I said and stuck my nose into the soft petals
and inhaled. "What's the occasion?"

"Starting over," he said. "I want to do this right. You said that
something was missing in our relationship. Well, I want to change
that. Tonight we are going out to have a romantic dinner and then
come home and get acquainted all over again."

My stomach tightened as I slipped on a pair of black silk slacks, lavender silk blouse, and strappy black patent leather sandals. I even put
on makeup, something I hadn't done in a long time, in an effort to become the "new and improved Mina, wife of the year."

When we pulled into the parking lot of the restaurant, the memories of when Regan and I had come here came flooding back.

"This place is supposed to be pretty good," Sean said, obviously un-
aware that I had been here before. More secrets. Dr. Metcalf would
not be pleased, but I didn't think this was the time or place to come
clean.

Sean and I waited at the bar for our table to be cleared. He ordered
a Corona with lime and I ordered a glass of wine. Our conversation
was light. We laughed and talked and things started to feel normal
again, at least until the hostess came to seat us.

The hostess was the same lanky brunette that seated Regan and I a few short weeks ago. I couldn't help but notice her ample bottom sway back and forth in her form-fitting sheath dress as she led us to our table. She set two black leather menus on the table and handed Sean the wine list. She snapped open the white linen napkin that sat on my plate and draped it across my lap. "It's nice to see you again," she said with a Martina Navratilova accent and a Linda Evans smile.

Sean looked up at me, confused.

I shrugged, feeling the under arms of my silk shirt pitting out.

The hostess unfolded his napkin as well and draped it across his lap and turned and walked away. I didn't dare look up.

"You know her?" Sean asked.

"No. She must have me confused with someone else," I said, picking up my menu and opening it to hide my guilt.

I perused the menu while Sean looked over the wine list.

"I saw you checking her out," Sean said from behind the wine list.

I didn't know what to say. I felt humiliated.

Sean closed the wine list and laid it down in the table. "You really can't help yourself, can you?" Sean whispered across the table at me.

I closed my menu and tossed it in the table. "I'm sorry, Sean. I don't know what you want me to do."

"Mina, can't you please just stop it?"

"What makes you think I can just stop it?"

"Because you've done it for this long. Why does it have to change now?"

"Sean, I wish none of this ever happened, but it did and now we just have to make the best of it."

"But you are not even trying," Sean said.

"Not trying? How do you expect me to try to make this work when I feel like your prisoner? You watch everything I do. I can't move. I can't breathe."

Our waiter appeared at our table just in time to quell a situation that could have turned ugly. I just wanted to leave, but I stayed. I didn't want to cause a scene. Sean ordered a steak and baked potato and I ordered another glass of wine. Whatever appetite I had previously had vanished. Sean ate his steak in silence as I sipped my wine.

At the speed Sean ate, this dinner would be over in ten minutes, and
we could leave with our dignity intact.

I looked around the room at the other diners. People sat at the bar,
laughing and joking. Couples sat close, engrossed in intimate conversation as they dined on oysters Rockefeller and crusty bruschetta. I
glanced over at the entrance and my heart leapt with joy when I saw
Rosetti coming in through the doorway of the restaurant.

Rosetti looked dashing in her tailored black suit and crisp white
dress shirt. She must have known about Sean's plan, knew it would be
a disaster and had come to rescue me. For a brief moment, I was convinced of this, but then I saw she wasn't alone.

A younger woman with shoulder-length blond hair dressed in a floral print summer dress stood by her side as they waited to be seated.
Tiny pangs of jealousy replaced the joyous fluttering in my heart. I
looked down, feigning interest in a packet of Sweet 'N Low when she
looked our way.

"Sean, Mina, hello," Rosetti said, approaching our table.

"Hey, Sarge," Sean said, putting down his fork. "What brings you
to this side of town?"

"I'd heard that this place had pretty good food," she said. "By the
looks of your steak, my informants were right."

"Yes, it was good," Sean said, wiping his mouth with his napkin.

"I'd like you to meet someone," Rosetti said. "Linda, this is Sean
Thomas and his wife, Mina. Sean is my new partner at the police department, and Mina takes care of my mom at the nursing home."

"It's nice to meet you," Linda said, smiling, exposing perfect white
teeth.

"Linda is a dispatcher at my old precinct in Cleveland," Rosetti
said, directing the comment more toward Sean than I.

The hostess appeared, ready to seat Rosetti and her date. "Well, I
guess our table is ready. Have a good evening," Rosetti said. The two
turned and followed the hostess through the crowded room. As Rosetti
walked behind Linda to their table, she placed her hand on the small of
Linda's back. I remembered the night at Bartoli's daughter's graduation party when it had been me who did the same thing to Regan.

I closed my eyes, feeling utterly miserable as Sean continued eating his steak until only the T-bone was left on his plate. Sean reached for the bread basket and the last of the dinner rolls when I peered over his shoulder to check out Rosetti and her date.

"What are you looking at?" Sean asked.

"Nothing," I said and took another sip of my wine.

Sean turned around and saw exactly what I was looking at. "Not her, too?" Sean said. "I know Rosetti's a dyke, but it looks like you're too late. I believe she's taken."

His comment infuriated me and I got up to leave. Sean grabbed me by the wrist and pulled me down. "Sit down," he said through gritted teeth.

I didn't want Rosetti to think anything was wrong, so I obeyed. My hands trembled as I picked up my near empty wine glass. I gulped what was left and wished I had more. I was so angry with Sean, I could hardly breathe.

"Sean, please take me home," I said, my voice quivered.

Sean signaled our waiter for the check. He paid it at the table and left a ten-dollar tip. When we got up to leave, Rosetti looked over in our direction and waved good-bye. I waved back, and I knew by the look on Rosetti's face that she knew things did not go well.

Sean drove home like a maniac. Apparently he wanted this evening to end as much as I did. The comment he made about Rosetti played over and over in my mind until I couldn't let it go any more.

"What you said about Rosetti . . . that was pretty mean," I said breaking the protective silence.

"What's Rosetti got to do with this?' Sean asked, defensively.

"You called her a dyke."

"I call 'em as I see 'em," Sean said.

"Is that how you see me?" I asked not knowing whether my question would infuriate him or humble him.

He didn't answer and I let it go.

"Rosetti doesn't think anyone on the force knows about her . . . orientation," I said.

"You're kidding, right?"

"No, I'm not. When I asked her how things were going at work, she told me rough at first, but that she thought it was because she was a woman, not because she's gay."

"Well look at her. That short hair, that deep voice, the way she dresses and the way she walks, a blind person could tell she's a dyke."

"Sean, she's a very nice person. You should see how she takes care of her mother," I said defending Rosetti's honor.

"She is a nice person and a hell of a police officer, but she's still a dyke."

"Sean, stop saying that word."

"You brought it up," he said.

"You make it sound like she's a bad person because—"

"Because she fucks women."

"Sean!"

"Jesus, Mina, what do you want from me? If you are such a big fan of Rosetti's you might as well go off and fuck her too. Go Mina, go fuck whoever you want. I don't care any more. I'm tired Mina, I'm fuckin' tired of all this. All I wanted to do tonight was to take my wife out to dinner and have a relaxing evening, but no, it has to turn into a big war."

Sean was right. It seemed like everything we did these days ended in an argument with one of us resenting the other. Once at the apartment, I got out of the car and rushed upstairs. I went into the bedroom and pulled down a suitcase from the closet and tossed in a clean uniform, a couple pairs of jeans, T-shirts, a sweatshirt, and five pairs of clean underwear.

"Where do you think you're going?" Sean demanded.

"I'm going to a motel. I can't stay here anymore, Sean. I can't live like this." My voice was fragile and shaky.

Sean stood hunched in the doorway of our bedroom. "Mina, don't leave. Please don't leave. I'm sorry."

"Sean. It's over. Our marriage is over. I am so sorry, but living like this is killing me, and it's killing you too."

I felt guilty and selfish and I couldn't look at him as I picked up my suitcase and backpack and headed for the door. I knew if I did look at him and see the pain in his eyes, I would change my mind and stay, but that wasn't doing either one of us any good anymore.

Chapter Eighteen

The Super 8 Motel on Route 82 rented rooms by the week. My room had a double bed, a TV with free HBO, and a tiny refrigerator that reminded me of a wall safe. For the first time ever, I was on my own.

Thoughts of Regan and Sean and Rosetti pounded through my mind, keeping me awake most of the night. I still felt guilty for leaving Sean like I did, but I felt liberated as well. Because I had to work for Brenda that night, I tried to sleep in that morning, but it was no use, so I got up and dressed and decided to spend the day exploring my new life.

I drove around aimlessly for about an hour and came across The Fireside Book Shop, a charming bookstore in Chagrin Falls that had three floors of books and a cozy reading area with a fireplace in the back of the store. I browsed the shelves for almost two hours and ended up making three purchases: A brown leather-bound journal, a softcover edition of *How to Pass the MCAT,* and a trade paperback edition of Alice Walker's *The Color Purple*.

I took my purchases down the street to a coffee shop, where I ordered a coffee and a blueberry scone. The delicious aroma of Arabica beans filled the coffee shop. I spotted a small round table, the kind you would see in an outdoor café or an ice cream parlor, near one of the picture windows that looked right out onto the main street, and made myself at home. I pulled out *The Color Purple* and began to read. The next time I looked up, it was dark outside.

I had read the entire book in one sitting. What an amazing story. Celie's life wasn't easy, but she knew how to survive. When she meets Shug, her husband's lover, Celie finds the courage to ask for more—to laugh, to play, and finally to love the other woman. If Celie could find herself, so could I.

The Choice
Published by The Haworth Press, Inc., 2007. All rights reserved.
doi:10.1300/5791_18

I returned to the motel in barely enough time to change clothes for work and head out. It felt strange driving forty-five minutes into work at eleven at night. I wondered how Brenda was doing it all these years. I was beginning to wonder if anything would ever feel normal again as I pulled my car into the practically deserted nursing home parking lot. By habit I scanned the cars wishing one of them would be Regan's, but again I was disappointed. It's funny, but I was beginning to expect it now, because in my heart I knew that Regan was gone from my life forever.

I gathered up my backpack and the MCAT book I had bought earlier. I needed something to keep my mind off of my crumbling personal life and figured that something this complicated would do the trick. As I walked through the parking lot I looked over toward the apartments. A deep sadness washed over me when I saw the light on in the dining room window of the apartment and wondered if Sean was home.

It had been twenty-four hours since I'd left. I did miss him and I hated to think things would end this way. I shook the thoughts from my head and went inside the nursing home to clock in.

When I got to the floor, the overhead lights had been dimmed, creating a peaceful atmosphere. Sandy was sitting in the lounge with three nurse's aides, watching the beginning of the eleven o'clock news. When she saw me she looked at her watch. "What are you doing here at this hour?"

"I'm working for Brenda. It's her anniversary. Charlie is taking her out."

"Oh. Okay," Sandy said, then got up and lumbered her large frame over to the desk.

Alberta would be my only aide tonight, as there were no treatments and only two short medication passes. Alberta was a good aide, and I was surprised and glad to see her since she usually worked day turn. I knew her husband was ill and unable to work, so she, like me, was doing what she needed to do to survive.

"I hope you brought something to read or crosswords or something," Sandy said. "The nights can really drag and the TV goes off at twelve thirty a.m. after Johnny Carson."

"Yes, I bought this today," I said and pulled out the heavy volume."

"MCAT? What's that for?" Sandy asked.

"It's to study for the entrance exam for medical school."

"Medical school?" Sandy said.

"It's just a thought. I wanted to see if I had what it takes to get in."

"Well, good luck. You're a lot more ambitious than I am. Sometimes it takes everything I have to do *this* job," Sandy said as she slung the strap of her bulging denim purse over her shoulder.

"Well, I better get out of here. I have to get the babysitter home by midnight. Have a good night," she said and crossed the shiny tile floor to the elevator.

The routine was the same for every night shift. Med pass, treatments if there were any, answer call lights. Alberta already had half of the midnight rounds done by the time I started the med pass. We were both completely done by one o'clock.

"So now what?" I asked Alberta.

"Well, I brought my knitting. It's the only thing that keeps me awake during these slow nights. That's why I like to work day shift—it's always busy," Alberta said, pulling red yarn and two metal knitting needles from a Kroger grocery bag. "We don't have rounds again until two, so you can take a quick catnap if you want."

"Catnap? That doesn't seem right."

"Well, it's hard to stay awake sometimes. Especially when it's slow like this. Sometimes you wish for a critical patient, something to keep you awake."

"Fine, well I'm just going to sit here and read," I said, opening the MCAT book. The first page was an application to take the test, which for students in Ohio was being offered in October.

I flipped through the pages and found I could answer a lot of the questions pretty easily. All those chemistry and microbiology courses I had taken in nursing school might just pay off.

After a half hour of answering questions I turned back to the front of the book and, just for the heck of it, filled out the application. After all, what did I have to lose?

I was really getting into the test questions when the elevator doors slid open and Sean appeared at the desk.

"Sean, what are you doing here?" I asked, shocked to see him and surprised at how awkward it felt.

"I saw your car in the parking lot. I hope you don't mind me coming up. Ray, the maintenance man let me in." He sounded almost apologetic.

The call light above Otis's room went off and Alberta tossed her knitting needles aside and sprung up. "I'll get it," Alberta said as she scampered past us.

"Of course I don't mind. How're you doin'?" I asked.

"Okay, I guess. I miss you, Meen. When are you coming home?" he asked.

"I don't know," I said. "I need some time alone to sort through all this."

"Meen, I know we can work this out. I'll look the other way; you go do what you have to do. Really, it will be okay. Mina, you're my best friend, you're my wife, and I can't bear to lose you."

Alberta returned to her seat in front of the elevator. Well within earshot of our conversation, making me self-conscious of what we were saying.

"Sean, living like we were, you watching every move I made and me afraid to do anything, we'd end up hating each other. I don't want that, do you?" I asked trying to keep my voice low so Alberta couldn't hear us.

Sean looked down. "No, I don't want that," he said, quietly.

Sean looked stricken. My stomach felt sick. "I just need some time, Sean. Can you give me that? I'm not saying that this is the end. I just need some time to sort things out."

Sean nodded. "Mina, we got married young, and maybe you think you're missing something, something that you can't get from me. I'd rather you have an affair and get whatever this is out of your system than end our marriage."

Otis's call light went on again and Alberta sprang up to answer it. "He's on the toilet," she said as she scooted past us on the way to Otis's room.

"Are you going to keep the appointment with Dr. Metcalf on Monday?" Sean asked.

"Yes, I was planning to, unless you want to go alone," I asked.

"No. I think it's a good idea that we both still go."

Teresa Rosetti's call light came on. "I better get this," I said.

"Okay. I'll see you Monday then at Metcalf's office," Sean said.

"See you then," I said and walked around the desk to answer Teresa's light.

Sean touched my arm and then bent down and kissed me lightly on the cheek. "Bye," he said, and then turned and walked away.

My throat clenched shut as I tried to hold back the tears. I leaned against the wall in the doorway of Teresa's room, trying to pull myself together. I had to, Teresa needed me and the rest of my patients needed me. I lifted the tiny woman onto the bedpan. The three diuretics she took each day to keep the fluid off her heart obviously kept her on the bedpan most of the night.

"Thank you, nurse, I am so sorry to bother you in the middle of the night like this," she said, reaching up and patting my face.

"Teresa, you are not a bother, honey. I'll be right outside, just put your light on when you are done."

I waited out in the hall until Teresa put her call light on, and then helped her off the bedpan. I tucked her in again and put an extra blanket at the foot of her bed because I knew she was always cold.

Alberta and I did two o'clock and four o'clock rounds together. The time between four thirty and six o'clock was the toughest. My head bobbed forward and my vision blurred as I tried to read the MCAT book. My eyelids felt heavier and heavier. I hated trying to fight sleep. I gave up on the book and decided to prepare the six o'clock med round early just to keep awake. I poured myself a second cup of coffee and set it on top of the med cart. I opened the medication book and began preparing the medications, signing the log as I went.

I shoved the last drawer into the cart when the elevator doors creaked open and Rosetti appeared carrying a small white bag from McDonald's. Her hair was still damp from her shower and she was dressed in her crisply pressed police uniform.

"Good morning," she said as she approached the nurse's station. "I wanted to stop and check on my mom before going in to work and I thought you might be hungry," she said and set the McDonald's bag in front of me on the med cart.

"Thank you, you didn't have to do that," I said and opened up the small white bag. The warm smell of egg and cheese wafted up, making my mouth water. "Would you like a cup of coffee or something? I think there is still some left in the pot."

"Yes, coffee would be great."

I started back to the tiny kitchen behind the nurse's station, and then stopped in my tracks. "How do you take your coffee?" I asked.

"Just cream," she said.

I returned minutes later with two silver Premarin mugs full of coffee. "Come on back and sit for a minute," I said, inviting Rosetti to sit in one of the desk chairs in the nurses' station. She took a sip of her coffee. "Wow, that's strong," she winced. "I thought the coffee at the police station was strong, but this stuff beats it by a mile," she said.

I leaned on the med cart and took a bite of my egg and cheese McMuffin. "Mmm, this is good," I said savoring the salty smoothness of the melted cheese and fluffy egg. I took a sip of coffee as well. "Working this shift, you need all the caffeine you can get."

"How was your night?" Rosetti asked.

"Not bad. It's something you have to adjust to. It was hard keeping awake after four thirty. I kept trying to find things to do."

"What kind of night did Mom have?" Rosetti asked, taking another sip of her coffee.

"Okay. She was up a few times to pee. Her water pills keep her up. I am afraid to get them decreased though, they are doing such a good job keeping her out of heart failure," I said and then took another bite of the breakfast sandwich.

"I appreciate you taking such good care of her," Rosetti said.

"It's my job. She's such a sweet little lady; I enjoy taking care of her."

"How was your dinner with Sean the other night?" Rosetti asked, blowing gently on her coffee mug.

I looked down. "Don't ask."

"What happened?"

"We got into a huge fight."

"Over what?" Rosetti asked, taking another sip of coffee.

"It's stupid really."

"It must be something if you fought about it. C'mon tell me."

I felt warm and uncomfortable. "He accused me of checking out the hostess at the restaurant."

Rosetti burst out in laughter.

"Oh, I'm sorry. I didn't mean to laugh," she said. "Oh my."

"See, it's stupid."

"No it's not, not really. Were you?"

"Was I what?"

"Were you checking out the hostess at the restaurant?"

My face felt on fire now. "Yes." I answered quietly.

Rosemary tried to suppress her smile.

"I'll bet that was a big blow to his ego."

"I guess. He wasn't too happy. We had a huge fight once we got home. I packed a bag and left."

"You left him?"

"Uh-huh." I nodded.

"Oh my God, Mina, for good?" Rosetti asked.

"I don't know. I need time to think. A lot has happened. Stuff we can't take back or change. I have to decide where to go from here."

"Things will work out," Rosetti said. "Would you like me to talk to Sean?"

"Oh, I don't think so. I don't know how he would react to that, and I'd hate to drag you into this."

"I understand," Rosetti said.

"Just . . . be there in case he does want to talk about it. I know you will be straight with him. I think that would be a big help."

"I will, I promise. But what about you? Who is your support system?"

"I don't know. Me, I guess."

"Any news from Regan?" Rosetti asked.

"Yes, I got a card from her yesterday."

"See, I told you that you'd hear from her. Did she tell you where she was?"

"Not exactly. There was no return address, but the envelope was postmarked Wheeling, West Virginia."

"West Virginia! Wow, I wonder what made her run down there." Rosetti asked.

"Being with me obviously."

"I'm sorry, Mina," Rosetti said.

"Hey, what can you do? I can't change the way she feels," I said, this time unable to hold back the tears. "Rosemary, my life is a real mess," I said.

Rosetti got up and handed me a bunch of Kleenex. I wiped my tears and blew my nose.

"Things will get better, Mina. You just have to hang in there. Change is never easy."

"But how do I know if I'm doing the right thing?"

"You have to go with your heart. You have to get real quiet and listen to what's going on inside of you. Inside of you is where all the answers are."

"How did you get so wise to the ways of the world?" I asked.

"I've had to make some tough decisions in my life. My decision to leave a job I loved in Cleveland to come back here and take care of my mother wasn't easy. And, I've had my heart ripped out and handed to me a few times."

"I see," I said. My thoughts went immediately to the woman I had seen her with at the Victorian restaurant. I wondered what part she played in Rosetti's life, but wasn't sure I wanted to know for sure.

"Are you going to be okay?" Rosemary asked.

I nodded.

"Where can I put this?" she asked, holding up the Premarin coffee mug.

"Here, I'll take it," I said.

"Thanks for the coffee. I'll have no trouble staying awake this morning," she said, opening her eyes wide.

I laughed.

"I better get moving. I want to look in on Mom before I go."

Rosetti got up and headed toward her mom's room.

"Thanks for breakfast," I said.

"You're welcome," she said and then disappeared into Teresa's room.

Chapter Nineteen

Lonely nights melted into lonely days. I had to do something to stave off the sadness, so I buried myself in work. It was nothing for me to work a twelve-hour shift, go back to the motel room for eight hours of sleep, and then return to the nursing home for another eight-hour shift. The money was great and it was enough to keep my mind occupied and my heart numb.

The sun was already up and blazing when I finished my last midnight shift. The air was thick with humidity as I walked out to my car. I reached for the door handle and discovered a folded up piece of white notebook paper tucked under my windshield wiper. Anxiety gnawed at my stomach as I cautiously removed the note, unfolded it carefully, and read it:

Mina, call me or stop by the apartment after work. We need to talk. Sean

I folded the note back up and slid it into my pocket. I didn't have the energy to deal with Sean right now, so I got in the car and headed back to the motel. I must have nodded off once or twice during the forty-minute drive, in spite of having the radio blasting and all the windows rolled down. I actually remember dreaming about being on a beach when the rough ride, from the car going off the road, woke me up. Thank God traffic was light.

Relieved to be back at the motel and in one piece, I pushed open the door to my tiny room only to find it sweltering inside. I pushed several buttons on the window air conditioner and it hummed to life. I stripped out of my uniform and panty hose and lay on top of the bed, not bothering to get under the covers. I was totally exhausted. The

The Choice
Published by The Haworth Press, Inc., 2007. All rights reserved.
doi:10.1300/5791_19

cool air felt good on my naked body. Sleep hovered and finally took over.

I woke up around three in the afternoon, shivering. The room felt like a meat locker. I pulled the polyester bedspread around me, got up, and shut off the air conditioner. I pulled back one of the room-darkening drapes and was blinded by the bright sunlight. I rubbed my eyes with my fists, trying to bring them back into focus.

I had the entire weekend ahead of me with nothing to do. Jacob's denied my last request to work tonight. She said I already worked sixty hours this week and she couldn't approve any more overtime for me.

I flicked on the TV. Nothing on but women's golf. I figured I'd work some more on the MCAT and rummaged through my backpack looking for the book. I pulled out the MCAT workbook and along with it, the forgotten copy of *Gay People's Chronicle*. I opened it at the entertainment section and found that there was a women's only bar on Arlington Street in Akron. Although I didn't recognize the address, I knew Akron pretty well, since I had done my pediatric rotation there in nursing school. Chances were pretty slim I'd run into anyone I knew there. And if I found out it wasn't for me I could always leave.

My stomach rumbled. I hadn't eaten since midnight when Alberta and I had ordered pizza delivered to the nursing home. Otis was rambunctious that night, putting the call light on every fifteen minutes, so Alberta got him up and he joined us for pizza with a Mylanta chaser. After that, he slept like a baby.

I looked in my wall safe of a fridge and found only two cans of Diet Coke and a brown banana. I needed to get something for lunch and some groceries for later. I picked up a six-pack of Diet Coke and a bag of Pepperidge Farm Mint Milano cookies, which are the ultimate breakfast food because their minty taste kills morning breath as well as satisfies hunger. They were great on vacation too, when brushing your teeth just wasn't convenient. Regan had introduced me to them. It made me feel good to buy them.

When I returned to my room, the red message light on the desk phone was flashing. Sean had called and left a message at the front desk asking me to call him as soon as possible. I dialed Sean's number.

"Hello?"

"Sean, it's Mina."

"Why didn't you stop after work this morning?"

"I was exhausted," I said, weariness crept into my voice. "What did you want?" I asked.

"Mina, you have to come home. I can't live like this anymore, it's killing me," Sean's voice broke.

I hung my head, feeling his desperation. "Sean, I need more time. Time to figure out what to do."

"Mina, please. I can't take it. I hate this apartment; it's so empty. I hate being here without you."

"Sean, I can't. Not yet. If I come home now it won't be because I want to; it will be because you are making me. That's not going to solve anything."

"Mina, you don't understand. The guys at work are talking. I'm afraid if they find out the real reason . . ." his voice trailed off. I could hear the pain in his silence. I didn't know what to say. I could only imagine how difficult this was for him.

"And another thing, your mom keeps calling here looking for you. I keep putting her off, but can't put her off much longer. You need to call and tell her where you are and what's going on."

Something else I had been avoiding needed to be dealt with.

"Okay, I'll call her and tell her what's going on," I said.

"What are you going to say to her?" Sean asked.

"I'll tell her we decided to separate for a while . . . that we are working on things but felt we needed some space. She doesn't need to know all the details," I said.

"If you tell her that, she'll think this was my fault. I don't think that's very fair. She needs to know the truth. You have to tell her what really happened."

"Well what do you suppose I tell her?" I asked, annoyed with him that he was being such a tight-ass about this.

"You need to tell her the truth."

"What's that supposed to mean?"

"I mean you need to tell her everything . . . about you and Regan."

"She doesn't need to know about that, besides, if I told her that, it would kill her."

"Well, if you don't tell her, I will," Sean said, his voice was cold as steel.

"You'll tell her?"

"That's right. If you don't tell her the real reason we are separated is because of your fling with Regan, I will."

"Sean, all that's going to do is hurt her. Don't drag her into this. She's had enough heartache in her life. She doesn't need this too."

There was silence on the other end of the phone. "Sean, are you there? Why are you doing this? I always thought you cared about my mother. God knows she cares about you. You're like a son to her."

"I do care about your mother, that's why I want her to know the truth. I don't want her to think I did something to cause our breakup. I want her to know what really happened."

"I still don't see how telling her is going to make this any better. All it's going to do is hurt her."

"Well, there is one way to avoid that," Sean said.

"What?"

"You can avoid her finding out if you just come back home. If you come home now, I promise I won't say a word to your mother."

I swallowed hard, trying not to reveal how angry I was with him for putting me in this position.

"It's your choice, Mina. You decide. We can make this work, I know we can if you'll just try."

I felt humiliated and defeated. I couldn't believe Sean would stoop this low to get what he wanted. I did try. I tried for six years, but the feelings kept coming back.

"So what's it gonna be? Are you coming home or what?"

"I'll come home," I said, my voice deflated.

Sean sighed in relief on the other end of the phone. However, his relief would only be short-lived.

"I'll come home tomorrow to pick up the rest of my things," I said, anger seething in my voice.

"What?" Sean asked.

"I'll be at the apartment tomorrow morning to pick up the rest of my stuff and I suggest that you not be there when I get there. You're not going to blackmail me into doing what you want. You think you've had enough? I've had enough, and this is the last straw, Sean. I thought I knew you, but for you to stoop so low as to try and hurt my family . . . Don't go anywhere near my mother or the rest of my family. I'm going to call her right now to tell her everything myself. This is my mess and my responsibility and I will take care of it."

"But—"

I slammed the receiver into its cradle before Sean could say another word. My hand shook violently as I picked up the receiver and dialed my mother's phone number, but then hung up, realizing that this was news that had to be given in person, like the death of a loved one. In a way this was the same. *I am sure my mother will feel like someone has died when we are through with this. Mina, the daughter she's always known and loved, will be gone in her eyes. I hope she can still love the Mina that's left,* I thought. I snatched the car keys from the nightstand and headed to my mother's house, knowing full well it may be the last time I'd ever be welcomed there.

During the forty-minute drive I rehearsed in my head what I was going to say to her. *"Mom, I have to tell you something. Mom I'm gay. Mom, I'm a lesbian. Mom . . ."* nothing sounded right. I pulled into her driveway half hoping she wasn't home. But her car was in its usual place. I took a deep breath and mustered up all the self-confidence I could manage. I got out of the refuge of my car and slowly walked up the driveway to the back door. I tapped on the screen door and let myself in.

"Mom? Are you home?"

My mother appeared, pink foam curlers in her red-penny dyed hair, faded blue seersucker housecoat, brown moccasin slippers, and the ever-present lit cigarette in her left hand.

"Well, if it isn't my long-lost daughter. To what do I owe this honor?

"I'm sorry I haven't called Mom. I've been pretty busy . . . with work and stuff," I said, feeling chunks of my confidence falling away.

"I talked to Sean the other day. Did you get my message?" she asked.

"Message?" I tried to remember if Sean said anything about a message.

"He said you called, but . . ."

"It wasn't important anyway. You didn't come to the calling hours for your Dad's cousin. I hadn't seen or heard from you in a while. I was concerned. Oh, I covered for you, by the way, with your father's family. I told them you were working and sent your condolences."

I looked down at the faded red linoleum of her kitchen floor. "Thanks Mom," I said.

My mom walked over and poured herself a cup of coffee. "You want some?" she asked, holding up the glass Mr. Coffee carafe.

"Yes, that would be great," I said and pulled out one of the oak kitchen chairs and sat down at the kitchen table. She set the sunny yellow Fiesta Dinnerware cup and saucer in front of me and opened a bag of Stella D'oro anisette toast. I took a sip of the coffee. Mmmm. Eight O'clock coffee. The aroma of fresh-brewed coffee was the thing that reminded me the most about being at my mother's house. She drank Eight O'clock coffee for as long as I could remember. As a matter of fact, she drank it all day long. Coffee and cigarettes, that's what she existed on. Her four-feet and ten-inch, one-hundred pound frame was a testimony to it.

I dunked the toast in my coffee. "Mina? Are you alright?" my mother asked, squinting through the smoke of her cigarette. "You look like hell," she said and then rested her Salem cigarette in the gray smoke glass ashtray someone pilfered from the Stardust Resort in Las Vegas. The white smoke rose from the ashtray in a sleek ribbon and dissipated into the air above her.

"Mom, there's something I have to tell you."

She closed her eyes, I'm sure bracing herself for the worst. The lines in her face seemed more prominent in the bright afternoon sunlight. She earned every single one of those lines dealing with life since my father had died nearly ten years ago, and I was sure I was about to add a few more.

"Mom, Sean and I have . . . separated for a while."

"Why Mina? What happened?"

"It's complicated . . ."

"Life's complicated Mina. You learn to deal with it. That's not reason to give up on a perfectly good marriage," she said. She lit another
Salem and forcefully blew a plume of smoke into the air.

"What I mean, Mom, is that there are a lot of issues Sean and I need
to deal with," I said, stalling for time.

"Issues! Everything is an issue with you kids. Marriage isn't always
easy, Mina. There are ups and downs all the time. You can't just quit
because of a little rough ground," she said.

"It's more than a little rough ground, Mom," I said.

"Well, what is it then?" Her voice was quiet now. I could see genuine sincerity and concern in her eyes. "What could be so bad that you
would have to separate?"

"Mom, I met someone," I said, unable to meet her gaze.

"What did you say?" my mother asked. She reached for the Salem
burning in the ashtray and took a long drag.

I flinched at the tone of her voice. "I met someone," I repeated.

"Mina, I can't believe this. You cheated on Sean? What the hell is
the matter with you?" my mother asked, rubbing her forehead with
one hand and crushing out her cigarette with the other. "Why would
you go and do something stupid like that? You weren't raised that
way. Thank God your father isn't here to see this."

"Mom, I'm sorry. Believe me, I didn't want this to happen. It just
did."

"Does Sean know?" she asked tentatively.

I nodded.

"So he asked you to leave?" she said lighting another cigarette.

I shook my head. "No, I left on my own. He wanted me to stay."

"He was willing to let you stay after you cheated on him, and you
still left?"

I nodded. "I needed to get away and think things over. I've learned
a lot about myself in the past few months."

"Mina, what the hell is going on?" my mother asked as she relit the
cigarette that dangled from her lower lip.

My throat felt like it was about to close off. I stared into my empty coffee cup, searching for the right words to say what I had to say.

"Mom, do you remember Regan, the nurse I worked with at the nursing home?"

"Yes, you two spent a lot of time together this past summer. What? She set you up with this other guy or something?"

"Mom . . . I fell in love with her." The words hung heavy in the air.

The knockout punch had been delivered. My mother sat across from me blank. I felt guilty and relieved all at the same time. A few minutes passed and then she got up and walked toward the kitchen counter. "You want more coffee?" she asked as if she hadn't heard a word I said.

"No, Mom. Thanks."

She refilled her cup, leaned against the counter, and stared out the kitchen window.

"Mom? Are you okay?" I asked hesitantly.

She didn't respond.

"Mom, did you hear what I said?"

"Huh? What?" she answered and turned toward me.

"Mom, I think I'm gay."

"No you're not," she said stoically, and then crushed her cigarette out against the white porcelain of the kitchen sink.

"Mom, how can you say that?"

"Because I didn't raise my daughter to be that way, that's how. You've been married to Sean for six years for Christ's sakes. Mina, Jesus, you must be going through some kind of early midlife crisis or something. What is it? Do you think you missed something? I know you had a lot of responsibility with taking care of your Dad and all, and I know you never really dated much in high school. Maybe if you would have got this out of your system in high school," she said, turning on the faucet and washing the cigarette butt and ashes down the drain.

"But Mom, I know how I feel. I fell in love with her. It was something like I had never felt before," I said, relief turning into embarrassment now.

"Mina, maybe you're confusing your feelings for that girl with something else. Maybe what you had with her was just a close friendship. You never had any close girlfriends in school. You always seemed to keep to yourself. I tried to get you more involved but you didn't seem interested."

I didn't know what to say. I felt her heavy gaze upon me as we sat quietly in the kitchen in the house that I grew up in.

"You know, Mina, when I was in high school, my best friend and I would go to slumber parties and sock hops and used to do stuff like wear each other's clothes and even practice kissing each other because we didn't have boyfriends yet. But just because we did those things, that didn't make us homosexual."

Those words sounded strangely familiar. They were Regan's words. Suddenly I felt sick to my stomach. And as if that wasn't enough, I surely didn't want to hear about my mother kissing girls in high school. Ironically, that thought repulsed me even more.

My eyes burned with weariness and fatigue. Across the table from me sat my mother, her thin, bony fingers tense in her lap and tears welling in her eyes. I wished I'd never come here and told her what I did.

"Mina, you don't want that kind of life for yourself," she whispered almost inaudibly. "Do you?"

I hung my head in despair. My own tears splashed onto the shiny oak tabletop.

She reached across the kitchen table resting her hand on mine.

"Those types of relationships never work out," she said. "It's hard enough for a woman to be on her own. Admitting that you are homosexual will make it twice as hard."

I didn't know what to say, because in my heart, I knew she was right. I knew it would be hard. But this didn't feel right either.

"Mina, you have a good husband who loves you. Why would you want to give that up?"

"Because, Mom, that's not who I am. I've tried being who everyone wants me to be and it isn't working."

"Mina, these feelings you have—that you think you have—will pass. Go home and work it out with Sean. I know he loves you," she said. Hurt gleamed in her dark eyes.

I looked away in shame. I should have just given in to Sean and be done with it. Who I was inside wasn't worth all the pain it was causing the people that I loved and who loved me.

I stood up and set my coffee cup in the sink. "I better go," I said and headed for the back door.

"Mina, wait," she said as I pushed the screen door open. "What if you and Sean talked to someone, like a priest or got counseling. Maybe that would help."

"We are, Mom. Sean and I are seeing a counselor in Akron."

"That's great Mina. See you two are working on it already. So what does this counselor say about all this?" she asked.

"She says she can't change the way I feel. That being gay is something I was born with."

"So this is my fault?" My mother asked defensively, her hand pressed over her heart as if she were having chest pain.

"No, Mom, none of this has anything to do with you. It's me. I'm the one who feels different, and I have to learn how to deal with it."

Her face was pale and drawn. She looked a lot older than her fifty-two years. I put my arms around her and hugged her tight. "I'm sorry Mom, I really am," I said.

We stood in her kitchen and cried. "I gotta go," I said and kissed her on the forehead. She nodded, wiping at her wet eyes with the sleeve of her housecoat. I closed the screen door gently behind me.

I drove back to the motel, tears distorting my vision. I thought about Regan and where she might be. I thought about what things would have been like if I had never met her. Would I be in the same spot I am in today or would Sean and I still be happily married? The thing that bothered me the most was the pain I saw in my mother's eyes. Regan's prediction was right: a lot of people did get hurt, probably more than she ever realized.

There was no going back now, only forward. Time is said to be the best healer, right? Only time would tell how my mother and Sean, and me, for that matter, would adapt to all this, if we adapted at all.

Chapter Twenty

I was exhausted mentally and physically when I returned from my mother's after our little talk. So I laid down for a brief nap. The motel room was dark when I awoke. My body felt stiff, my eyes were swollen from crying, and I had a throbbing headache. I forced myself to get up and dressed. I needed to disappear into the night. Go somewhere where no one knew me. Maybe I would just take a ride to Akron and see where the bar was, but not go in. No need to rush things, right? After all, my only experience with gay bars was the disastrous evening at the bar in Youngstown with Regan. I hated to think about that night. It had been my last night with her.

I pulled on a pair of Calvin Klein jeans and a pink Izod polo shirt and checked my look in the mirror. Before I left the motel room, I pulled off my wedding ring and put it in my backpack for safe keeping. I did it fast, like ripping off a Band-Aid. If I was going to do this, I needed to do it for real. No in between and no going back. I grabbed the *Gay People's Chronicle* on my way out and headed west on the highway to a new and different life.

The bar was pretty easy to find, as Arlington Street is one of the main drags in Akron. I pulled into the crowded parking lot and couldn't believe my eyes. This place was unbelievable. The bar was housed in a building that used to be an old Kmart department store. A neon sign blazed "Quest" over the glass double door entrance. It was nothing like the bar in Youngstown, where there was no sign, and it seemed you had to belong to some sort of cult or club to get in.

I sat in the parking lot for nearly a half an hour, watching as women from all walks of life filed into the bar, before finally getting up the courage to go in. As I walked through the glass doors of the entrance I was greeted by a woman sporting a snow-white crew cut. She sat at a card table with a rubber stamp in one hand and a bottle of Miller Lite

The Choice
Published by The Haworth Press, Inc., 2007. All rights reserved.
doi:10.1300/5791_20

beer in the other. She was wearing black leather pants that strained at their seams and a black leather vest that exposed her voluptuous pale cleavage. Her doughy white upper arm was encircled in a tattoo of barbed wire connecting with two interlocking women's symbols.

"Hi," she said as I approached her card table. I felt her eyes appraise me. "Two dollar cover tonight," she said. Her voice was soft and feminine and did not match her exterior at all.

I pulled two crumpled dollar bills from the front pocket of my jeans and handed them to her, hoping she couldn't see my hand tremble.

"Thanks, honey. Have fun," she said as she stamped the underside of my wrist and directed me down a glass-block-lined corridor to the entrance of the bar.

Bright lights swirled all around the club. The aluminum-covered dance floor was two tiered, with running lights flashing on each tier. Same-sex couples, all women, gyrated to the music. A woman dressed in a Laura Ashley print dress and black leather Army boots danced with a woman with long blonde hair dressed in a man's business suit.

I had never seen this many gay women in one place in all my life. There were women of all sizes, shapes, and colors. There were butch women, wearing leather. There were businesswomen in pant's suits who probably stopped off for a drink after work. There were women in tight, high miniskirts and women dressed in softball uniforms. The whole scene made me dizzy.

There were actually four bars in the place, one on each wall, each being about twenty feet long and three people deep. Huge white marble columns with plastic ivy running up and down them supported the painted blue and white sky ceiling. I walked over to the nearest bar and got in line behind a woman wearing a chiffon blouse and a pair of skin-tight hip-hugger jeans. Her long, dark hair cascaded down her back, brushing the top of her hip-huggers. The woman standing next to her caught me looking at her friend and gave me a look that said she could easily punch my lights out. She slid her arm around the woman's waist, pulling her to her, claiming her, letting me know she belonged to her.

I stepped back, giving them some space, realizing I had done something wrong, I just didn't know what. It dawned on me that I might have to learn a whole new set of behavior, like visiting a foreign country. I guess my first lesson to be learned in this foreign country is that lesbians can be pretty possessive.

I finally made it up to the bar and ordered a Diet Coke. There was nowhere in the place to sit as all the bar stools were taken. So I picked up my Diet Coke and moseyed around the place, taking in the sights, as the same Gloria Gaynor song, "I Will Survive," that had played in the Youngstown bar, blared from the six-foot speakers that flanked the dance floor. *Must be some gay theme song,* I thought as I leaned against one of the marble columns and sipped my soda.

I was surveying the room, taking it all in, when I noticed a woman, standing alone, close to the dance floor. She was handsomely dressed in beige slacks, a black T-shirt, and black blazer. When our eyes met, my face flushed. She smiled and I smiled back. Her smile was affectionate and relaxed. A few minutes later, she was standing next to me.

"Would you like to dance?" the woman asked.

I looked up at her in surprise. She was tall and fit and seemed comfortable in this environment.

"Excuse me?" I said, not sure I heard her right over the blaring music.

"I said, would you like to dance?" she repeated and held out her hand to me.

My heart raced with excitement. I nodded.

I set down my soda and followed her to the dance floor just as Madonna's "Crazy for You" began to play. She gently took my hand and rested it against her shoulder as her arm encircled my waist. She smelled of hairspray and cigarettes and men's cologne. Paco Rabanne, I think.

It felt weird to slow dance with a woman. Regan and I never got the chance. But it also felt wonderful to be held in someone's arms again. She was a head taller than I and I comfortably rested my head on her shoulder. Her body felt strange and familiar at the same time. I was getting lost in the music and the sensation of the slow swaying of our bodies. She whispered in my ear that her name was Devon.

"I'm Mina," I said but before I could say anything else my throat closed off in panic. Sean was standing just inside of the bar entrance, staring straight at me. Fear and then anger welled up inside of me. Afraid of what might happen next, I broke our embrace.

"What's wrong?" Devon asked as I pulled away.

"Uh . . . I have to go. I'm sorry. Thank you for the dance, but I have to go," I said and turned to leave the dance floor.

"Wait—" Devon said reaching for me. But I was already off the dance floor and headed toward the door.

I tried pushing my way past Sean without a scene, but he caught me by the arm and shoved me against the glass block wall. "What's going on?" he asked.

"I guess I could ask you the same question," I said through clenched teeth.

Sean tightened his grip on my arm. I was sure it would leave a bruise.

"Mina—"

"Sean, I can't believe this. You followed me here?"

He nodded and looked around the bar.

"Who the hell is that?" he asked gesturing toward the dance floor where Devon still stood.

"A friend," I answered.

"It looked like more than that from here," Sean spat out. "Jesus, Mina, is this what you want? Do you want to throw away our life together for this?" He looked around at all the different women.

Sean grabbed both of my arms as if he were going to shake some sense into me. "Mina, you're not like these people. Look at them, they're freaks," he said as a woman with a purple Mohawk walked by.

I felt sick and was having trouble breathing. "I need to get some air," I said and broke free from his grip and headed toward the door. Sean followed close behind me.

"Everything all right?" the crew-cutted door person asked as we passed by her card table. She got up from her post and followed us outside into the sticky night air.

"Is this guy bothering you, honey?" she said, flabby white arms crossed in front of her chest, sizing up Sean.

"No, it's okay," I said between gasps. "He's my husband."

"Whoa . . . okay, as long as you're alright honey," she said and then went back inside he club.

I still felt dizzy and sat down on the curb. Sean sat down next to me.

"Sean, why did you come here?" I asked.

"I followed you because I needed to see for myself what was really going on with you. I don't think you belong in this lifestyle. I wanted to think that maybe you were going through a phase or maybe there was something I wasn't giving you. I wanted to prove Metcalf wrong. I don't know. But I'm beginning to think she's right. She said a lot of people try to live with the charade for a while, but it definitely takes its toll and eventually ends up destroying them as well as their relationship."

"Sean, I don't want to destroy you or me or our relationship. I love you and I always will, but—"

"I know, I know," he said holding up both hands.

Sean hung his head. I slipped my arm over his shoulder, rubbing his back, trying to comfort him.

"It's just so hard to let go," Sean said wiping his eyes with the back of his hand.

"I know," I said choking back my own tears. "But ending our marriage doesn't mean we have to lose each other. We can still be there for each other. Sean, I will always love you. There will always be a place for you in my heart."

Sean looked down remorsefully. "Did you tell your mother about you and Regan?"

I nodded.

"How did it go?"

"Not well. She seems to be in denial about the whole thing."

"I'm sorry, Mina. I'm sorry I threatened to tell her. I just felt so desperate."

"I know. I'm sorry, too."

Sean took my hand and held it in his. He gently rubbed his fingers over the place where my wedding band used to be. "When did you stop wearing it?" he asked.

"Tonight. Just tonight," I answered.

Sean lifted my hand it to his lips and softly kissed it. My heart ached, as I knew it was his kiss good-bye.

Sean stood up and brushed off the back of his jeans. "I better get going," he said. "These people are staring at us as if *we're* some kind of freaks. As if they never saw a man and a woman who truly loved each other." He was smiling at me. Even in his pain, he was trying to make me feel better.

"Were you still planning on coming to get your things tomorrow?" Sean asked. "I can be out of the apartment for a while if it will make things easier."

"No, that won't be necessary. It can wait," I said. "If that's okay with you."

"It's okay. Call me when you are ready," he said and turned to walk to his car.

He waved good-bye and I stood in the parking lot and watched as the red taillights of his car and our six-year marriage faded into the night.

Epilogue

Sean and I filed for dissolution of our marriage in August 1986, and it became final on November 22, 1986. We shared the same lawyer and split fifty-fifty everything we had accumulated in our six years together. Our lawyer said it was the most amicable divorce he had ever handled.

The only thing we didn't agree on was my taking back my maiden name, but I thought this should be a clean break, and holding onto Sean's name would be like holding onto him. Reluctantly he agreed with me, and so I went back to being Mina Caselli again.

Sean offered me the apartment because he said it was too hard for him to stay there without me. I accepted his offer.

On October 2, I passed the MCAT on my first try. The cheap rent at the apartment would work out great financially for me when I'd have to cut back my hours at the nursing home to start medical school the following fall.

Sean rented an efficiency apartment across town. I went with him on several occasions to help pick out paint and furniture to get him set up in his new place. We both stayed at our old apartment until his apartment was painted. The night before his actual move day, we made love for the last time.

The most heart-wrenching thing of all was watching him pack up his clothing and personal belongings. We had moved together three times during our marriage. But this time he was moving without me, and it was more than I could stand. I told him I had to run some errands and would be back later. He nodded and understood why I couldn't watch him leave.

I sat in the car for a while, watching him through the dining room window as he packed. My life as a police officer's wife was over, and what lay ahead of me was uncertain, to say the least. I started the en-

The Choice
Published by The Haworth Press, Inc., 2007. All rights reserved.
doi:10.1300/5791_21

gine and slowly drove out of the apartment complex, knowing that when I returned, he and all the familiar things about him would be gone.

I drove downtown and pulled into the police station. The dispatcher buzzed me in. I walked into the reception area and tapped on the thick bulletproof glass. Rosetti looked up from her paperwork and, by the look on her face, was happy to see me.

"Mina, what a nice surprise. What brings you here?" Rosetti said, her voice sounding mechanical through small round opening in the center of the glass.

"Moving day," I said.

"Oh, I see. How ya doin?"

"Okay, I guess," I lied, and she knew it. "I was wondering if you got a break soon . . . maybe we could go for coffee or something?"

"Sure, I'd love to. Give me a few minutes to finish up this report and I'll be right out."

"Great, I'll wait out here," I said and took a seat on one of the plastic orange chairs in the lobby. I looked around at the familiar surroundings of the police station. Memories of my life with Sean hung all around me. I used to come down here many times to pick up Sean after work or bring him dinner when he worked afternoon or midnight turn. That seemed like a hundred years ago.

Ten minutes later Rosetti appeared at the side office door. "C'mon in," she said holding the heavy steel door open for me. "My car is in the sally port. We can leave through the back."

One door closes and another one opens, I thought as I followed Rosetti through the gray-walled corridor of the police station and through the door leading out to the sally port. In life, there will always be choices to make. Some are more difficult than others, but the key to a good life is to be true to yourself. Always.

ABOUT THE AUTHOR

Maria V. Ciletti is a registered nurse currently working as a medical administrator and is the president and owner of MVC Medical Consultants in Niles, Ohio. She writes nonfiction medical articles, short stories, and literary fiction, as well as gay/lesbian fiction. *The Choice* is her first novel. She is currently working on a sequel.

The Choice
Published by The Haworth Press, Inc., 2007. All rights reserved.
doi:10.1300/5791_22

HARRINGTON PARK PRESS®
Alice Street Editions™
Judith P. Stelboum
Editor in Chief

Past Perfect by Judith P. Stelboum

Inside Out by Juliet Carrera

Façades by Alex Marcoux

Weeding at Dawn: A Lesbian Country Life by Hawk Madrone

His Hands, His Tools, His Sex, His Dress: Lesbian Writers on Their Fathers edited by Catherine Reid and Holly K. Iglesias

Treat by Angie Vicars

Yin Fire by Alexandra Grilikhes

Egret by Helen Collins

Your Loving Arms by Gwendolyn Bikis

A Donor Insemination Guide: Written By *and* For *Lesbian Women* by Marie Mohler and Lacy Frazer

From Flitch to Ash: A Musing on Trees and Carving by Diane Derrick

To the Edge by Cameron Abbott

Back to Salem by Alex Marcoux

Extraordinary Couples, Ordinary Lives by Lynn Haley-Banez and Joanne Garrett

Cat Rising by Cynn Chadwick

Maryfield Academy by Carla Tomaso

Ginger's Fire by Maureen Brady

A Taste for Blood by Diana Lee

Zach at Risk by Pamela Shepherd

Order a copy of this book with this form or online at:
http://www.haworthpress.com/store/product.asp?sku=5791

THE CHOICE

_____in softbound at $16.95 (ISBN-13: 978-1-56023-638-2; ISBN-10: 1-56023-638-8)

209 pages

Or order online and use special offer code HEC25 in the shopping cart.

COST OF BOOKS_____

☐ **BILL ME LATER:** (Bill-me option is good on US/Canada/Mexico orders only; not good to jobbers, wholesalers, or subscription agencies.)

☐ Check here if billing address is different from shipping address and attach purchase order and billing address information.

POSTAGE & HANDLING_____
(US: $4.00 for first book & $1.50 for each additional book)
(Outside US: $5.00 for first book & $2.00 for each additional book)

Signature_____

SUBTOTAL_____

☐ **PAYMENT ENCLOSED: $**_____

IN CANADA: ADD 6% GST_____

☐ **PLEASE CHARGE TO MY CREDIT CARD.**

STATE TAX_____
(NJ, NY, OH, MN, CA, IL, IN, PA, & SD residents, add appropriate local sales tax)

☐ Visa ☐ MasterCard ☐ AmEx ☐ Discover
☐ Diner's Club ☐ Eurocard ☐ JCB

Account #_____

FINAL TOTAL_____
(If paying in Canadian funds, convert using the current exchange rate, UNESCO coupons welcome)

Exp. Date_____

Signature_____

Prices in US dollars and subject to change without notice.

NAME_____

INSTITUTION_____

ADDRESS_____

CITY_____

STATE/ZIP_____

COUNTRY_____ COUNTY (NY residents only)_____

TEL_____ FAX_____

E-MAIL_____

May we use your e-mail address for confirmations and other types of information? ☐ Yes ☐ No
We appreciate receiving your e-mail address and fax number. Haworth would like to e-mail or fax special discount offers to you, as a preferred customer. **We will never share, rent, or exchange your e-mail address or fax number.** We regard such actions as an invasion of your privacy.

Order From Your Local Bookstore or Directly From

The Haworth Press, Inc.

10 Alice Street, Binghamton, New York 13904-1580 • USA
TELEPHONE: 1-800-HAWORTH (1-800-429-6784) / Outside US/Canada: (607) 722-5857
FAX: 1-800-895-0582 / Outside US/Canada: (607) 771-0012
E-mail to: orders@haworthpress.com

For orders outside US and Canada, you may wish to order through your local
sales representative, distributor, or bookseller.
For information, see http://haworthpress.com/distributors

(Discounts are available for individual orders in US and Canada only, not booksellers/distributors.)

PLEASE PHOTOCOPY THIS FORM FOR YOUR PERSONAL USE.
http://www.HaworthPress.com   BOF06